MW01076311

WITHDRAWN

Slepyng HOUND to Wake

Small Beer Press Books by Vincent McCaffrey

Hound
A Slepyng Hound to Wake

Slepyng
HOUND
to Wake

a mystery

VINCENT
McCAFFREY

Small Beer Press
Easthampton, MA

Small Beer Press
150 Pleasant Street #306
Easthampton, MA 01027
www.smallbeerpress.com
www.weightlessbooks.com
info@smallbeerpress.com

Distributed to the trade by Consortium.

Library of Congress Cataloging-in-Publication Data

McCaffrey, Vincent, 1947-
A slepyng hound to wake : a mystery / Vincent McCaffrey. -- 1st ed.
   p. cm.
ISBN 978-1-931520-26-3 (alk. paper)
 1. Booksellers and bookselling--Fiction. 2. Murder--Fiction. 3. Boston (Mass.)--Fiction. 1. Title. 11.
Title: Sleeping hound to wake : a mystery.
PS3613.C3435S54 2011
813'.6--DC22

                          2011004627

First edition 1 2 3 4 5 6 7 8 9

Printed on 50# 30% PCR Natures Natural recycled paper by Thomson-Shore in Dexter, Michigan. ·
Cover by Tom Canty.
Author photo © 2011 by Adam H. McCaffrey.
Text set in Baskerville 12pt.

For my Thais; the mystery continues.

Chapter One

The books were like corpses, the ink of lost dreams dried in their veins. On a bad day, Henry Sullivan felt like a mortician salvaging the moldering flesh of small decaying bodies to be preserved for a proper burial. But on a good day, though there seemed to be fewer of those of late, he might save something which left him giddy.

Henry pulled the second box free from a mat of cat hair and dust beneath the bed, and peeked beneath the lid.

"Yes!"

The foul odor of the mattress too close to his face made him swallow the word along with the impulse to gag.

A month before, after lifting the spoiled leaves of disbound volumes abandoned in a basement beneath the seep of a ruined foundation, he had uncovered loose pages sheltered by a collapsed box of empty Croft Ale bottles. Separating the layers until the fetor of mold had made him dizzy, he had salvaged a bundle six inches thick of cream colored rag paper broadsides, announcements, and advertisements, all in French. They had been discarded by a print collector interested only in the engravings originally meant to illustrate the words. And in the heart of that, Henry had found a first printing of *The Declaration of the Rights of Man and the Citizen*.

Those rare sheets were sold now to the highest bidder, but they were a part of the romance Henry imagined about himself. It was still his belief that long before Foucault and Derrida, when words still offered a common meaning, the world could

1

be changed by the content of a few fragile pages. And this was why Henry Sullivan loved his job.

And this happened every once in awhile, more often to him than others, he thought, because he had a nose for it.

Henry pushed a broom handle into the depths of the crevice below the bed frame. Again he heard the hollow strike on a box.

It had to be done. He lowered himself onto his belly and reached further with his hand. The cardboard lip of the box broke free as he attempted to pull it to him. He lay still then and considered other options as he sipped breath at a small stream of fresh air flowing close to the floor from the wide open window. The drone of cars on the interstate obscured all sound.

Sometimes, flashlight in hand, the breath of mildew could be imagined as the stench of cheap oil burning low over the blackened brass of a lamp. Sure, he had as good an eye for value as any other book dealer, but it was his nose he depended on. Like a good hound, he was drawn by the smell of books, and a rare book seemed to smell that much sweeter to him. Usually his finds were little more than some early work of a once popular author, like the Patricia Wentworth he had snagged at a church rummage sale a couple of weeks before. But just the previous Saturday, he had picked over a yard sale conducted by Harvard graduate students and found a single ex-library volume of bound *Harper's* magazines from 1852 with the first published portion of Melville's *Moby Dick*.

What were his options? He could think of no other way.

Henry stood, braced himself, and lifted the wide bed free at one end, wheeling it toward the open space before the door, blocking an easy escape. Dust and odor wafted upward.

The lids of the remaining boxes made him think of small coffins exposed amidst a graveyard of settled refuse. He lifted them carefully one by one to avoid a further stirring of dust as much as to contain the possibility that they would break suddenly under their own weight.

This morning's discovery in Medford, only blocks from Tufts University, was slightly less literary. Here an embankment of three-story houses guarded a patched asphalt trough of road, narrowed further by parked cars and uncollected mounds of trash, all in the shadow of Interstate 93. What once were single-family homes now housed two and three loosely tied human gatherings, but none who cared enough to trim a shattered hedge or paint a rotting sill. It was here, cocooned in the faded green asbestos shingles of a post–World War Two renewal, he had found shoe boxes filled with paperbacks from the late 1940s and early '50s—as new as the day they were bought, read once and stashed away beneath a bed.

How could a human being sleep in the same bed for fifty years? The books beneath the bed and in the closet were the only ones not soaked by the spray of cats who had lived in the house as feral lords over the old fellow who had been found dead the week before. Choked by the smell, Henry wanted to leave from the first moment he entered. He gagged more than once as he pushed at lumps of old clothes with the broomstick he had grabbed from the kitchen below.

Books were stacked everywhere; the too frugal accumulation of years of library sales, yard sales, church sales, and probably curb side pickings. Magazines swam loose from broken bundles over the pilings of book club editions and chunky Readers Digest condensed volumes.

The man's sister was adamant.

"Garbage. What you don't take is goin' in the dumpsta. I think the peoples next door is goin' ta buy the place and tear it down."

She had called Ready Refuse Removal and hired Albert Hamilton to dispose of the junk. Albert had called Henry, as he always did when he found books.

"The place is crawling with books," Albert had said on the phone, leaving out more important detail. Henry had to discover for himself that it was mostly just the cockroaches that moved.

But the only books he could salvage were the ones in the shoe boxes—twenty-four shoe boxes in total—pushed beneath the bed years ago, perhaps forgotten, and thankfully ignored by the cats. The cats, gone now, had once belonged to the man's wife. She had occupied the rest of the small house until she had passed away herself only the previous year.

In the closet of the bedroom, wrapped in plastic grocery bags and scotch taped against the ambient filth, were hundreds of pornographic novels. Henry left those behind. He was not up to the numbing process of checking each title to see if it had been written during the struggling years by some now famous author. Nor was he interested in getting calls from the sleazy types who dealt in that subterranean literary world. Pornography was the paper-thin gratification of a life spent in a room. It was a part of the book trade he could live without.

Henry shifted the mattress back again into its corner and carried his meager find to the open air of the porch to wait. He didn't bother to look more closely at the books for fear of soiling them with his hands. Instead he studied the line of equally broken houses across the street and considered the nature of things from this angle in his life.

Things were not so bad. Not at all. But what was he up to? In the longer run, was something like this really worth it? Perhaps he would be happy with a real job. Then again, maybe not. Probably not. Definitely not.

Junior Hamilton, a white dust mask splayed like a bandage over his dark face, came by again and again with barrel loads of trash headed for the big truck. Usually talkative, Albert's son was silent in his unhappiness. This was not the kind of job even a curious seventeen-year old could appreciate.

Finally, Albert took a break from the stench of the house for lunch and drove Henry home, leaving Junior on the porch with the brown bag of sandwiches Alice had wrapped for them in wax paper. Albert hunched forward as he drove, the black skin of one forearm resting on the steering wheel highlighted by dried sweat. Though Henry was not a small man and only two years younger, sitting beside Albert made him feel like a boy riding with his father.

Henry's idle thoughts about the house made him more than a little sad for the human race, and a dispirited silence had overcome Albert as well. Henry looked for something better to talk about.

"It was the cover art that saved them. The titillation. They're mostly Popular Library editions. With some Dells I think. Odd. He kept them away from the rest because he was probably a connoisseur of Earle Bergey and Rudolph Belarski pulp art. Busty women in lurid color. Beautiful stuff but pitiful to think about in the context."

Albert was unsympathetic to Henry's prudishness. "At least he kept 'em whole. Not like the print collector you told me about who dumped the books in his basement after he razor cut all the pictures out to sell."

This was true. What was the difference between the copper plate engraving of William Hogarth and the four-color process of Earle Bergey, when reduced to the commerce of interior decoration? What was the difference between a street hooker and the call girl who worked the Ritz? The smell?

Still, Henry wondered, could the final value of a lifetime be a bunch of cheap paperbacks? He had to ask, "What's happening to all the furniture? Can it be salvaged and refinished?"

With the big truck stuttering in low gear as it drifted in the midday traffic, Albert let out a long unhappy breath and squinted against the sun. "Sure, I guess. But it's cheap stuff. Machine-made for factory workers a hundred years ago. Looks nice from a distance, but the veneer's peeling up. It's worn out. I made a couple of calls. Bernie got over there pretty quick this morning when he heard you were coming to look at the books. He's still sore—you know?—about you snagging that Morris chair last year. But he told me this stuff is all worthless, and I couldn't find anybody else interested in coming over to salvage it."

Albert would know. Albert could see the value in things. Henry knew there was no need to worry over what couldn't be saved.

"I like my chair. I think of Helen Mawson every time I sit in it. And I like my lamp. It puts the light right down where I want it when I'm reading. Bernie can shove it."

Albert grunted in perfect harmony with the motor.

"Yeah, well. I'll tell ya what. You won't believe what Alice is up to. She's gone out and bought a great big album. She's got all of Helen Mawson's letters mounted in mylar, like Junior and Danny do with their comic books. This is the woman who won't let me keep a newspaper more than a week. She's read some of those damn letters five or six times. She reads them in bed at night. I wish to hell sometimes I never found that stuff."

Henry looked out over the roofs of the cars on Massachusetts Avenue all the way to Harvard Square. More even than the filth, the sheer quantity of human congestion got to him sometimes. It was easy to imagine Helen Mawson's world and feel it must have been better than this. And still, every time Albert called him now, there was that momentary thought that maybe this time would be like that. It was foolish, of course. Most of the houses Albert cleaned out were not as bad as Medford, but they were seldom even nearly as precious as the little room in Dedham had been.

"Funny. I don't think I've been the same since I read those letters. I'm with Alice on that."

Henry tried to rub more of the crust of dried sweat and filth from his hands onto his pants. He said, "Anyway, thanks for giving me a call. I'll see you at Tim's tomorrow. And thanks for the ride."

Albert's squint became a frown, the direction of his thought clearly changed. "Your little truck fixed yet? You want to try and save any of that furniture, you can have it. Although I don't know where you'd put it. That place you live in is too damned small."

Henry knew where this was going.

"Not yet. The garage isn't done with it. Benny's ordering a part from some guy in Louisiana." Henry paused before adding the important detail—the detail he might as well get out now while they were both depressed. "And I told him to put his garage name on the side so the commercial plates would be good."

Henry's 1952 Chevrolet truck was a sore point between them. He had outbid Albert for the truck at an estate auction that spring.

Albert groaned unhappily. "I could have done that. You could have parked it with me and I could have put *my* name on the door."

There were already three trucks parked in the driveway at Albert's house in Dorchester. His son, Junior, drove the old Grumman delivery van. Alice had taken a liking to Albert's new Ford 150 since her old Buick died, so Albert drove the 350 pretty much everywhere now. He never had that far to go in any case.

Henry objected, "I don't think Alice would approve of that."

"Alice doesn't have the final say."

"No, you have the final say. And your final words are 'Yes, Alice.'"

Albert hit the palm of his hand against the steering wheel.

"That's a fine little truck…"

It was. That 1952 Chevy wasn't as bulky as the newer trucks, but it rode as high as most, and it was prettier. It would haul any lot of books Henry wanted to buy, but his desire to own it had come from somewhere else.

Henry had not known how much he wanted an old pickup like that until he saw it in the driveway at the house where the auction was held. He had grown up with a picture of a truck just like it. Even now the picture was on the desk where the bills were paid at his father's house in Brookline—a black and white Kodak picture with deckled edges of a young girl, trapped in time between glass and a plain wood frame. She was perhaps twelve years old then, standing on the running board of that truck, waving with one hand at the camera, smiling, her teeth already uneven, overalls worn white at the knees, the fingers of the other hand locked on the wood of the side gate. His grandfather Mac was in the driver's seat, stern as ever, his gaze straight ahead over the steering wheel. Henry knew he would have paid as much as he had to for the truck that day at the auction, and been happy with the price.

Henry said, "You want to get a beer now instead?"

Albert's face went from irritated to unhappy.

"Junior's waiting on me back at that pit. I can't. And Myron's in the hospital again. I'm going over for a visit later."

"That's not good."

"No."

"Any idea how long?"

Albert shook his head. "Myron never was in a hurry. He'll string it out. He's discovered daytime TV. Never made it to the golf course this summer. He uses that new nine iron I bought him to turn the TV off and on and to scratch his back…. A month, maybe."

Myron had been retired for almost twenty years. At least he had made the most of it since he passed the business on to Albert. He lived year round on the Cape now, where the snow melted earlier, and Henry had heard him brag last year that he had taken to using fluorescent golf balls so he could find them in the last drifts.

Henry could think of nothing more worth saying before Albert pulled the truck up by the gate at Mrs. Murray's.

His apartment filled the second floor of the small clapboard house, and he carried the shoe boxes up in four loads. Mrs. Murray had waved at Albert as he turned the truck around and then watched Henry skeptically from her garden at the side after he said only "Hello." She was not a nosey sort of landlady, and she had spoken only one additional word, "Shoes," with no hint of question or irony, when he made his third trip down to the porch to collect his lot.

Henry washed his face and hands in the sink before spreading a blue cloth over his kitchen table. He then opened several of the boxes and placed the small paperbacks nearly edge to edge with their covers face up. Standing on a chair with his digital camera suspended in a rigging of thin rope which he otherwise used for drying his underwear and socks, he could fit about twenty covers into a single frame with all important detail preserved. He steadied the camera and snapped his first shot, corrected the height, and took another. In less than an hour he had twenty-four good shots of all four hundred and ten books. Another five hours was spent typing up the publisher's number, the title, the author, and the illustrator. This and the digital photographs he posted on his website almost immediately—but not before eating a liverwurst sandwich and drinking a beer while again admiring the lurid color covers. He posted a link to the books in an email he sent out to his regulars customers. The email was cryptic. There was no need for lengthy descriptions in this case.

"Some bodies of books for somebody to love." He said the words out loud to be sure.

When he returned home that evening, he would probably have an offer—or several. After a week he would take the highest bid, or the one he wanted to take, or none, if it suited him.

The bookshops and dealers who bought books from Henry knew his style. He had cultivated that. There was no sense in sounding like everyone else. There was no reason to do business like other dealers, so long as it worked. He knew they joked about him. It did not matter. He was odd. So what?

Henry had borrowed his sales method from an old catalog he had found years before—the inventory of one Elmer Watkins, Books and Printed Matter. Elmer had constructed a mimeographed list of books each month and sent it out to his clients, offering them a chance to buy anything for the price of their own choosing. They could bid any price on any book. At the end of the month he notified those who had been high bidders of their purchase when he mailed his new catalog.

This was the same method Henry had used when he started selling on his own. The only change in his methods had come with the internet, when he had shortened the bid period to a week.

The internet had changed everything. Through the late 1990s, the web had taken business from most of the larger bookshops, but it had been good to him. It had made his life easier and increased his turnover. Henry sold almost exclusively to other dealers, those with state resale numbers, so that he did not have to contend with sales taxes. But though the web giveth, the web also taketh away. There had been a tenfold increase in the number of people selling books each year since, year after year, many of them small and specializing in specific areas, such as vintage paperbacks. Henry had refused to specialize, and in the odd world of bookselling, this had become his limitation.

Now he wanted a shower and a change of clothes to eliminate the lingering traces of the house in Medford. He could not as easily wash away the images of decay in his mind. That kind of thing had never been part of his plan.

He had begun on his own in 1987 with about forty clients—every one of whom he knew personally from his years working for Barbara Krause at Alcott & Poe. Her bookshop had been his college. Barbara had learned to manage by first managing him, and he had learned the book trade. Though he had almost eight hundred regular customers now, many in England, Germany, and Japan, there were still too few for him to ever get rich.

In fact, Henry had always assumed that he would never be rich. Getting rich had not been part of his plan either. He had wanted to make an honest living, and he simply liked books. Most books. He liked their shape and size and weight and smell. He liked the look of the type set upon the page, and the subtle grain of fine paper. He liked the neat crimp and curve of a Smyth sewn binding and the textures of cloth. And ever since his eyes had begun to race just ahead of his mother's hand on the page as she read aloud, he had loved to read. With the work done, he stacked the paperbacks on a shelf in the closet that filled the space beneath the stairs to the third floor. This was where he kept most of the titles he was selling. There were seldom more than two thousand books lining those walls or stacked in the file boxes on the floor. In the months since he had moved in, he had found the time to build shelves to fill the space there, but not to find a better place for his clothes, which he hung now on several rolling racks salvaged from a bankrupt clothing store. These he kept to one side of his mattress, in a bedroom already too small.

The rest of his books—the ones he kept for himself—filled a mismatched assortment of shelving on one wall of his living room, gathered around his desk. That left enough space for a couch, his Morris chair, a record turntable set over a stereo receiver on top of a narrow record cabinet, and two tall speakers in opposite corners. Most of his records were collected in small gatherings which still leaned against the single open stretch of wall opposite the books, just as they had since he moved in during the winter. He often examined the empty space of that wall with his eyes, calculating the most efficient system of shelving to hold both the records and perhaps an additional thousand titles for sale.

He stuffed the clothes with their sour smell deep into his laundry bag.

Now he deserved a treat. A reward. A week of false leads and empty promises had left him feeling a little down. It was good to have pulled something small out of all the crap he had been through of late. Way too much crap.

Especially from Della.

He let the water in the shower run cold.

She had wanted to come by again.

She had called almost every day since the last argument. But it was not going to happen. That was history. He was not that desperate. Almost, but not quite. He was getting too old to be changing his life to suit someone else's idea of how to live. He had given it a try. She was not the right one. And he was not going to end up like that old guy in the room in Medford.

He was going to go to the movies instead.

For lack of space, he stood on his bed to change clothes, and idly calculated as he buttoned his shirt. He could sling a hammock between the window frame at one end of the room and the door frame at the other. He had always wanted a hammock to sleep in. It might be cooler in the summer heat. Or it might just be a good place to dump his dirty clothes. That bag was stuffed now beneath the clothing rack closest to the door.

At last he stuffed his wallet in his back pocket and dropped down the stairs.

Della Toth was sitting on the top rail of the wooden fence of the house across the street when Henry came out. She was wearing a dress instead of her usual pants, and swinging her legs. She had turned thirty-three just two months before, but she often seemed to him like an overgrown school girl. She had nice legs. She knew that.

She jumped and trailed after him. "Where you goin'?"

He tried to ignore her. "Out."

Della came up right behind him. She smelled good, and she knew that too.

"They're running some heartfelt documentaries at the Coolidge. The Capital is just doing last month's action retreads. The Brattle has Preston Sturges. You want some Preston Sturges, I can tell."

One thing that always bothered him was that she somehow knew what he was up to. He had habits. He liked habits. They were comfortable. They made things work. She was always taking advantage of his habits.

He said, "I need air-conditioning and popcorn."

She came up along side of him. "So do I." She said this as if it should be obvious.

It also bothered him that she could look him in the eye. It was not that he was that short. It was just that she was that tall.

He said, "Why don't you leave me alone?"

He looked over at her as they walked. He liked her hair cut shorter. It curled on its own and picked up the light in the yellow. It reminded him of someone.

She said, "Because you need me. You're a loser without me. I am your muse."

He really hated the fact that she was so direct. He wished he knew a girl who could be kind—a little more gentle—with the facts of life. That was not Della.

He said, "Why don't you go find Bob? I'll bet he likes action films."

"He's on my shit list."

"Put me on that list too, will you?"

"But I love you. I don't love Bob."

"Anymore."

"Anymore."

He had never before had to compete for a woman with another man. He was not about to begin.

Bob—the world's authority on nearly everything. He had met Bob once, by accident, and it still made Henry's toes curl.

They walked several blocks in silence. The pale evening light of June caught high in the trees. It was too bad he was with Della. It was a nineteenth century kind of light. Romantic. Overlapping variations of green parted into chasms of evening blue. With his eyes high, his shoe caught an edge and he stumbled awkwardly on some sidewalk bricks turned up by the roots of a tree.

She seemed to have missed his near pratfall when she spoke. "It's kinda European out. The way it stays light late in the evening, just like England."

She knew he had never been to Europe. Why would she bring this up? It was another sore point.

He said, "Ah, to be in England—" but he was not good at sarcasm.

She interrupted, "We could go together. I have two weeks vacation coming. We could go in September or October after the tourists are gone."

He could not tell her that he liked the idea. She would have everything planned within days, right down to the room numbers at the hotels.

"I don't have any extra money. I don't want to go into debt just to take a vacation."

Della had often spoken of seeing Eastern Europe. Her mother had escaped from Hungary in the revolution of 1956. She wanted to see Budapest. She still had family there. This brought back to Henry the question of who it was her short cut hair reminded him of. She looked a lot like Ingrid Bergman in an old film he had seen—*For Whom the Bell Tolls*. He had not liked Hemingway's book. It was not Hemingway at his best. The Old Man was trying too hard. But Henry still liked the film because of Bergman.

As they approached along Brattle Street, it was Henry who saw Bob first—the large figure occupying the very front of the line waiting to enter the theatre. Bob was getting a belly. Football players always ended up with bellies. His hair was longer since the last computer company he had worked for had shut down. Henry thought the long hair was probably more to hide a bald spot.

But this was no accident. Bob had managed to find out that Della wanted to see the Preston Sturges. Bob was that kind of competitor. Bob knew the laws of supply and demand. There was only one Della. And Henry was not going to sit in a row with Bob.

Henry abruptly turned and headed back. Della hesitated, but she kept going. She said nothing. It bothered Henry more than he liked that she kept going. He did not look back.

The world appeared suddenly darker as he walked. The sun was gone from the treetops. The distances seemed to have grown.

The narrow three-story building where Henry lived had once been a single-family house and later been divided as simply as possible by Mrs. Murray after her husband had died. She lived on the first floor. Sasha, a music student who was seldom home, lived above Henry on the third. The front door, which gave access to the first floor as well as the stairs, was often left unlocked during the day when Mrs. Murray was there. It was a quiet dead-end street, occasionally disrupted by arguments over parking spaces, but not often visited by strangers. Henry was surprised to find someone sitting on the stairs in the half-dark as he entered—a small man he thought he knew.

"Henry. Been waiting for ya…. Got a deal. Hav'a friend who's just laid a good item off on me. It's over at my place in Central Square. A nice item."

"Hello." Henry said, and waited for him to respond. There was a beat of silence before the fellow spoke again.

"Hello. Like I said. It's real nice. Some good money. The guy needed the cash. I'm willing to sell it quick for cheap. Can you handle it?"

"Your name is Eddy?" Henry remembered him now. He had aged quite a bit in a few years. Thinning hair was combed over from the side of his head. His face was lean and he had lost weight in his shoulders. He had not shaved for at least a couple of days.

The man responded without a hesitation. "Right. What do you think?"

"I think it's kind of odd for you to be waiting for me this time of night to sell me a book. Is it stolen?"

The shake of the man's head came attached to a shiver of his body. "No way. It's only eight o'clock. The night's still young. And it's only one book. If you can't do it, I gotta get movin'. I gotta get my cash back tonight."

Henry answered with unnecessary sarcasm. "For food, right?"

There was no shake of Eddy's head this time. "No. I work at a restaurant now. I eat fine. I'm clean. I'm off the stuff…. That's a fact. But there's a book auction tomorrow—you know. In Newton. And all my money's tied up. I gotta get a little back so I'll have somethin' to use tomorrow."

Henry had decided not to go to Newton. It was an estate auction. Perhaps he had made a mistake. Maybe there was something there to see. Eddy seemed very intent on it.

Henry said, "Why didn't you bring the book with you?"

Eddy leaned his head to the side and examined the wallpaper. "I didn't plan it out that way. I was over this way for something else. The idea just hit me to check with you before I went home."

Henry smiled at the evasion.

"I don't keep cash around Eddy."

The man's eyebrows rose in perfect arcs. "You got a card for the bank machine, right?"

Henry tried to see what was in the man's eyes. Was he desperate? Was there any panic?

"What kind of book is it?"

The eyebrows fell. "Arkham House."

That was a limited market, Henry knew, but it was steady.

17

"Recent?"

"Nah. From nineteen forty-three; *Beyond the Wall of Sleep*, in jacket."

A rare book, limited market or not. Henry had never cultivated a taste for the hothouse atmosphere of H. P. Lovecraft's world of horror fiction.

"How did you come by it?"

"A friend. I said a friend before, didn't I?"

There was a hint of irritation in his answer, as well as the sound of New York. Henry guessed that Eddy had been raised there.

The last Henry knew, Eddy was a drug addict. Eddy Perry had once run a small used bookstore right in Harvard Square, above the old Wursthaus. That was years ago.

Henry considered the possibilities.

"I don't deal in stolen books, Eddy."

Eddy's cheeks puffed where he had lost teeth. The unshaved grey stubble there made him appear older than he was. "Don't shit me. I'm not a thief. I got this legit. I passed two Benjamin's for it. The guy needed the money and I saw I could double it. What's wrong with that?"

Henry shrugged, as if unconcerned. There was no point in upsetting this man. He seemed to remember Eddy upset easily.

"Was the book his to start with?"

"Yeah. It was me who sold it to him in the first place—once upon a time…" he hesitated, and repeated the words. "Once upon a time, I bought it as part of a collection, years back. I sold it to the guy when he was flush."

Henry was not in the mood for sitting alone at home. "I'll take a look."

He began to regret his decision from that moment.

Eddy was out the door with his words. "Follow me."

Henry stayed a step to the rear. Eddie chatted, his questions broken by long silences as they made their way to Central Square.

"How's business?"

"Quiet."

Eddy said, "Summers were always quiet at my old place. Didn't pick up till the Harvard students got back in August. Tourists don't buy books."

Henry noticed the man's feet as he answered. Eddy's black cloth sneakers were worn through in places above the rubber soles.

Henry told him, "I don't have to deal with the public anymore. I'm online. Just dealers."

Eddie blew air into his cheeks. "Whew. It's a new world out there. The machines talk to each other and the people watch TV."

Henry was surprised by the comment and considered it silently as they circled to a street behind, and a narrow house sandwiched between several others just like it. The smell of spoiled milk and coffee grounds filled the hall. Eddy opened a double-locked door which had clearly been kicked in several times before and repaired with a metal plate.

Paperback and hardcover thrillers were piled in a jumble on a mantle above a fireplace which had long since been plastered over. The apartment was small, but still bare of any real furnishing. A grey metal office desk filled the space below the single window. Yellowing newspapers partially buried a heavy black Royal typewriter, a relic of the 1930s. The bed had been left unmade and covered with a blue wool blanket that showed the lumps of wadded sheets. There was no television set. No radio that Henry could see. No pictures on the wall. A cheap plastic frame sat on the desk behind the papers, but he could see little of the picture it contained.

The book in question was face up on a card table at the center of the room. The dust jacket had been carefully encased in clear plastic, making it look very neat. On the endpaper, a penciled name had been erased, but the indentation remained visible. He knew the name immediately.

"I remember that sale…"

Eddy nodded. "Can you imagine people with that kind of money who don't take care of themselves?"

"Yes." Henry answered. He had gone to such auctions many times over the years.

He had always thought it was a funny name—Hale Peabody. It made Henry think of the phrase "Hail, Caesar." The family had once been among the rulers of business in Boston and Salem. Henry had also been in that house at Prides Crossing on the North Shore during the auction about fifteen years before. The prices were way above his head that day, but Henry had managed to buy one book, a small vellum volume of Cicero for twenty dollars. He had been the only one to spot the pale brown ink inscription and the numerous notations throughout the text for what they were. The book had once belonged to Thomas Jefferson. From the notes, it appeared Jefferson had sent it to John Adams some time shortly after the War of 1812, with the intent of making a point in an ongoing argument. Jefferson's signature was clear, if crammed a bit below the notation on the flyleaf. This page had fastened lightly over time to the free endpaper, and gone unnoticed. Only God knew how Hale Peabody had acquired it, or why he had owned a book collection of weird horror stories by the likes of H. P. Lovecraft.

Eddy leaned in over the table. "He had all the good ones. I only paid about nine hundred dollars and I got twenty-five early Arkham House editions that day." It sounded like a boast, but then it might just be a fond memory. All booksellers kept such moments in mind to tide them over the bad decisions.

Henry asked, "What happened to the rest?"

Eddy shrugged his shoulders. Bones pressed against the cloth of his shirt.

"Sold 'em all. Sold 'em at my old store. You remember that place, don't you? It was the science fiction fans who used to pay my rent there. Nobody gives a damn about Cervantes anymore. Had a set of the Boswell journals when I opened up. I was there twelve years. Managed to read through the whole damn thing during slow times. Knew it was time to close the place for good when I finished the last volume."

Henry nodded and Eddy let him inspect the book in silence. This copy of *Beyond the Wall of Sleep* had been read more than once. The binding opened freely. But there was no significant wear. The paper was cream white and without a dirty fingerprint—unusual enough for the war years when the paper used was of a lower grade. The black cloth had the sheen of its original state, the bottom edge was unscuffed by shelf wear. The book itself was still in fine condition, but the dust jacket was better described as near fine—no visible soiling, slight yellowing, with a small nick at the top of the backstrip and a closed tear of less than a quarter inch. When Henry finally spoke, he was only saying out loud the thought in his head.

"Funny thing is, that the Peabody family fortune was made on the opium trade in China."

Eddy shrugged. "Is that right. Is that so? What goes around comes around, don't it? Hale Peabody liked the horses and the horse they say. Well…so. What will you give me?"

Henry had not heard the term "horse" for heroin since he was a kid. He looked at Eddy's eyes. They were clear.

He said, "Three hundred."

Eddy did not wince. "It's worth two thousand."

Henry nodded. "I could go four."

Eddy wagged his head. "Four-fifty."

They both knew it would be less than five at the start. The dance was only a sort of handshake, to make it official. In fact, Henry would be selling the book again wholesale for less than half its potential value to the right dealer.

Eddy now followed as Henry carried the book wrapped in a brown grocery bag back to Harvard Square, purposely skipping a closer branch of his bank, just to be in a more public place when he withdrew the money.

The Square was busy. The plaza at Holyoke Center was thick with an evening mix of students and street people. The drum of a musician on overturned buckets punctuated the din of talk and traffic.

A policeman, one foot up on the curb and head half turned, seemed to be keeping an eye on the underage crowd gathered in the brick-lined "pit" behind the subway entrance.

"June 24th, 2003," flashed in green from a glass strip in the stainless steel face of the bank machine. Another insisted on the time. It was 9:37.

The machine sucked in Henry's bank card with the purr of an animal, but then refused his request. He punched in half the amount. The tongue of bills Henry pulled from the slot were new and stuck together in the warm air. He used his credit card to extract the rest in the same fashion. Eddy counted it twice, hunching his shoulders as he did, and using his scrawny frame to block the view of anyone interested. Henry saw the cop turn toward them and then away again.

Eddy said, "Deal."

Henry nodded. "Good. Have fun at the auction."

They parted at the enclosure for the bank machine, going in opposite directions. Eddy's last words were, "Catch ya later."

Henry walked back slowly, trying to enjoy the night. Recent days of rain had left things clean. A small wedge of moon held a cloud apart long enough to overcome the city lights. On narrow sidewalks he stepped aside for couples. The fleeting thought crossed his mind that he had forgotten something or was headed in the wrong direction. He was going home alone, with a book in his hand. It did not seem enough.

He arranged the book on his kitchen table, as he had done with the paperbacks earlier, but photographed it several times from different angles. He removed the jacket and photographed the book standing up with the title page visible. Then he uploaded the images to his computer and sent out his second email of the day, this time including the basic bibliographic information cribbed from an old catalog. His collection of catalogs on the specialties he was less familiar with filled two shelves beside the couch. This left him hungry again and he put his mind on a cool beer.

Someone knocked on his door—a familiar knock. He opened it without asking. Della was there, and came in talking.

"Is that your landlady on the front porch? She seems nice— like somebody's aunt. The movie was good, but Bob can be a real jerk. Likes to control everything. Take charge. But I've told you that before. What are you doing?" She made a direct line for the book on the table. Henry had not yet spoken, or even smiled. Her string of banter continued. "Cool…Always up to something. Busy, busy, busy. Did you get this while I was watching your namesake trying not to fall in love with Veronica Lake? He didn't succeed. Neither will you."

Henry opened his arms dramatically. "That's what I really ought to do. I ought to run away. Take a trip—Like *Sullivan's*

Travels. See what the world looks like on the other side of the Connecticut River."

She did not pause. "But you've been to Northampton. You want to go in the other direction. You want to go to Budapest." She paged the book. "This stuff is weird."

She was suddenly ignoring him, reading random paragraphs. That was another thing he did not like. She was a speed-reader. He had failed to convince her to read more slowly, to enjoy the use of words. But then, she read such crap—why dawdle?

"You're right. I've been all the way to Northampton. What I really want is a beer, and the fridge is empty." He motioned her toward the door again.

"Good idea…As always." She kept reading, without making a move to leave.

He said, "That's not your kind of stuff," and nudged her. "Lovecraft was a misogynist."

She finally turned to him. "What are you doing with it then? You love women. What's it worth?"

Why did she suddenly want to know that? She seldom expressed any interest in his books.

"Enough to bother with. The dealers will make their offers, and I'll take the best I get. Come on."

She turned her head a little sideways and raised her eyebrows at him. He wished she wouldn't use color on her eyebrows. She did not know how to use makeup. She was a natural blond, and she had the silly idea that her eyebrows disappeared without additional color.

She said, "Books are not a living. They're a hobby. You want to make a living—you get a job and I'll marry you and we'll have two and a half kids and you can do this on the side and we'll live happily ever after."

"With Bob?"

"Bob is a jerk. He tried to feel me up while we were watching the movie."

Henry shook his head. "That wouldn't be because you gave him the wrong signals or anything, right?"

"Right! I just wanted to go to the movies. I knew you weren't going to sit there with him on the other side of me, trying to feel me up or not. Now, if you both had been feeling me up, that would have been different, but you just can't share, can you?"

"No."

"See? That's why I love you and not Bob. It's a Solomon kind of thing."

"A what?"

"Like Solomon. Like the two women and the baby. You're the mother who wouldn't share, and I'm the baby."

"So now you're saying I'm a mother?" He exaggerated the look on his face. She always had the oddest analogies.

But he never had the chance to analyze that idea further.

There was another knock on the door—not familiar. Then a voice.

"Cambridge Police. Henry Sullivan?"

Henry looked at Della, who looked back at him without expression. He liked the idea that she was slow to panic.

He opened the door on two uniformed officers standing at either side of the frame, as if he was about to shoot his way out.

Chapter Two

His eyes followed the perfect arc of Varitek's home run and stopped at the sweeping edge of the lettering on the John Hancock sign as the ball fell to the bleachers. The sign did not have the same comfortable feel as the old red and white Hood Milk billboard. And Henry could not remember just then what standard had been replaced by the pale colors of the Dunkin Donuts sign. Everything was changing, and he had not been to as many games lately as he would have liked. He felt a wave of complaint rise inside of him.

He wished he were a snob. Why didn't it bother him that he was nearly forty years old—very nearly—and his best friend was a garbage man? He should have gone to college, if for no other reason than to have a better grade of friends to hang with. Why should he be satisfied with this? He should have season tickets. Box seats, maybe. He could have been a snob, if he had tried. Albert hated snobs. It was worth at least an hour's ranting. Henry was about to disclose this newly discovered wish when Albert spoke first.

"You stink."

Henry started from the reverie which overlaid his concentration on the game. "What?"

How could Albert distinguish Henry's smell amidst the hot breath of Fenway Park? The kid with the cardboard tray of nachos directly behind them was chewing with his mouth open. The kid's father had spilled half his beer onto the cement, and it was drooling among the peanut shells at Henry's feet. Because

Johnny Damon could slice a ball their way any time, Henry wanted to keep his eyes on the batter.

And that was another thing. That was a complaint for the ages. He had never gotten a foul ball since he was a kid, not even close, and he was almost forty.

Albert leaned Henry's way. "Just something I noticed. I think it's the books. It's the mildew. It's the rot."

Henry defended himself without turning. "All I smell is beer and peanuts—and garbage. You can't smell anything because you're so used to the garbage."

Albert reacted as if he were hit.

"What garbage? I changed my clothes. I took a shower. There's no garbage on me."

Henry had an answer, but he wanted to keep his eye on Johnny Damon. The Detroit pitcher was really letting his fastball ride up. But Henry had a good comeback, even if it would be a waste to use it just now. He could say, "How would you know if you had any garbage on you? You can't smell worth a damn."

Or he could mention Teddy Morris. Any mention of Teddy Morris was worth ten minutes of Albert's ire.

But Henry didn't feel up to it. He was not on his own game today, much less the real deal in front of his eyes. Henry decided to appease, instead.

"I knew a girl once who worked over at the Necco candy factory. She always smelled so sweet. You just wanted to lick her."

Albert's answered as if uninterested in deténte. "You mean Mandy. I remember Mandy. She didn't smell. That's just your dirty mind."

Damon swung beneath another fast-ball and was gone.

Henry was not in the mood for any more verbal wrestling. The real problem was that Albert was still unhappy with Henry about buying tickets for seats so far beyond third base. Henry had drawn the short straw to stand in line with several hundred other fools during a freezing rain in February, and he had screwed up. He had overslept. He had never overslept for anything else in his life. Not that he could remember. Even in December he was one of the first in line at the Hubley book auction, huddling in the early morning dark at that metal gate and stomping his feet against the cold. He couldn't even blame Della. They had just started dating at the time, but she had gone home early that night. It just happened. And this was their fourth game of the year and Albert was still complaining.

Albert seemed to swell in his seat. This was part of the punishment. Already too large for the narrow seats offered by the cheap Red Sox management, Albert grew larger at times like this, his elbows and forearms overlapping the metal armrests, his knees hard against the seat in front of him. Children often cried if unfortunate enough to be stuck behind Albert. Grown people whispered and whined to their partners. In fact, Albert was not over six foot four—only a couple inches taller than Henry. It was the breadth of his shoulders that made the difference.

Henry leaned forward so that their shoulders did not meet. He said, "Things get in your pores. You can't get them out. It's like a coal miner with the black grit beneath the skin. They can't get rid of it. You can't let it go. You can't get over it. Like some people are with other people's mistakes. So, you think I smell like books—"

"Nasty old rotten books," Albert added.

"…but you smell like—"

"Dove soap. It's the only kind Alice ever buys."

"…garbage."

They both stared out at the field between innings. Henry knew Albert's mind was working on something more and he waited on it. Let him make the next move.

Albert poked a finger into the air. "Now, not like my boys! That's a real smell. Pure locker-room. That's what Alice calls their bedroom. The locker-room. They stuff their dirty clothes under their beds. Danny has taken to using a hair gel that draws flies. Junior is doing three sports at school this year. Alice makes him do his own laundry, so he waits until things get stiff before he washes them."

Henry let out a short laugh. "It's all in your mind. Like those guys you read about who lose a leg and still think they can feel their toes. The stench of ripe garbage has numbed your senses. You wish you could smell, so you imagine it. You wish you could smell as good as I do."

Albert ignored that line of reasoning. "Coal grit? Missing legs? It's that book leather I'm talking about. Leather comes from dead bodies. It's just rotting skin."

Henry had to admit, that was good. He liked that. He had no verbal maneuver to better it. Henry was not going to be able to win this one.

"You've never even smelled a dead body. How would you know? The leather is tanned. It oxidizes."

Albert turned to Henry suddenly, his voice a little lower. He had been reminded of something. "Do they know yet what happened to that poor guy?"

Henry was glad for the change of direction. "I called the detective back after they questioned me the last time. It was probably just a robbery. Eddy had my four hundred and fifty dollars on him. People have been killed for less. God only knows what Eddy had hidden in that apartment. They asked me more than once if I had noticed anything when I went in there. I guess the place was ransacked afterwards. They have no idea what might have been stolen. Eddy hung out with the wrong people. And I guess druggies get killed all the time." He paused and then added, "The cops don't seem to care as much as I do."

There was another fly ball and the inning was over.

Albert said, "There've been a few of those type of things in Cambridge, lately. Someone's killing druggies, like they're not going to die soon enough on their own."

Henry studied the Boston bullpen again. A reliever was up but he could not quite see the number on the shirt. He was a righty. They needed a lefty. "That's another reason not to read the papers," Henry answered. "The auction announcements are the only section worth looking at."

Albert turned to him, "Are you ever going to get the book back?"

Henry shrugged. "Cops still have it. I think they'll return it to me at some point. I have an order on hold already."

"Stinks."

"Right."

Albert shook his head and stared out at the field. "Lot's of things stink."

Henry held back an additional thought and looked toward the bleachers, as he often did, to find the seats he and his sister and the old man used to sit in.

Albert nudged him with his shoulder.

"You want your beer now? It's my turn."

Henry nodded.

The fifth inning had started as Albert rose from his seat and someone behind them shouted for him to sit down. Albert glared back and moved down the row without waiting.

Henry took the opportunity to look past him and peek again at the redhead directly behind the visitor's dugout. She was amazing by all standards, and it was not a coincidence that he had to look over the backs of so many other heads along the line of sight. The tall fellow beside her was George Duggan, twice her age, and not her father. Some authors lived better than others. It was the way the system worked. Some authors lived better than a hundred others, Henry thought idly. Henry had sold Duggan's very first novel about Boadicea at least a dozen times over the years, each time for more. A fine copy was now going for a thousand dollars and up, online. He could still remember the first one he had sold for Barbara at Alcott & Poe sometime around 1984, for twelve bucks, and glad to get it.

The batter for Detroit put a ball into the bullpen, just short of the outstretched arms in the bleachers.

Henry recalculated the trajectory of the ball as if it were coming right at him, just as it did when he used to bring his glove—Shelagh used to wear his father's old glove to the games, because she liked the look of it, and he was always jealous of that small and beaten thing, even as proud as he had been of the new mitt he had bought for himself. The three of them used to sit in the bleachers just there above the bullpen and look in at the box seats.

The old man called them the swell seats, but he meant the seats for the swells. His father earned decent money. He was union, but he always had extra work. They were not poor, in any case, and all the seats were a lot cheaper then. They could have afforded better. But it was part of a way of thinking. It was something Henry hoped he had left behind. "Use it up. Wear it out. Make it do, or do without," his father used to say. Always buy what was on sale. Never pay full price. Henry hated it. It was like an infection in his blood. It was somehow the exact opposite of greed or avarice. Not frugality, but parsimony. Niggardliness. It was the compulsion not to want. The desire not to have. The need not to wish. It was one of the things which had made his sister Shelagh run off with Rick long ago.

She had been Henry's buddy. After their mother died, it was Shelagh who had taken over the house. It was Shelagh who had coached Henry through algebra and chemistry. Except for the money, she could have gone to any school she wanted, but the University of Massachusetts was the only one the old man would allow. She had tried that for more than a year, taking the bus each day out to Dorchester, taking care of homework and housekeeping at night, and waiting tables at Vinnie's on weekends. She had managed it all until the day she ran away.

Not long after that, it was Albert who had first taken Henry to the ballpark one July, and had bought the better seats. "Why sit in the bleachers if you don't have to?" These came as words of revelation. It had become something of a motto with Henry since then. "Why sit in the bleachers if you don't have to?"

Nomar Garciaparra launched himself from his position at shortstop and extended in the air for a ball, flipping it to the second baseman before his own feet touched the ground again. The crowd erupted. But the Sox were still down by two.

Albert was right, of course, but Henry was given to twisting it around a little. In the new world of city-bound SUVs and three-dollar cups of coffee, it was an easy motto to lampoon. "Why sit in the bleachers?"

What if Henry had pulled a "Teddy Morris"? There was no stink on Teddy Morris any more. Henry could have gone to college and worked for a big corporation, owned a second house on the Cape, a condo in Vermont, and two cars, supported his second wife in better style than his first, raised a teenage daughter who was pregnant with no idea who the father was and a son who stole money from his wallet, had a fifty-inch plasma TV with all the channels, and died young after the second bypass.

Henry usually raised Teddy Morris out of the grave when drinking beers with Albert at the Blue Thorn, just because it was worth more even than the mention of a snob. The only thing worse to Albert than a snob was somebody who had it all and threw it away.

Henry considered this bit of dark fantasy now as an alternative to his riff on snobbery. It was certainly a better topic for idle ballgame chatter than whether Henry stank. Someone might overhear that and misunderstand. Whatever device Henry chose, Albert needed a jolt. Albert was being too smug. He needed a hit. He needed a cold chill down the spine of the cozy little world he had made for himself, if for no other reason than Albert had not given up on his fit over the tickets. He had raved about it for half an hour before the game. Henry was tired of it. Albert had brought it up a dozen times in the past month. Henry had paid. He was paying. He would stick it to Albert when he returned because he knew Albert's weakness.

Albert had gone to college. Albert could have been a lawyer and filled the affirmative-action slot at some big firm downtown and made a fortune. He had passed the frigging exams, for Christ sake. He had the freakin' scholarship. He could have gone to Yale. But what had he done? He had stuck with Myron Evans. He had taken over Myron's refuse removal business. He was a garbage man. A big, smug, and happy garbage man.

But it was Albert who spoke first again as he handed Henry his beer.

"Sweet Mother of Mercy, that girl is stacked."

Everybody was looking at the redhead. Diverted, Henry sipped his beer and considered his knowledge of the subject.

"You think they're real?"

Henry could never tell at a distance. Mandy, the girl he had dated from the Necco candy factory, had been blessed by God and they were real. But how could you tell from a distance?

Albert shook his head. "Nah. It's the lift. See the lift? Real ones that big would droop."

Henry turned and studied the matter. The crowd around him rose to their feet. He turned toward the field in time to see a fly ball enter the upheld hands of the fellow directly in front of him.

Sweet Mother of Mercy! Henry closed his eyes on the thought.

"You could'a had that," Albert said. "It was yours."

It was his, the one he had been waiting for.

He kept hearing Albert's voice well into the night, well after they stopped at the Blue Thorn on the way home. They sat at the bar and leaned into the wood. The Red Sox had lost. They had lost to frigging Detroit.

"You were at least a foot higher." Albert raised a hand above Tim's head across the bar to dramatize that matter. "It was on your side. It was yours. I should have reached over myself, but it was yours."

Henry pleaded his case to Tim's unforgiving eyes. "I didn't see it."

Albert repeated, "It was in front of your face."

Tim said, "I know you. You were looking at some girl. I'll bet you were staring at some girl."

Tim wiped the already clean counter once more for effect and walked away.

Tim could be annoying. He was taking his new role as a father too seriously. Bartenders could not afford to be prudes.

Albert nursed his glass with a smile caught in his cheeks. Henry finished his own beer as he re-imagined the moment yet again. The ball was right there.

Henry reconsidered his plan to put an elbow into Albert's soft spot as a way to get him back. But Albert beat him to the punch once more.

"Will they have a funeral for the book junkie?"

It was not Henry's day. He must have missed some sleep. Albert had been one up on him all the way. He gave up.

"No. I don't think he had a family. No prayers for the book hound."

Henry had not known whom to ask.

Albert looked at Henry in the mirror across the bar. "What happens? Cremation?"

Henry shook his head. "I don't know."

"Alice's mother was cremated," Albert added. "She wanted it that way. She was cheap to the end."

Henry shook his head again with nothing to add.

His own mother's funeral had been short. His father would not have it drawn out. She was buried at Mount Auburn near a cluster of chestnut trees. His father had picked that spot himself. Give the old man credit for that, at least. He hadn't been cheap when it mattered most.

Henry remembered little of it. Probably because he was bawling his eyes out. Twelve is too young to lose a mother. Shelagh was the one who had always said the ceremony had been too short. But Henry had been up there a hundred times since, and he had always thought his mother would have liked the spot. When she was alive, she had kept a few dried chestnuts, collected during her frequent walks, on the little table near her bed. For good luck, she said.

Henry put his finger up to catch Tim's attention for another beer and pushed the image of his mother out of his head. Albert seemed to be waiting for more detail.

Henry said, "Eddy Perry was an odd little fellow. Looked like one of those guys you see at the racetrack."

"You ever sell anything to him?"

"No. He lost his store not long after I quit working for Barbara. But I saw him around a few times."

Albert squinted at him. "But something still bothers you about it?"

It was true. Something was still bothering Henry about Eddy Perry. Why?

"Yeah…. Maybe it's just the image of an old bookseller coming to a sad end. I saw his apartment. He had nothing left. I don't know how he was getting by, but it seemed so damn desolate. And then there's that place we went to—the guy with the shoe boxes—seeing them both the same day. It was a pretty bleak picture."

Albert grunted, finished his beer, and shook his head. Henry prepared for the inevitable rant. "I see it every damn week. You've seen it before yourself. It's just people who don't take care of themselves. They don't know what to do with their lives. They're lost. Life is really so simple. You either fish or cut bait. But these days it looks to me like half the people out there just want to eat. They don't want to fish. They don't want to cut bait. They just say, 'Fry it up in a good cornmeal batter please, and cut me a lemon for the side, thank you.' They don't have the faintest idea even how to fish. They don't want to learn. They won't get out of bed in time to cut bait. They just want to eat. And then they make a mess. Don't even clean up after themselves. I worked sixty hours last week. You know that. Sixty hours. And half of it went to taxes. City of Boston raised the taxes on my house again last year just because I keep it up. Doesn't pay. I ought to let it fall down."

Albert stopped talking long enough to drink the rest of his beer in one long swallow. Henry took the opportunity.

"What does that have to do with Eddy Perry?"

Albert answered, still irritated.

"Everything!"

Albert's unified trash-field theory was not Henry's favorite.

Henry said, "Eddy was just a drug addict with a love for books—"

Albert interrupted. "Another lost soul."

"A lost soul, maybe." Henry kept talking. He wanted to make his point now. "I wonder about that. I'd like to find out. I'd like to find out what happened to his soul."

Albert turned and looked at him with a big eye.

"You only had two beers. You're not ready to talk like that."

Henry hunched his shoulders with both forearms on the bar, and grasped his glass between both hands. He felt like hunkering down. He might be getting sick. He was never sick, but this might be the time. It was that kind of day.

He said, "I had one more at the game."

Albert's voice was not forgiving. "That was no better than water. It's too early in the evening to be talking about finding souls."

"I just wonder who he was."

"You're feeling your mortality. It's just you turning forty."

"I'm not forty yet. You don't have to be religious to believe in a soul."

"Damn near."

Henry persisted. "It's just what a person is, without the ugly details of dental floss and toilet paper."

"A dirty stinky person."

"The essence—"

Albert interrupted again, "The perfume of a week's worth of garbage."

Henry answered, "A person is more than the sum total of their garbage."

Albert raised an eyebrow at him. "Is that *your* philosophy then?"

Henry sat back. "Eddy Perry was a bookseller. How did he become a bookseller?" He looked at Albert as if the question might be guessed.

Albert scowled. "You can't expect to understand what motivates everyone. It's usually just the path of least resistance that takes folks along."

Henry said, "I'd like to know.... Someone has to bother."

Albert said, "I guess it doesn't hurt me, one way or the other. You've heard me say it before, ninety percent of everything is trash. Sooner or later, I'll have to haul it. I'm in the only business there is with a guaranteed future."

Henry turned his head to look at Albert's face. "Doesn't that depress you a little?"

Albert grimaced a bit with the thought. "No. Yeah. Sometimes. Not often. Sometimes you can see a life there. You can see the geology of a person's life in the layers of trash they accumulate. You see what they cared about. Their taste in clothes. The cereal they liked to eat. The kind of music they listened to. It's no different really than the rest of mother nature. Layer after layer. It's just the turning forty thing that's got a hold of you, Henry. You're starting to feel like things don't last forever. Time to start living before you start dying."

Henry blew a low whistle at the image. "A pleasant thought. I don't think Eddy had enough to speak of geologically. It didn't look to me like he had anything at all."

Albert worked Henry's thought a bit further. "And you're wondering what you'll have in the end. Aren't you? Who is going to say a prayer for Henry Sullivan when he goes?"

Tim spoke from the far end of the bar. "You know, Henry, you ought to get married. You need a wife."

Henry shook his head in disbelief. "Jesus, you are something else, Tim. It took the combined efforts of both Albert and myself to get you out of that one-room studio in Charlestown. I still have a piece of the wedding cake in my freezer. You have no authority on the subject. Not yet."

Tim looked back directly at Albert and spoke in tones of pity. "He's going to die a lonely man, all by himself. Who's going to come to his funeral when some shelf of books falls down on his stupid head?"

Henry sat up straight from his slump. He knew the right answer to that.

"Alice will come. Alice will be at the funeral just to be sure I won't be coming over afterwards for any fried chicken."

Albert's laugh quieted the voices behind them in the bar.

Chapter Three

Henry."
It was Barbara's voice. She never said "Hello" when she called on the phone. He pretended not to know who it was, just to irritate her.

"Who is this?"

She ignored him. "Wake up. I read in the papers that you were questioned by the police."

She could tell by his voice that he had been sleeping.

He chided her. "That's old news. You're behind on your reading."

"You're right about that. Time has been a little tight around here. What happened?"

He took a breath to get a bit more oxygen into his brain for a good answer.

"All I did was buy a book. I don't know. But Eddy Perry is dead."

Barbara had known Eddy, though Henry could not help but wonder if there was some other reason for her call. Henry had not been in Alcott & Poe in weeks, and he could not remember when they had last spoken.

"Very sad.... I guess he'll never write the book he used to talk about."

The concern in her voice was real. She cared about Eddy, but then she cared about almost everyone. "Earth Mother," he used to call her.

Henry remembered seeing the typewriter on the desk in Eddy's apartment. "What kind of book?"

"I don't know. Just something I heard him say more than once. I only saw him in the store now and again. You know, I was afraid he might be stealing, because of the drugs and all. But he was always friendly. I think he liked to talk to me. I never heard him say more than a few words to Sharon or anyone else, but he always seemed to like me."

Her assistant, Sharon, was a different story—an ice queen by comparison to Barbara. Most people liked Barbara. She was the nosy, assuming, irritating, opinionated, outspoken, well meaning type that everyone was fond of. She had easily over-whelmed Henry during the years he had worked for her.

"He was a sad case. Had he sold anything to you recently?"

"Not in a while. You know we've been a little short on capital lately. But someone else told me they saw Eddy making the rounds with a few items some months back. I think he was trying to get something going again with selling books. I think he might have been getting back on his feet."

"I guess that makes it even sadder."

There was a silence that made it clear Barbara was trying to work her way toward another topic.

She said, "But, you're okay. You didn't lose much?"

"Fine. No. Everything is fine. I might be out four hundred and fifty dollars, but I have enough coming in to cover it."

She paused. He knew the amount was not important to her. She was working toward something else.

"If you need any help, you can ask, you know. I won't bite."

"I don't remember any biting."

He was sorry he said it, as soon as the words were out.

"You're being nasty."

"I didn't bring it up."

There was another brief silence.

"How's Miss Toth?" Barbara's tone of voice had somehow changed. Just a nuance. It was funny how she remembered names. The second time he had taken Della out on a date they had bumped into Barbara at the Gardner Museum.

"She's fine." He knew she would want more.

"Are you still going out with her?"

"No." The less he said, the better.

"That was quick. You looked pretty serious."

"It didn't work out."

"Sorry. I know you only take the girls you're serious about to the Gardner."

"Is that so?"

"It's where you took me, the first time you took me anywhere."

"I guess so."

"It was sweet."

He was not going to say anything else. He let a moment of silence break the chain. He could see the pattern and knew where this was headed. She finally spoke.

"You want to go to dinner sometime and talk?"

"Thanks. No."

"I'll bite."

"Thanks. But no."

"All right…. But, you can still come up and see me sometime."

"Okay."

She hung up without saying goodbye.

Barbara was getting better looking as she got older. Was that just him or was it true? When he had worked for her, back in the '80s, she was just a skinny little rich girl out of Boston University with the want to run her own business because she could not stand taking orders from anyone else. It had taken Henry months to convince her she should mix used books with her new stock, but in the end she had listened. Unfortunately, as much as she liked dealing with people, she had failed to convince him in turn that the human race was worth saving.

Still, they had learned a lot together. She was a good lady, but she had never learned how to give in when the time came. As much as he had liked it at Alcott & Poe, he had never regretted leaving. He had made so many stupid moves. Breaking with Barbara had been a right one. She liked being the boss a little too much. She had never understood his craving for a simpler way of doing things. Or why he was so easily aggravated by customers. He could forgive people their ignorance— he certainly forgave himself for enough of that. But he could not forgive meanness. She did not understand why he would rather work sixteen hours a day instead of only twelve. She had wanted kids. Probably still did. How would he have been able to take care of kids? He would have been as bad at that as his own father had been.

Barbara was a survivor. He could not have known that then. Little rich girls come and go. Very few learn the right lessons in life before they run out of their parents' money. Barbara had. Her personality hadn't changed, but she was a lot more woman now than she was then, in many ways—and he liked the extra weight. "Zaftig" was the word she used, but she exaggerated.

The morning sunburned, even through the curtains.

Henry lowered the back of his Morris chair and closed his eyes again. He had been reading most of the night, caught in the wave of a story he had picked up casually the night before with no expectation. He loved it when that happened. The author, Robert W. Chambers, had been the Alexander Dumas of his time. Much like George Duggan was today. After reading through a collection of historical romances that he had picked up for next to nothing at an auction, he was coming to the conclusion that Chambers was underrated. Maybe one day he would be rediscovered. Perhaps it would be worthwhile putting together a small set of first editions in dust jacket. It would not cost all that much.

He was startled when the phone rang again. He had begun to dream again. The sun was into an afternoon slant against the wall.

"Sorry to wake you." It was Della.

"I was reading."

"Why do you always say you were reading when you were really sleeping? Are you guilty about sleeping? Everybody does it."

She always knew too much, and let him know it.

"Why did you call?"

"I wondered what you were doing."

"I was sleeping."

"You want to go out? We could get ribs at the Blue Ribbon."

"I'm feeling poor."

"Pulled pork sandwiches then, on me."

"Sounds messy, but interesting."

"I need to get out," she said.

"All right. Pulled pork on you, and then we go out."

"Stop it! It's too early. I'll be there in fifteen minutes."

He climbed in the shower and stood with his head right below the nozzle, as if he could wash the dream he had been having from his mind. He had been dreaming about Barbara, and that surprised him. They had worked together for seven years. In his memory now he had worked harder at keeping the distance between them than he had worked at selling books. Their romance had come only at the end, the year before he quit. Even if he was glad he had left, he had never shaken the heat of their relationship just before it was over.

When he turned off the shower, he could hear the phone ringing again.

Barbara began to speak before he had a chance to say hello.

"Henry, I thought about this before calling you back. I had something else on my mind, and I shouldn't have hesitated before. But what are my options? I need your help."

Barbara always had something else on her mind.

"What do you need?"

As he said it, the image of Barbara from his dream came back again. It was funny to him how he often imagined her naked, but always as she was now, never as the skinny kid she had been when they were together.

"A friend of mine needs some help. You know her—Sharon. Well. The problem is…. You know how these things kind of work off each other. The idea occurred to me when I read your name in the story about Eddy Perry getting murdered."

A bit of warm June air blew through the curtains at the window and cooled his skin. He looked down at the puddle of water at his feet.

"What can I do for you, Barbara?"

"Do you remember reading about the murder of the Harvard instructor on the street a couple of years ago?"

"No. I don't." He seldom read the papers. She knew that, just as he knew she read both the local papers and the *New York Times* as well.

"Well, his name was James Frankowski. He taught ancient history. It was a tragedy. He was mugged one night on his way to his office."

"Yeah…" He thought again of Eddy Perry. And hadn't Albert mentioned something about others who had been killed in Cambridge in the last few years?

"Well, he was Sharon's boyfriend. They were, like, married, only without the certificate. They had been living together for years."

"Yes...."

"It's Sharon who needs some help. I can't really do so much. I've had to let half the part-timers go. Sharon and I are at the store at least ten hours a day. More! Seven days a week. There's no time left. And the police can't do anything. They haven't done anything, or they won't do anything."

"You mean, about his murder?"

"Yes, but that's not it. She thinks that—"

There was a familiar knock at the door, probably Della's.

"Hold on." He held the phone in one hand as he pulled the coils in the cord straight and opened the door. Della was wearing the same dress again from the night before. He let her in.

"Who's that?" Barbara said on the phone.

"It's Della."

"I thought you weren't seeing her anymore."

"I wasn't."

There was a brief silence. Henry looked at Della, who was shaking her head without even knowing what Barbara was saying.

Barbara took a new breath that was clearly audible. "Well, look, can we get together over a cup of coffee this evening and talk about this? It's important to me."

Whatever it was, Henry was not in the mood for Barbara's pushing.

"Not tonight. Tomorrow. We can have a cup of coffee before you open in the morning."

She hesitated. "Eight-thirty. At the place next-door to the shop."

"Right." Henry managed to fit the word in before Barbara hung up.

Della stopped shaking her head.

"You're not eating enough fatty foods. You need some bar-beque. You're getting too skinny."

When he looked down, the first thing he noticed were his wet footprints.

Chapter Four

Barbara was not alone. Sharon was taller, as blond as Barbara was brunette, and as thin as Barbara had once been. They were sitting at a table at the rear, and their eyes reflected the bright sun from the street behind him as well as his shadow, as he approached.

It was Sharon who had taken over Henry's job at Alcott & Poe years before. She had done a better job of it, he had to admit that. Henry had always liked finding the books in the first place, while Sharon seemed to enjoy the detail of research. Barbara was the one who ran the shop day to day, ordered the new books, and bought the used stock that people carried in the door. Both Sharon and Barbara went to the book auctions together, but it was Sharon who cataloged the old ones and worked on the displays. Customer relations had always been Barbara's strong suit. Because of that division of labor, Henry had spoken to Sharon very little over the years, and had not formed much of an opinion about her.

The chairs in the cafe had thin wire backs to discourage staying too long. He ordered a cup of coffee as he sat down. Sharon seemed to be studying him as if she had never seen him before. He hoped he had remembered his zipper.

He said, "I'm here at your command."

Barbara did not skip the beat. "We need some help…Sharon needs some help."

Always sincere, Barbara could express concern with the look in her eye better than most people. Everything was always important. She was not given to joking, which was why Henry tried so hard not to be serious when he was with her.

Sharon smiled. Henry's eyes were captured by the look of her mouth. Her teeth were perfectly set within full lips. Her lips had the fine edge of sculpting. The pale blue of her eyes did not hold his attention in the same way. She certainly was not a match for the usual picture of a used book merchant—nails manicured, hair styled fashionably short. He did not think the blond of her hair was natural. A very good-looking woman, Henry thought, even if she lacked Barbara's assets.

Sharon said, "I'm trying to avoid getting involved in something I can't afford, but I do need help," Her diction was precise.

Barbara quickly added, "She thinks George Duggan plagiarized the last book Jim wrote."

Henry actually felt his jaw drop a little. He had been prepared even to hear of some unfortunate connection between Eddy Perry and James Frankowski. After Barbara's call, he had tried not to imagine himself involved somehow in the work of a serial murderer stalking the side streets of Cambridge. He had unsuccessfully suppressed the image of himself, Walter Mitty–like, lurking at dark corners in pursuit of a fiend. It had been at least twenty-five years since he had filled the imagined shoes of Sherlock Holmes in the dark alleys of London, but the fantasy had come back to him easily. He had no idea what Barbara wanted, and he smiled now at his own foolishness. She misunderstood his smile.

"I'm not kidding Henry. It's serious."

Barbara was a contrast to Sharon in most ways. Her brown hair was pulled back too severely to the grip of a rubber band. "Unmanageable," she always said. Her nails were cut short and darkened underneath with the soil of book dust. The weight she had put on over the years was not unpleasant, but she hid her bosom behind a vest jammed with pencils and erasers. She wore jeans, as she had the day he had first met her in 1980, just a few months after she had opened the store.

"Duggan?" Henry asked. He could not help the escape of a short laugh, and tried to squelch it with words. "As a matter of fact, I just saw him at a ballgame the other day. Looks like he's enjoying the good life. He has a gorgeous redhead for a gal pal. What makes you think he's a plagiarist?"

Sharon spoke now, holding her hand up as if to keep Barbara silent. He looked at Barbara's blank face and knew this bothered her. Sharon's voice was not calm.

"It was something out of the blue. We received an advance reader's copy of the new George Duggan book a few months ago. I just threw it aside. Why would I need to look at it? We don't order new bestsellers. We can't compete against Barnes & Noble discounts. He'll sell another million copies anyway. But a name caught my eye. The main character is named Scipio. Not a lot of Scipios running around."

"Nor Hannibals." Henry offered.

Barbara laughed. "I told her you'd know who Scipio was."

Henry shrugged off the implied compliment. "There were actually several. I just guessed."

Sharon held her hand up again and continued her story.

"So I started reading it. Well, the words are different, but the story is the same as the last novel that Jim wrote before he died. Just the same! Jim's book was called *Hannibal's Dance*. Duggan's book you know is called *Dreams of Bithynia*. They both take place for the most part around the court of Prusias." Henry sat back and held up his own hand to interrupt.

"That's just history. If the words aren't the same, that's not plagiarism. Anyone can write about the same subject."

Sharon leaned forward, her thin neck extended above the table, her face pulled tight. He thought he could see a flare of her nostrils. She had a very pretty nose.

"But wait. It is. Jim wrote the whole thing first. He set most of the story after the battle of Magnesia, with Hannibal alone in defeat, encountered by Scipio in a goatherd's shelter during a storm. The two generals had never actually met face to face before and never met again. Jim used to get very excited about things. Obsessed, really. He thought it was too much of a coincidence that both Hannibal and Scipio, the great lifelong enemies, men of such honor and mutual respect, died within a year of one another. The rest of the story is divided between Scipio's farmhouse in Italy and Hannibal's refuge in Bithynia. Jim imagined it like the deaths of Jefferson and Adams, both men wondering if the other still lived. Except in this case, instead of being elder statesman, they were hounded to their deaths. Scipio, by not taking up the reins of Counsel after his great victory, and thus not becoming the ruler of Rome, had unleashed the forces of politics. Hannibal, by continuing to support the enemies of Rome, had ensured the ultimate destruction of his beloved Carthage and the domination of Roman culture." Both her hands rose now, fingers spread. "And in their final moments, each separately recall, and retell, to an illiterate female servant slave—the only ears to listen—their own version of the one time they met face to face—alone—when there had been a climactic contest just between the two of them, which had determined the future of Rome and thus the Western world—how they had only recognized each other in the heat of the struggle. And that Hannibal had won, and then chosen to let Scipio live, which becomes the reason the Roman had refused to take the mantle of power when he returned…" she paused for dramatic effect. "Jim staged that moment as the end of the ancient age of myth and heroes and the beginning of the modern world of politics and mediocrity. That's not actual history. There is no real record of that. That was Jim's idea."

Barbara raised an eyebrow and tilted her head down far enough to put folds in the skin of her neck.

"Now, you have to admit, that's not a likely coincidence. What are the options? Mr. Duggan somehow manages to put out more than a book a year. He's like a machine. Is it a coincidence he would write a book with that story at the same time as Jim, with goatherd huts and female servant slaves and all? And it's Duggan's biggest book in about four years. Number one on the *New York Times* bestseller list, first week out. And he's already sold the rights to some big movie outfit and it's going to make him millions more."

Barbara was always too worried about money. The idea that Duggan might be making a fortune off the work of James Frankowski would infuriate her. But Duggan stealing another man's work still seemed difficult to comprehend.

Henry shook his head, "But you say he didn't use the same words. Then it's not plagiarism, is it? Don't the words have to match, or something close to that?"

"He wouldn't be that stupid," Sharon said. Her tone went from sarcastic to hurt. "But it's the same material. And it was Jim who made it all up. It never happened. It's not history. The story never existed until Jim created it. It was Jim's answer to a gap in historical knowledge that might reveal the cause of something that changed everything that came after. And George Duggan stole it. It's not fair. It's not right."

Henry had to ask, "But how did he get it?"

"From one of his publishing friends, I think. Jim had sent the book out a bunch of times to be read."

Henry was confused.

"What do you expect me to do?" He realized as he said it, there was a tone to his voice. He was sorry for that. He could not help but wonder if Barbara might be using this problem to get him involved with her again. Still, he owed her a great deal.

"Help us find out when he stole it," Barbara jumped at the question. "Find out how he stole it. We need to know the way it happened, in order to make a case. This can be settled out of court. Lawyers will just see it as a feeding frenzy. Duggan has a reputation to protect. And who knows how he got hold of Jim's idea? Who knows what goes on? He might have gotten the idea from someone and not even realized the source. There's no reason to make a stink, if it can be settled. It's a matter of fairness to Jim and Sharon. But we need a little help. Sharon's not much of a hound. Behind that smile, she has a temper. She gets angry." Barbara raised an eyebrow and looked at Sharon. "That's why we keep her doing the cataloging and research and I take care of the customers.…"

Sharon had begun to smile before Barbara's final words brought her forehead to a frown.

Henry leaned back in his chair. The thin wire of the chair back sagged uncomfortably behind him.

"I'm not a detective. I am a bookseller." It was a weak defense, he thought.

Barbra was ready for more of an excuse than that. "You're a hound. You see stuff other people don't. I know that. You notice things. You always have.… And we'll pay you. I can't afford to lose Sharon to all this. She's done too much for me. I need her work in the store. And Sharon has agreed."

The two women exchanged glances and smiled weakly at one another. There was friction there, Henry thought. Barbara could be overbearing. He imagined Sharon had to work to keep her reactions under control if she had a temper.

"You agreed to what?" he asked.

"To let you help," Barbara said. She might just as well have added "of course!"

"Help what? What am I supposed to do?" He had asked the wrong question again. This would only give her an opportunity to tell him.

"Figure out how it happened."

Sharon held her hand up again.

"After Jim's previous publisher rejected it, he sent it to half a dozen other places. Duggan must have seen a manuscript. One of those people Jim sent his manuscript to must have shown it to Duggan. He must have read it."

Henry thought this made little sense. Was Barbara too quick to think badly of Duggan just because he was—Duggan? The Duggan. Duggan the great. Duggan the powerful. Duggan the rich.

He asked the obvious, "Do you have a particular publisher in mind?"

Sharon's eyes widened. The pale blue caught the sunlight reflected from a car on the street and suddenly flashed.

"Tremont. They're right here in town. They were the last ones to see the manuscript, and I think they kept it the longest."

Henry felt trapped. "I have a business of my own. I can't stop work for something like this."

He hoped there was no whine to his voice.

Barbara leaned in on the small table, her ample bosom as close to him as her face.

"Henry. I know you. You are not the most ambitious guy I ever met. Work a little harder for a while. You can do this on the side. Help me. Otherwise Sharon is going to end up with a bunch of lawyers, and they'll take whatever they find."

Barbara's eyes had become darker in the shadow of her own frown. Henry looked at Sharon again, but there was nothing to read there. He decided they were robin's egg blue. He had seldom actually seen eyes of that color, as often as he had read of it in novels. More, there was no silent plea there for help. She looked at him as if she already knew what he would say and was simply waiting for him to say it. Henry did not like the feeling. He had to get this under control—at least part of it.

"But it's not really plagiarism. Duggan will know that. Why would he be worried by any accusations?"

"Maybe it's not legally. But it should be. Maybe it's some kind of conspiracy. It's at least a fraud. And there is his reputation. He's at the top. He doesn't need this kind of thing to get out."

Once, less than a year before, Henry had watched as George Duggan had delivered a eulogy for a mutual friend, Morgan Johnson. He had watched the big ruddy man in the dampened light of that church and thought well of him for clearly seeing in Morgan the woman that Henry had known, and not offering the false testimony so common at funerals. Henry had liked Duggan then for his honesty, and it made no sense to Henry now that George Duggan, already successful, would steal another man's work.

"But Tremont is not his publisher," Henry argued.

"No, but you know that redhead you saw Duggan with at the ball park?" Barbara countered. "She is the editor at Tremont."

Henry shook his head. Sex and money. He supposed it could happen.

His defenses weakened, he tried again, "But what am I supposed to do?"

Barbara answered over Henry's last few words. "Draw the connection. Make it obvious. If they think it looks bad enough to the eye, they might settle the thing."

Henry looked back to Sharon. She did not seem to have the strength for battle. She was the kind of woman that men liked to protect. It was that urge which discomforted him. He changed the subject.

He said, "You were never married, but you were the beneficiary of Jim's will?"

Sharon smiled. The contest was over. Her teeth appeared translucent at the edges, porcelain jewels aligned and formed, as if intended for a toothpaste commercial. The pink of her tongue passed at the edges as she spoke, unharmed. He had already considered the pale rose red of her lips, and wondered how soft they might feel. He knew that she used that smile as a weapon.

"He had no will, really." She paused, pressed her hands together, and looked back directly into his eyes. She would not be denied. "But when we bought the condo together, the insurance was a problem and the lawyer made us sign something which basically said that if anything happened to one of us, the other was the beneficiary and responsible for the mortgage and any other expenses. So when he was killed, I ended up with everything. Jim's parents are pretty old. He has a married sister who lives in California who is very well off. So, it's left to me…to see to it that Jim is given credit for his work."

Barbara was looking intently at him as well. He was not going to wiggle out of this. "Just help us to put things together. It won't all be on your shoulders. But we need the help."

He usually had difficulty defending himself against one woman. Two women were overwhelming.

He moved to escape. "I have to get going. Let me think about it. You call me later."

He left his coffee untouched. He would just have to get another somewhere else.

Chapter Five

W hat do you think?"

Barbara's voice was too eager for so early in the morning. He held the phone away from his ear. His eyes found the clock. It was not yet nine. He hoped waking him first thing in the morning was not going to be a habit.

"I'm not thinking. I'm too tired."

"Come on. What do you think? You read them both, right?"

"Yes. I finished the Duggan yesterday."

He had just spent the last hour rereading bits and pieces as he drank his coffee.

"And?"

"I'm tired. The Punic wars were very tiring."

"But do you think it's plagiarism?"

He once had a teacher in fifth grade who asked questions in that tone of voice. She usually got the same answer out of him.

"No."

"Why?" Her first word was almost a yelp. "Why not? It's the same story. It can't be coincidence."

Henry held the phone away from his ear. "You asked me. I'm not a lawyer. I'm tired and I have to go to a book sale this afternoon and I want to take a nap."

Was he whining again? He had not slept well. He had spent the early hours of the morning filling orders, sending out emails to buyers and packing books on his kitchen table. Barbara blew air at the phone in exasperation.

The decibels of Barbara's voice suddenly dropped and Henry brought the phone back to his ear to catch her words. "What is it then? Duggan is sleeping with the editor who read Jim's book and you think it's just coincidence? That's absurd. You think she talks in her sleep? He stole Jim's story. They thought Jim was dead and they could get away with it. It's a conspiracy!"

Henry was not ready for jumping to such conclusions.

"Stop! You asked me to help. I'm trying to help. You aren't talking about plagiarism here. Not technically, anyway. Not as far as I know it. And I'll agree that it can't just be coincidence. I will accept that. I think Sharon might already understand the problem. It's in her letter to them. She didn't really accuse them of anything. I think she knows."

Sharon Greene wrote very well. Her initial letter to George Duggan had been polite, concise, and convincing. She had made each of the points Henry would have made. She did not say Frankowski's book was plagiarized. She suggested it. She did not accuse him of theft. She only pointed out that it appeared a theft had taken place—that something had happened, and with James Frankowski dead, it was in her hands to see that some fair compensation was made.

Reading the letter after finally getting the chance to read Frankowski's book, he was confident Sharon had taken the right tack in making her case. Henry slipped her letter behind the manuscript of *Hannibal's Dance* in his lap. This copy was the one originally returned from Little, Brown and had been addressed to Frankowski's previous editor there, Jean Parsons. It had been inscribed to her on the title sheet. Unfortunately, Parsons no longer worked at Little, Brown at the time it was submitted, and it had been returned unread. As luck would have it, that was the week Little, Brown had reduced its Boston staff by another twelve people in its migration to New York City. Henry had tracked Parsons down the day before at Houghton Mifflin, where she was now in the textbook division. She had been very apologetic that she had never had the chance to see it. She did not think it was appropriate to speak with Henry about the book—but she had said the same thing to Sharon.

The note James Frankowski had written to Jean Parsons was still paperclipped to the front of the manuscript. "Jean— you will like this even better than the last one. I'm very excited. Let me know your thoughts as soon as you can. Jim."

Frankowski had reason to be excited. It was a very good piece of work. Henry had read it through nonstop. Historical fiction was seldom that compelling, because the imagined elements usually took the hard edge off the fact. Henry had never considered Hannibal beyond a cockscomb helmet and metal-clad elephants.

Duggan's *Dreams of Bithynia* lay on the couch. Perhaps the comparison was unfair. Henry had started reading the Duggan book only a few hours after he had read the Frankowski story. Duggan's writing was clean and clear, but lacked the emotion which carried the Frankowski novel. Duggan's own voice was seldom heard over the methodical progress of the narrative. Frankowski had invented a style for *Hannibal's Dance* which avoided most objective description and dwelt in the minds of the characters. It surprised Henry that a historian would spend so little time on the background detail of a period and so much effort to realize the personalities of individuals. Where Duggan spent twenty pages relating the historical hierarchy of Roman politics, Frankowski struggled with the internal demons of giants beset by the adversity of political enemies. Frankowski's Hannibal was a somber and brooding character haunted by the ghost of his father. Duggan's Carthaginian was a dynamo wielding his powers with relish. Frankowski's Scipio was a philosopher and politician thrust upon the events of his time. Duggan's Roman was a schemer and master of gamesmanship.

Accusations of Duggan writing too quickly were justified. But he also moved his story along at a faster clip. The climax was more fierce and compelling as it projected the magnitude of the events. In the end, it was the same story told by two different authors. The plagiarism, if that was what it should be called, was in the story itself, not the exact words. It was in focusing so clearly on the imagined last moments of those two men, Hannibal and Scipio, that they overlapped. It was in the character of the servant slaves that they differed most. Duggan used the device as a reason for the men to speak their thoughts. Frankowski used the female slave as a counterpoint to their fears.

Henry's own guess, not being a lawyer or wanting to think like one, was that a case of plagiarism would not hold. Sharon was going to lose. Whatever had happened to transfer the idea for this story from the manuscript of James Frankowski to the mind of George Duggan was lost in the shuffle of circumstance. However, it might be in Duggan's best interest to settle—to avoid the negative publicity of some kind of a suit against himself or Tremont. There was some chance a case of conspiracy would stick. Some effort should be made. It seemed a terrible pity that Frankowski's good book might be buried in the process.

He explained this as best he could to Barbara, who listened with little comment. When he was finished, the eagerness had left her voice.

"All right. Do you have any ideas?"

He could only say, "I'll have to think about it."

Barbara said, "Thanks."

And then the phone was dead.

He did not want this job. He would do it for Barbara, but he was not going to pretend he was happy about it.

Shelagh had once told him something—no, she had told him more than once. His sister had said it whenever he had complained out loud about some unpleasant work—"It's all in the effort. Do not count on the results. Make the effort count."

Where had she gotten such an idea? Henry had never heard his father use those words, and the old man had a habit of repeating himself. Henry sat back and wondered if this was something his mother had told Shelagh, but he had missed.

He would have to call his sister. He had not spoken to her in weeks. He could ask her. But there never seemed to be a right time.

Henry awoke to the sound of a violin, clear and close above. His neighbor Sasha was practicing in her kitchen. He had dozed. The afternoon breeze was from the side of the house, and it carried the smell of tomato leaves and freshly turned earth.

He jolted upward. He had a book sale to get to.

Chapter Six

There was a hum to the warm air, or perhaps it was more of a continuous sigh, but the early morning dark was not silent. He was seldom out at this hour, in any case, and it was not a sound he was used to. With what little traffic there was passing a block away at Central Square, few cars disturbed the haze of streetlights on this back street. One distinct noise was the clink of deposit bottles and the accompanying timpani of cans as trash pickers rifled the repeated knots of garbage set out on the thin rope of curb which trailed beneath the lights.

Albert, lodged in his seat in the truck, rubbed his hand over his face to bring the blood back, as Henry leaned toward the open window from where he stood on the curb.

"I got a full day ahead of me, Henry. Would you please hurry it up?"

Henry's first couple of guesses had been wrong. The houses looked too similar in the dark. Street numbers were too often missing or obscured. His investigation of the first two piles he had chosen had been fruitless.

"Maybe they didn't put the stuff out."

"Maybe."

"Then it's got to be the one closest to the mailbox. It's the only one left on this side."

He pointed to the larger mound of black plastic bags piled loosely there. As he did, he could see the movement of another garbage picker with a "borrowed" grocery cart slant across the street toward the spot, undoubtedly drawn by the same magic that brought flies to a piece of pie. The metal of the cart rattled on the uneven pavement. Albert gunned the engine of his truck, shifted gears, and moved forward faster than Henry expected. Henry ran in the street after him. The truck stopped short of the cart by a foot or two. The startled eyes of a child stared over the top of the already full basket.

Albert waved at him through his open window. "Sorry kiddo."

The wide bulk of the mother wearing a yellow cloth coat, perhaps to be better seen, already hovered over the bags. Henry moved as quickly as he could, grabbing the bulging plastic without inspection and tossing the bags over the gate of the truck into the back.

The woman scowled. "You a garbage man?"

Henry answered, "Yes, ma'am."

"You too early to be a garbage man." Her tone had not accepted his answer for fact.

Henry pointed at the words emblazoned across the truck door as he spoke. READY REFUSE REMOVAL.

Albert had gotten out of the truck now and grabbed several bags at once. The women bent over the bag she had cut open with something in her hand.

She said, "Just books."

Henry pulled a thin fold of bills from his jeans and handed a twenty to her.

When she stood erect and grabbed the bill, he scooped the torn bag up and tossed it over the gate. The thump of loose books drummed in the silence as they broke free and hit the bed of the truck.

He answered, "Just books."

They stopped the truck ten minutes later beneath the streetlight which illuminated the dumpster behind the Blue Thorn. Tim had given Henry his okay earlier. It took them until the grey of dawn to open each of the bags and discard most of the contents.

Henry did not know exactly what he was looking for. It was instinct. Eddy Perry was not likely to have anything of value he had not already sold for cash. But booksellers were odd people. Eddy was odder than most.

When phone calls had produced nothing but malfunctioning answering machines on the previous Friday, Henry had gone around to find out what was happening to Eddy's stuff. It was the tenant on the first floor who had tipped Henry off to the fact that the room was already rented and that Eddy's property was in plastic bags in the basement, ready to be tossed. The basement door was locked. Wednesday was garbage day. So they had taken the chance.

The books were mostly thrillers: several Thomas Harris titles, every one a book club edition; a dozen Jack Higgins and Clive Cussler titles, all hardcover and discarded from the Cambridge Public Library. Obviously Eddy had liked Tom Clancy, because he had at least a dozen of those. Six or seven other authors were less familiar, perhaps forty books in all. In the fifteen years since Henry had stopped working in a bookstore, it was clear that the end of the Cold War had ruined a thriving industry of cover art incorporating the Soviet hammer and sickle. More recent titles had drifted back to the old standby of the Nazi swastika and evil Germans. Henry put them aside to donate to the Salvation Army. He was never able to throw a book away.

Then there were bills. Unpaid bills. Yellow notices. Pink notices. Blue notices. One bag alone was primarily bills. Not a single personal letter.

Four bags held all the clothing Eddy had worn, summer and winter, most of it was probably too cheap to even donate.

Henry finally found what he was looking for with a pile of magazines. Whoever had cleaned the apartment out had obviously piled things by size. The slick covers slipped away, and in his hand was the manuscript.

"*Penny Candy* by Edward Perry," Albert said out loud as Henry held the binder up to the light.

Henry flipped the thick pack of paper to the last pages and turned. "Look here—it says, 'End.' I guess he finished it."

A small clear plastic frame fell from a bag filled with newspapers. It was a picture taken at a beach. The woman in the picture, slightly overweight and wearing a bikini which did not fit well, was not familiar. It probably was not Eddy's mother. Henry put the frame in his pocket.

Henry wondered what had happened to the typewriter. He had always liked old typewriters.

After breakfast at Charlie's Sandwich Shop, they reorganized the day. Albert wanted to go home and make up with Alice for skipping out at three in the morning without telling her where he was going. Henry wanted to get rid of the rest of the stuff in the truck before going home to bed.

An hour later, having waited with an unhappy Albert until the doors were unlocked at nine, he carried the bags into the Salvation Army store, two at a time, and set them by the desk as the clerk watched stolidly—making three trips back and forth before the women finally bothered to tell him they "weren't taking any more books at the present time."

He stared at her, wordless.

"Books don't sell," she said in explanation. "We have too many already."

Henry began to carry them back to the truck.

Albert had stayed behind the wheel to keep an eye on the parking-meter bee who was visiting her metal flowers in the morning sun, one by one.

He said, "Leave the clothing here. We'll bring the books to the library. They still have sales at the library, don't they?"

The cover of the top book in the last bag made Henry hesitate as he set them back into the bed of the truck. It was covered in clear plastic like the other ex-library books—but the plastic was clean and new like the Arkham House title Henry had purchased from Eddy. Henry had actually looked at the book before and dismissed it as another book club edition. No price on the dust jacket. No printing stated. He realized suddenly how tired he really was, and pulled the book out now, and sat in the cab with it in his lap, unopened.

"You going to read Clancy?" Albert said. "You need thrills and adventure in your poor book-hound life?"

"No." He did not have to look at the book again. He knew the joke. "But Eddie didn't read Clancy either. I'll bet you a thousand dollars on that."

All the other books he had seen piled on that mantle in Eddy's apartment were there to hide just this one: Clancy's first, and the only one that was rare. Albert turned the key in the ignition, his eye sliding over to the black, red, and grey of the cover in Henry's lap, then he shifted, let his foot off the clutch, and wheeled the truck smoothly into traffic.

"I'll pass."

Chapter Seven

Henry was awakened by the sound of pounding from downstairs. Half consciously calculating that Mrs. Murray must have gone out and locked the front door, he stumbled through his own door, grabbed the stair rail, and bent down to see the face through the glass. It was Bob. What in hell was Della's Bob doing at the front door?

Henry went back to bed before realizing he was completely awake and then got up again to take his shower. The phone rang. He ignored it.

He was not in a good mood. He wished he still smoked as he drank his coffee. It had been less than six months since he last quit, and for him, mornings were the hardest.

Eddy's manuscript lay on the floor beside his Morris chair. Henry had finished it less than twenty-four hours after pulling it from the trash. Now his sleeping schedule was completely off. Reading all night was a student's game. He was getting too old to do that and then have the energy to hit the road.

There was knock on his own door, and his first thought was that Bob had come back and found the front door unlocked, but the knock was hesitant and not very strong. Henry guessed correctly that it was his landlady, Mrs. Murray.

She said, "You woke me up last night."

"I'm sorry. I was just reading."

"You were tapping your foot. You told me you'd stop doing that." She was smiling. It was her joke. She told him when he moved in that she would cure him of all his bad habits, for no extra charge. She got him to quit smoking the very first week.

He looked over at his chair. He had not promised to stop tapping his foot when he read, only to take care of the problem. The rug he had used to cut down on the sound was gone—still at the cleaners.

"Sorry. I spilled my coffee the other day. I haven't gotten the rug back yet."

Her smile grew almost to a grin, with her eyebrows slightly elevated. He had never noticed her do that before.

"I heard that. Your friend was here, wasn't she?"

He wondered what else Mrs. Murray had heard. He said, "Yes." He could think of no other response, given his mood.

She spoke each word with care, as if preparing to spell it afterwards. He imagined her as the teacher she had been before she retired, driving her students crazy.

She said, "I have a rug you can borrow."

"Thanks, but it'll be fine. I'll take care of it today."

"You've been up at night a lot lately."

"Right. Well…I'll get another rug for the middle of the floor." There was some tension he had not noticed before between them. He smiled back.

"If you need anything, you know you can ask."

"Yes, ma'am."

She frowned. The wrinkles on her face darkened. She was a handsome woman. Her eyes were a sapphire blue. He once had a teacher in the ninth grade as pretty as Mrs. Murray was. He had been so infatuated with her, he had raised his grade in English from C to A. One of those small matters of fact that had changed his life. The question was, why should he be suddenly remembering old teachers? Her eyes still studied him.

"Sarah. I've asked you to call me Sarah. I'm not that much older than you, I believe."

It was a gentle scold.

"Yes, Sarah."

The phone rang, and this time he picked it up as a means of escape. It was Della.

"Have you seen Bob?"

He hesitated before he answered.

"Why should I see Bob?"

"He came to my office, looking to take me to lunch. Goofball Diane said I was having lunch with you. She doesn't like Bob."

"Why would he know where I live?"

"Because I told him. Once.... It was a mistake. It's a long story. I'm sorry."

What story? Why would she have given out his address? Especially to Bob? Had he forgotten something?

"Were we supposed to have lunch today?"

"No, but it's a good idea. You want to have lunch?"

"No."

"Well, what are you doing?"

"Talking to you."

"Besides that."

"Trying to make a living."

"You'll have to get out your door to do that."

A small cry of the floorboards made him turn. Mrs. Murray was still there. She was looking at his kitchen, one hand fingering the clothesline he had rigged above his table.

"I'm trying." He said into the receiver.

"Is someone else there?"

She had great instincts.

"No—well, Mrs. Murray."

Hearing her name, Mrs. Murray turned and looked at him. "Yes…" she said.

"Nothing." he answered.

Della said, "She's too old for you, Henry."

He could think of no witty answer for that.

"I have to go. See you later."

He turned again to Mrs. Murray. She smiled.

He had to ask. "Is everything okay?"

She sighed. "Just fine. But you have so little food. You should cook more."

"I like to eat out. I don't like doing dishes."

She put her tongue against her teeth and made a sound of teasing disapproval. It was a habit he had noticed before and seemed sort of girlish and cute. It occurred to him suddenly that Mrs. Murray was in some ways a mature version of Sharon Green—a bit more developed, and a lot more interesting.

She said, "Men never change, do they?" as she made her way to the door and turned. "My Sam used to say things like that all the time. Why don't men cultivate the gentle habits of everyday life? Doing dishes is like gardening. It's a measure of the daily experience. It's a repetition of the process of life—the turning of the wheel. Why don't men appreciate that more?"

The image of turning wheels made Henry think of an old hippie song. It was easy to imagine that Mrs. Murray was once a hippie.

He answered in defense. "Because there is always something better to do?"

Her face fell, her head tilting sideways.

"Like a child. You're forty aren't you? You must appreciate by now that every moment cannot be an adventure."

"Why not?" He felt silly saying it.

She shook her head, then smiled again as she left.

Now he was late. He had wanted to be out the door before this. Tomorrow he had an appointment to look at an estate in Salem. He liked Salem. He had always been lucky getting good books there. John Marquand was from Salem. And Nathaniel Hawthorne. For now he had to get to the garage and make sure Benny had the truck ready. And he wanted to get copies made of Eddy's manuscript.

Mrs. Murray had left her door open, and he heard some piece of classical cello music he could not identify as he passed on his way out. She was sitting, turned away from the door, in a high-backed chair, with the light from the window illuminating a book open in her lap. It reminded him of his mother.

This thought, and knowing that he found Mrs. Murray more than a little appealing, disturbed him. Della's warning was not lost. She had warned him about Barbara, as well. But there was no way he was going to avoid that. His conversation with Barbara from the day before was in his ears again as he walked.

Why did people get themselves into such messes? Life was complicated enough.

The situation with Sharon was not simple, and it was coming at a bad time for Barbara. But then, there was usually a reason such things happened all at once. The bottom line, though she had never completely admitted it to him, was that Barbara was badly in debt. He jerked his head at the thought. No, the bottom line was simply that she had asked for his help.

During the years he had worked for her, she had rarely mentioned money. He had never seen her be careless, but never especially concerned with it either. Now the internet had combined with other changes in the market and stolen over a third of her business in just the past three years. She had admitted that much in conversation months before. In the late '90s, when times were flush, she had spent everything she could to renovate the store—additional shelves, added space in the basement, and increased stock. Wasn't that what a good business did—reinvest capital? The internet then looked like a bonus.

She had the best used bookshop in Boston. No contest. Other stores were bigger, but with nowhere near the general quality. She specialized in the good stuff. She had a few rare books, but most of her stock was simply the best writing she could find. Over time, twentieth-century authors had become her specialty, despite the store name, because she had learned as she went along. For the most part she had left the antiquarian trade to the older crowd of Boston booksellers who had frowned on her when she started out.

When Henry had begun working at Alcott & Poe, she had just rented the first-floor space. By the time he had left, she had taken over the second floor as well. She had opened the basement about ten years ago and filled it with cheaper books. This had been a big success, and a way to dispose of stock which had not sold well otherwise. For awhile, sales had continued to climb.

Now this was all in jeopardy.

She could no longer afford to keep prime real estate space on Newbury Street in Boston and remain competitive with mom-and-pop booksellers on kitchen tables in Indiana and Arizona, who sold their books over the internet with little or no overhead. Even relatively local customers had stopped braving the parking conditions in Boston and started ordering online. Then her largest clientele, students, had discovered the joys of the laptop computer, which had become commonplace. Whole course lists could be ordered online. Customers who used to come from out of state, where few good used bookstores could be found, no longer waited to visit Boston to buy, while browsing their favorite websites weekly.

But her greatest mistake was to go into debt, rather than close. She had believed, with the false hope of a mother in a bad child, that she could turn it around.

Sharon was there through all of this. Unlike Henry, Sharon had stuck by her. Sharon already knew, by the time she had lost Jim Frankowski, that the store was losing money. Why did Sharon turn around and invest $50,000 dollars of Frankowski's life insurance in a lost cause? She must know as well as Barbara that the days of big old bookshops were numbered. Obviously there was more to Sharon than good looks.

Now Barbara was in debt to Sharon, and Sharon needed a favor, and that was the end of the story.

When he dropped Eddy's manuscript off at the copy service, the place was empty. Students were gone for the summer. Business was slow. Two of the employees stood on the sidewalk, smoking. They told him to return in an hour.

At the garage, Benny was all smiles and few words. This had Henry on his guard immediately.

The truck was parked at the very front of the lot, where it could be seen by anyone passing. The paint job was perfect. The green was alive. The pits in the chrome were miraculously gone and the metal polished enough to make his eyes ache. BENNY'S GULF was emblazoned on the door in gold letters.

Henry felt like this was the best thing he had done in memory. He had known that letting Benny put his name on the door would insure the quality of work done. Henry did not need his name there. He could not overhaul an engine if his life depended on it. Yet he had always wanted an old truck, whether he knew it before or not.

He had been without wheels since the winter, when his old Ford van had encountered a Mercedes Benz in the worst way. But Barbara still had hers. He had helped her buy it, years ago.

Those boxes on wheels were good for carrying off a house full of books. Henry had no such constraints now. He seldom bought more than a hundred at a time, let alone a thousand.

The rounded bumpers of this old Chevrolet looked like a woman to him. The chrome around the headlights seemed to wink. The flat lines of the grille wanted to smile. And now he could park it for free, the insurance paid for, just for the cost of the advertising. He pulled open the door and put a foot up on the running board. Benny had even polished the brown Bakelite knob at the top of the gear stick. The musty smell of cotton batting in the seats wafted from the sun-heated interior.

"Where's the key?" He put out his hand.

Benny frowned. Benny had always been overweight, but in recent years he had gained a lot around the neck. When he frowned, the sag appeared to reach the top of his work shirt. It was a frown of true sadness.

"It's not ready. The new distributor just arrived yesterday. Anthony has to install it. He's the only one. He won't be back for at least an hour. He promised to do it tonight. You'll have the truck by tomorrow morning. I promise."

"Promise?"

"Promise." Benny smiled again.

Henry imagined putting a natural wood gate around the open bed and having a green tarp to keep the rain off books he had purchased. He stepped back, admiring the truck again.

"Nine o'clock?"

"Nine o'clock." Benny's hands went up as if to say, "Of course."

Henry had planned to drive the truck around town for the afternoon—perhaps drive by Albert's house three or four times, or drive around Brookline Village to see if anyone he knew was out. He would have to do it another day now.

The copy service had three copies of the manuscript ready and bound when he returned. He flipped the pages of the first, more than slightly awed. He was holding someone else's life in his hands. His thumb stopped the turn of pages at the dedication. Eddy had written it as a kind of poem.

"To Janet Fowler, for love, this gift, too small, is given. Our precious time, for certain, still dear, too late, forever given."

Was the picture of the woman at the beach in the plastic frame Eddy's Janet? Where was she now?

By the time he was home again, Henry had another idea.

In the phone book, he found the address for Tremont Press on Arlington Street in Boston. He put Eddy's manuscript in a shipping envelope, made the letter he enclosed short and sweet, and then decided not to mail it.

The urge was spontaneous, and it appealed to him. There were so few independent presses left, and Tremont had a reputation for publishing new authors. They even published poetry, a thanklessly small market. From others, Henry had often heard the rule: query first. But he did not have the time to be sending letters around, or a good idea of how a query was written. What happened to the days when Thomas Wolfe could show up at Scribner's with an armful of manuscript? Besides, it could be interesting to approach the business of books from the other side for once.

The real matter to him now was Edward Perry. It was a damn shame someone with that amount of talent had never found a safe haven for himself in the world. *Penny Candy* was not a happy work, but it was poetic and at times elegiac. Though rough in sentiment because the subject was harsh, it was beautifully and carefully written. Perry had grown up in New York City during the 1950s. His father had been an abusive alcoholic. His mother appeared to have been schizophrenic, alternating between being obsessively caring and totally cold—forgetting to buy food or, at other times, to cook the food she had bought. In the midst of this, Eddy had lived the life of a carefree child. The streets of New York had been his playground, day and night, and his memoir of that time was something new to Henry. Perry had roamed with fearless abandon. Shopkeepers had given him odd jobs for pocket money. He had befriended an old used book dealer on Second Avenue and spent afternoons carrying loads of books from place to place in return for the knowledge that would one day be his trade. A brokendown whore, with the odd name of Pissy, had even given him a bunk out of the cold on Houston Street one winter when his father had failed to make the rent and they lost their apartment. Eddy had pushed a broom in the wet slop at the Fulton Fish Market and eaten like a king. His small stature had given him the security of being a child until his hormones had finally made life difficult. His first love, a Puerto Rican girl already addicted to heroin, had brought his childhood idyll to an abrupt end in the emergency room at St. Vincent's Hospital. Henry could not help but compare this to his own childhood, which had been safe and secure and never lacking in either love or care. His own father may have been hard-nosed, but he was fair, and home every night at six. His mother, as long as she lived, had been given to frequent kisses, had read her Yeats out loud to them, and even in her sick bed had sewn his clothes back together. She had put a good meal on the table every night until the day she could no longer stand.

Henry had run away from home the first time at the age of twelve, shortly after his mother had been buried—all the way to Boston from Brookline on the Green Line trolley. Then he had walked home in the dark, lacking the return fare. His sister Shelagh, just sixteen then, had left a brown paper sack of dinner in his room, so that his father would not see.

They may have both followed the same drummer in the end, but there was more difference between Eddy and himself than they had in common. Henry had been a difficult and reluctant student, while Eddy had been the favorite of almost all his teachers. Rejecting what little authority he could find, Henry had refused to go to college, or even into the army. Eddy had been stationed in Germany and received a scholarship to NYU. After three years of odd jobs in high school, it took Henry little time to know what he wanted when he found it. It was on the base in Germany that Eddy had really discovered drugs, not on the streets of New York. Eddy had flunked out of NYU in his second year, his mind numbed by heroin.

Yet none of Eddy's book was an apology. There were no excuses. Eddy had lived his own life and paid the bill. He was thankful. He was not bitter, or resentful, or jealous. He had his chances.

The thought occurred to Henry that Eddy Perry was a better man than himself. It was a thought he could not shake.

The brownstone of the building on Arlington Street was melting with the years of weather, every detail rounded like a sand castle. The front steps had been replaced with mud-colored cement in an attempted match, but were square and edgy in harsh contrast.

The door to the building was locked. A nicely hand lettered sign above a wide brass-lipped slot commanded, LEAVE ALL PACKAGES HERE. There were three buttons followed by names. Tremont Press was at the top. Henry went out to the sidewalk and looked up at the face of the small building again. There was nothing to see but decorative blinds. A thick clot of traffic from Storrow Drive gushed into Arlington Street behind him with the change of the traffic light. He heard a horn and turned.

A UPS delivery truck had stopped a few doors away, and a driver in a Toyota was upset at getting caught behind.

Henry went back to the door and pushed the top button. A voice cracked through a small brass grill.

"Yes."

He said, "UPS."

The buzzer sounded and Henry opened the door. The first-floor offices were closed behind carved mahogany. Brass plates offered the name of a law firm Henry had heard of, Boyle and Doyle. He imagined this was the origin of many water-cooler jokes. He started up the stairs. Behind him he heard a noise. The brown shirt of a UPS driver was visible through the glass of the door. Henry moved faster. On the second floor, doors were open, but a plastic sign announced the offices of the Pine Comb Charitable Fund. A secretary looked suspiciously over her glasses at him and asked if she could help. He pointed upward and continued to climb.

On the third floor a single door offered a name in small letters. TREMONT PRESS.

Behind him he could hear heavy steps on the stairs.

Henry opened the door.

There, facing him in a large room of unoccupied desks, each overflowing with manila envelopes and piles of correspondence, was the amazingly endowed redhead from Fenway Park.

Chapter Eight

So what happened?"

Della was impatient. He had begun the story at the wrong turn of events. He leaned back farther in his chair and switched the telephone to the other ear.

"You've got to read it. I can't tell you everything. But you know he ended up in Boston. You know that. And then I got this idea."

"You people are all weird. I think it's the mildew. It's the spores of the mildew in the old books that gets into your brains and starts rotting you from the inside out."

"A pleasant thought."

"You're supposed to be a bookseller. You're not Humphrey Bogart. If you want another job, you should get something that actually pays a salary."

Logic had no place in this, he thought. This was a matter of reason.

"This way I can kill two birds with one stone."

He immediately heard his father's voice in his head warning him about "a lazy man's load." Carrying too much was as bad a carrying too little. Della heard something else.

"An unfortunate turn of phrase. The redhead will have you arrested. UPS will have you in jail."

"They can't do anything. I told him I just said yes, not UPS. The redhead just misunderstood, with the truck sitting outside and the noise."

"I'll bet she bought that. You look like a sneak thief to me."

She was being flip. This was important.

"The problem is, you should see the place. The UPS guy was carrying in ten or twelve packages—I could tell they were all manuscripts. FedEx envelopes were stacked a foot deep on some of those desks. Eddy's book would just get lost in there. But if Barbara's idea about Duggan is right—"

"Barbara has given you too many ideas already. I thought you were staying away from Barbara."

"—if Barbara's right and Duggan is the money behind Tremont, it explains why they can publish so many new writers. That's why they have such a backlist. They don't depend on making much of a profit. And that's why he was at the ballgame with Nora."

"I thought she just yelled at you. How did you get her name?"

"The UPS guy. They know all the girls by their first names. He called her Nora when he came in."

"Maybe you should work for UPS. You could meet a few more girlfriends that way.... So what is your idea?"

If she was not going to be serious, he wouldn't either.

"I don't like to wear shorts."

"What kind of idea is that?"

"The UPS guys all wear shorts." She was not going to let him get away. "But my idea is to try to get Tremont to publish Eddy's book."

She did not even pause at the revelation. "You have nice legs. You'd look good in shorts. But if this Nora stole the idea from Frankowski's book and gave it to George Duggan, why would you want them to publish Eddy's book?"

"You'd look better in shorts than me. Why is it only the UPS guys that wear shorts? I never see the women drivers wearing shorts."

Della blew a breath of exasperation. "I've never seen a woman UPS driver. Just the ones for FedEx. Is that because the FedEx packages are smaller?"

"I don't know. But I wouldn't let Tremont have *Penny Candy*, if that turns out to be what happened. It just gives me a good excuse to try to talk to them. And if it's all some kind of mistake, then Eddy's book might get a chance."

"What kind of mistake?"

"I don't know. I told you Duggan doesn't seem like the kind of guy who would steal somebody else's ideas."

"But, you said you only saw him once before."

"Yeah. Well. That was the impression I got."

"You trust a guy you only saw at a distance once before. Kind of like love at first sight?"

A sudden change of tone in her voice worried him.

"No. He just seemed like a decent guy. Didn't you ever see somebody you liked right off?"

"Yes. But it's causing me a lot of trouble."

Henry ignored the remark. "Besides, I don't have any better ideas."

"We could go someplace for dinner."

There was a knock at the door—a knock he knew but could not identify.

"Hold on."

He put the phone down and opened the door to the small figure of Sasha. Dressed in what appeared to him to be thin black pajamas, she was carrying a suitcase almost half her size. Her violin case was strapped across her back.

"I'm locked out. Can I go through your window to the fire escape? I left my kitchen window open…. Mrs. Murray can't find her key."

"Sure." That was easy enough.

She had been crying. He could see the puffiness around her eyes. From the telephone he could hear the small thin voice of Della.

"Who is it? Henry, who is that?"

81

Henry opened the kitchen window and moved the plants away. Sasha scampered through with the nimbleness of a child. When he went back to close the door, he lifted the suitcase she had left behind. It seemed far too heavy for her to be carrying. He found himself grunting as he pulled it up the stairs to her door. She opened her door as he arrived.

"Thank you. Thank you. Thank you.... It has been a very long day. Thank you."

"You're welcome."

He had never seen her apartment before. He stepped forward unconsciously. It was stuffy from lack of use, and sparsely furnished. The polished wood floors were bare except for a large pillow at the center of the living room. Sasha was half Japanese, and the minimal decor was clearly in that direction.

Astonishingly, on the wall was a life-size photograph of a nude—Sasha—holding her violin to play while seated on the very same pillow now at the center of the floor. With one leg folded beneath and the other extended, her back arched, small breasts almost touching the bottom surface of the polished wood, face tilted to the side toward the camera, mouth open just enough to force her jaw against the edge of instrument, elbows up and out, the fingers of one hand grasping the end of the bow and the fingers of the other curved around the thin neck toward the strings, the pose could have been stolen from a ballet. It had to be the most erotic photograph Henry had ever seen.

She asked, "You like it?"

She was smiling, not happily, but showing no embarrassment. He said, "It's beautiful."

"I am going to burn it. It was taken by my ex-boyfriend. Ex-Ex-Ex. He is a cheat. He is a creep. I don't ever want to see him again. And I don't ever want to see this picture again."

She was still smiling. It unsettled him.

"But it's so beautiful."

"He is a great artist. But he is a creep. You take it."

"What?"

"You take it. It's yours. I never want to see it again."

She lifted it from the wall, her arms spread to full width, and presented the picture to Henry, her smiling face peeking over the top of the frame.

He took it in both his hands, as if grasping her body, while looking down at the face in the picture with the violin propped hard against the jaw, and then he looked back at the artificial smile on Sasha's face before him. Then he remembered Della.

He thanked Sasha several times as she shut the door behind him, took the stairs carefully with the frame tilted to fit the narrowed space, and set the picture upright on the floor against the open wall of his living room wall. The phone was silent when he picked it up.

He said, "Hello?" There was a moment more of silence before Della answered.

"What was that all about?"

"Sasha. The girl on the third floor. She was locked out. I had to help her."

"Really.... You are a very helpful sort of person." Her voice turned on edge. "Do me a favor, will you?"

"What?"

There was a pause. Finally a sigh.

"Never mind. You can't help yourself. You want to go out to dinner?"

Henry thought he had better say yes.

Chapter Nine

They had first played chess together in 1979. Little had changed since. Then it was on Thursday nights at the small second-floor chess club on Newbury Street where they had first met; a place long since gone. Now it was usually at the Blue Thorn, and any night that Albert needed to get away from Alice, which was often once or twice a week. Then Albert had just graduated from high school and Henry still had two difficult years left. But their strategies had remained the same. Albert always plotted to kill the queen, with the assumption that the king would follow. Henry always took the shortest path to the king.

"Why did Hannibal wait so long to attack Rome?"

Albert had asked the question without preparation as he moved his bishop forward, perhaps because of their conversation the week before about James Frankowski's book, but probably only to distract Henry, because it was just the kind of question that got him going.

Henry studied the board, hesitating a few times as he stopped himself from making moves he thought better of, and finally answered with the advance of his bishop and his own question.

"Why did I wait so long to try my luck with Miss Stinson?"

Albert frowned, grunted, and moved to block the bishop's next advance with a pawn.

"I'm serious, now. I've always wondered that.... Thousands of miles across rough terrain—this is before the Romans had built their marvelous system of roads, remember—across countless rivers, through the Alps, with elephants—defeating one army after another. He is now at the very gates of Rome. This was the dream of his father's life, as well as his own— if Hannibal had taken Rome, he would have ruled the world. Scipio would never have been able to organize his troops in Spain in time. And we'll never know what went on in Hannibal's head, because his enemies wrote the history books.... You have to take my pawn. You can't just ignore it."

Henry moved quickly in response.

"I'll take your knight instead. Your diversion did not work.... But I'm serious too. I've thought seriously about Miss Stinson for almost fifteen years. Usually at night."

Albert's frown was frozen in place as he studied the board. Finally he moved his bishop forward again.

"Miss Stinson...She was the teacher at the Harvard Extension course you took that time. Why didn't you make a move on her? That wasn't ancient history. That was Pre-Raphaelites or something, wasn't it?"

Albert seemed annoyed now. Henry smiled.

"Very good. I'll take your other knight for that.... It was 'The Conflict and Influence of Carlyle and Emerson on the Pre-Raphaelites and William Morris and the Beginning of the Arts and Crafts Movement in England and America.'"

Albert's frown broke.

"Your queen is in check."

"Only if you don't mind losing your king."

The frown came back and he grunted.

"Right...so, what does one thing have to do with the other?"

"Rome."

"Yeah."

"You've been there, Albert. I haven't. According to the books, it's gorgeous. It was the greatest city in the world. The New York of its age. You think Carthage was so fine? Carthage was a great city, but it was a city of merchants. It was a port city, built by the Phoenicians. It probably looked like any other stinky port city of the time, only bigger. Do you think another city on Earth was so beautiful as Rome in 217 B.C.? This is before the urban sprawl and the hordes of immigrants. This was the Rome of the Republic."

Albert sat back from the board without making his move.

"Hannibal was in awe? You're saying he was spellbound? He couldn't bring himself to the final assault because he was agog? He was dazzled? After working that hard all his life to fulfill the dreams of his father and avenge the honor of his country, it wasn't the walls that held him back, it was awe?"

Henry could make no move on the board and sat back as well.

"Miss Stinson—You saw her. That one time you went over there to meet me before the movie. Tell me you can't still remember her. Tell me you can't see her in your mind at this very moment."

"Right…Maybe you're right." Albert shook his head and sat forward to study the board again. "So what happened to her?"

"She married a hot-shot doctor who was never in awe of anything in his life. I heard somewhere later on that she was engaged again. A lawyer this time…. And I'll always wonder why I held back. Just like Hannibal."

"I think he's stopped wondering a couple of thousand years ago…. Now your queen is in check."

The gloat in Albert's voice trailed off as Henry moved quickly again.

"I'll take your bishop in trade."

There was bravado without confidence in Albert's answer.

"Bad trade.... With all that drooling, did you learn anything in her class?"

Henry leaned back just far enough now to display satisfaction with the eventual outcome of the game.

"Yes, as a matter of fact, but not the point of the class. I got a glimpse of why the younger generation of 1850 were all rebelling against that hero-worship the Germans were exporting through Carlyle. It was a bag of bones. It was just another religion. All the secular idealism of the eighteenth century— Carlyle was a Scot, you know, a product himself of the Scottish Enlightenment—all of that was being sold down the river by another religion. Hero worship!" Henry kept a straight face. "Hand me that pawn please."

Henry moved his knight. Albert sat back with a jerk of his chair. "Crap. How did you do that?"

"The same way I did it last time."

"Last time I beat you," Albert objected.

"That was two times ago. That was Thursday. That was after Alice threw the fit 'cause I kept you out all night."

"Right…you want another game?"

"No. I want another beer…. So, what did you do about Alice?"

"What about Alice?"

Henry sat back now. "You gonna tell her about every bit of extra money you make under the table? She's not just upset with me. I don't even pay you. It's the other jobs. You're working too much."

Albert rolled his eyes.

"You know. You don't give a damn 'cause you don't have kids. You've got no responsibilities. You die, and they'll dig a hole and dump your stinky books in on top of you and that'll be that. I have to put something away for a rainy day."

Henry persisted. "So. Are you going to listen to her? If you die from overwork are the boys better off?"

Albert tilted his head at the thought, and then dismissed it.

"It's the principle. She's right about that. I told her. No more under the table."

"And you'll be okay if you lose a few jobs? Some people won't bring you in, if you won't work off the sheet. You've told me that."

Albert weaved in his chair a bit.

"I'm busy enough. I'll have to take the loss. She's right. How would I explain it to the kids anyway?"

Henry continued to take the devil's part. "Say, 'Here's a new bike'?"

"You know what I mean." Resignation lowered Albert's voice.

Henry pressed at the sore spot. "Say, 'Let's take another week of vacation'?"

"Get off it...." Now there was a touch of irritation.

"You'll be the only trash collector in Boston who doesn't take a little extra on the side."

"Let it be, then. Let it be."

"You're a lucky man." Henry relented, collecting the chess pieces left on the board and putting them back in the coffee can.

"You know it." Albert snapped the answer.

Henry said, "Every guy needs an Alice."

Albert sat back again and gave Henry the steady stare.

"What? You having problems keeping your accounts straight?"

That was the real problem, wasn't it?

"Yeah."

"How? What's up?"

"The book I bought. From Eddy Perry. If I had said no, he'd be alive."

"You buy books. It's your job. Why? Was it stolen?"

"No. I told you. No. In fact, it once belonged to Hale Peabody. Eddy bought it at an auction years ago. After that it belonged to a guy named Ferris—an MIT computer whiz. He had to unload it because EMC Corp. cut its work force and he couldn't pay all the bills he'd run up living large. He sold it back to Eddy for two hundred dollars."

"And the problem is?"

"It's all such a cycle of misery. Ferris is one of these geeks they turn out at MIT who has no social skills and no life outside the lab, and no moral compass—like if the Nazis were recruiting for brains, he'd be their pick. His ethics are all from movies and videos and Coca-Cola ads. In his best moments he lives in this sick fantasy world dreamed up by H. P. Lovecraft with its own mythos. Now, there is a real piece of work—Lovecraft's a truly sad piece of human genius gone bad for lack of fresh air and sunlight and a female hand…. So, after this guy Ferris graduates and gets hired away by the big computer company, he invests all his money in what?" Henry looked directly at Albert. "New clothes? A dental program? Dance lessons? No. He buys first editions of H. P. Lovecraft and the rest of the Arkham House weird fantasy crew. So really, where does the money go? It goes to Eddy Perry—to a little guy who has no more control over his life than Ferris—an introverted little book dealer who lives from library sale to yard sale, lives in a barren little tenement in Central Square, dreams beautiful dreams about a rotten childhood, and finds what joy he can in—what is the fashion right now? Is it cocaine?"

"I think I read in the papers that they're back to heroin."

"Heroin…. And I buy the book from him knowing he'll use it for heroin?"

"Someone was going to buy it."

"It didn't have to be me."

"It was book dealer to book dealer."

"I knew he was a addict. I was taking advantage."

"You told me you paid him what he expected."

"I could have paid more. He was probably desperate. I could have guessed that."

"It would have ended up with the person who killed him. You're not obliged to pay people what they expect. You pay what you think you can afford and make a profit. You didn't know he was going to get killed. You were doing him a favor just by going out in the middle of the night to look at a book and then going to get the money for him."

"Evening. It was still only the evening."

"Doesn't matter. Your job is to pay low and sell high, otherwise you're out of business. How many mistakes do you have to eat along the way? The week before that, you had nothing. You told me yourself you had nothing. How many books are in that closet of yours that you'll have to sell at a loss. You pay fair. You play fair. Don't start to second guess yourself. Don't be a chump."

"I need an Alice."

"I got Alice. You get your own."

"Right."

Chapter Ten

Her television was off, but it bothered him to see his own reflection on the darkened glass of the screen. With both of them sitting on the couch, he had to turn awkwardly as he sat back, in order to see her face.

Sharon asked, "Why do you live alone?"

It was an attack. He fumbled in his mind for the right answer. She did not wait for him to regroup.

She said, "It has been so very difficult to be alone here since Jim died. I've cried myself to sleep too many times.... It's not healthy for people to live alone."

Henry looked again around the periphery of the living room. There was no picture of James Frankowski for him to call attention to as a defensive measure. More surprising to him, the only bookcase in the room was small, relative to the size of the cabinet that held the TV and stereo. Most of the books in the case he had quickly scanned, out of habit, when he had first arrived. It was an odd collection of self-help and psychology books mixed with a few historical novels and a shelf of ancient history. One of the historical novels was Duggan's *Dreams of Bithynia*. Henry noticed that Frankowski's first book, *Epaminondas,* which was there as well, had been rebound in green leather.

From tall speakers came the sound of some currently popular song he did not understand the lyric to. Sharon was looking at his eyes, as he refocused on her mouth. He resorted to old lines.

"I like things the way they are. I do what I want. I enjoy the freedom."

One eyebrow went up in critical emphasis.

"You broke Barbara's heart, you know."

Henry shifted on the cushion without finding a more comfortable position. "That was my fault. I have always regretted that part. But she would have hated being married to a guy like me."

Without obviously moving, perhaps it was the way her body was turned, she had somehow edged noticeably closer. With one finger she drew a crease in the fabric of the cushion between them, as if marking a line in the sand.

"What's so bad about a guy like you?"

He had been so stupid. When she had asked him to sit down, he could just have easily chosen one of the side chairs.... No, he thought again. She had directed him to the couch, hadn't she?

He opted for self-disparagement as a defense. "I'm selfish. Much too—"

She shook her head once in dismissal before he was finished. "We are all selfish. It's human nature. That's why love is so important. It overcomes all that selfishness."

She leaned toward him, her face even closer.

It was not only because she was a good-looking woman that he was uncomfortable. It was because she seemed to have more of an idea why he was there than he did. He had managed to put the meeting off for a week. He had run out of excuses. They were supposed to be finding some way to make a case against Mr. Duggan. They were not getting much closer to that.

The blood color of her lipgloss pulled at his eyes. Perfume thickened the air he was trying to breathe—breathe as slowly as possible. He searched for another defense.

"When exactly did James finish the manuscript?" he asked.

Her eyes shifted. Did they roll just a little?

"Oh…About three years ago. We talked about that, didn't we?…He wanted to finish it by the Millennium. That was his deadline."

She moved away again, slightly.

"2000 or 2001?"

"2001. James was very precise about things like that."

Henry rested the ankle of his right leg on his left knee as a kind of block, but that was even more uncomfortable.

"How long was it after you finished your research?"

She shrugged and made a face, excusing herself for not remembering exactly.

"A year perhaps…. But I was correcting the manuscript right up to the day he mailed it out the first time."

"And you're sure he mailed it to the Tremont Press? When?"

"Must have been March 2001."

"But you are not sure."

"I'm sorry."

"Did he change it at all after he got it back?"

"No. He was pretty unhappy about that rejection, and he put it away…. That was just like him. He wanted to think about it for awhile. I wanted him to send it out again immediately. I don't see how a manuscript gains anything from aging inside a drawer. But Jim had his way. And then everything went bad with his death, and I forgot about it completely until I saw the advance copy of the Duggan book."

"But you are pretty sure that Tremont was the last place he sent it?"

Her voice went flat. Perhaps with exasperation, he hoped. Woman never liked clueless guys.

"Yes."

It was his advantage now.

"When was the first time again?"

"Well, he sent out a number of queries after Little, Brown declined to look at it. They were very unhappy about the lack of sales on his first book. I think someone lost a job over that, but I can't say. I'm not sure. Perhaps Knopf or Viking. I'm sure it was one of them."

"And he never contacted an agent? I thought everyone used agents these days."

"He really didn't know about all that. It was Little, Brown that contacted him first, you understand, about writing something, after hearing of him from one of the other people at Harvard. He was very happy with Little, Brown...until they declined."

"You did not type up the letter. It's not on your computer now?" Henry looked over at the computer on a desk in an alcove.

She shook her head. "I bought that one myself. I had to get rid of his old Mac. I had no reason to keep it after he died. It didn't work well with the computer at the bookshop. Besides, it was filled with his personal notes. He was so disorganized. He had grocery lists in there next to notes about sheep herding in ancient Galatia. I couldn't stand to look at it. I even had the apartment painted. Most of his personal books are gone now. I'm sorry. I didn't know, when I did it, that they would matter. You don't know what it's like after you lose someone. I needed to start all over."

He could hear her taking breath as if her throat was tightening with emotion. Henry worried that the conversation may be going in another wrong direction.

"Did he keep any of the rejection slips?"

Her eyes searched Henry's face. "No. That wasn't like him. But I remember one, at least. It was a letter. I saw it briefly. It was from Knopf, I think. It said they liked it—thought it had promise. But it wasn't right for them at the time. Just the usual kind of thing publishers say."

He pressed the thought. "How about the one from Viking?" She shook her head. "Do you remember the letter from Tremont Press?"

Her head shook again as her eyes narrowed, as if the memory were lost.

"Tremont said something like Knopf had. She might have said she liked the subject…I can't remember exactly."

"She? Nora Lynch?"

Sharon stared blankly at him for a moment, as if trying to understand some other motive in his questions. The robin's egg blue was darker in the lower light of the apartment.

"I suppose so."

"And the version on that computer—is it the last version?"

She stared at him a moment longer, her eyes opening wider, then began to shake her head again.

"No…no. That's the version I put on a disk and transferred over.… Probably the week I bought it."

"When was that?"

"Oh—after I got back."

"From where?"

"From Europe. I went away just after Jim's funeral. I needed some recovery time."

Henry paused. Her lips had thinned now with the tightness in her cheeks and she was staring down at her own hand on the cushion. He worried she might be getting close to a more emotional response.

"Do you have any kind of notes at all from the editors? If we just had some confirmation from a third party about the content of the book, it might make a difference."

Her index finger continued to work the trough she had made in the loose fabric of the cushion.

"I wondered about that, of course. I wrote to Knopf. But there have been so many changes over there, the last few years. They had no record. No one remembered it."

Somewhere there must be an editor or a slush pile reader who read *Hannibal's Dance* and liked it as much as Henry did. It was not a story that would easily fade from the mind, but more than that, it was good. Good stories were not easily forgotten.

"What did Viking have to say? No one has a record there either?"

A frown dipped the corners of her eyebrows in a plea of mercy. Her voice sounded weary of his questions.

"Well, there were only a few. Just two or three publishers before Jim gave up."

"And Little, Brown—they have no record?"

"But remember, they declined to even read it. It was very unusual because they had the option from the previous book."

Henry looked back at the reflection on the television which now included them both within the frame. "Barbara thinks Nora Lynch is the key to all this. She thinks Lynch passed the idea on to Duggan. He might not have had any idea where it came from."

She answered weakly. "I know. I thought of that."

Was there resignation in her voice?

Knowing Barbara's doggedness, Henry wondered how many times she had gone over this with Sharon before. The first time he had actually met with Sharon, at the café, he had thought she was a little cold. The second time, the fiasco at Barbara's apartment, had made him think she was a good sport with a quick sense of humor, which was something he had always liked. Life was full of human error, folly, and mischief. A lack of humor was deadly.

On that occasion, it was Barbara's idea that they meet for dinner. Barbara had made her great spaghetti—something she had learned to do originally for him, to please him, back when they were going together. Sharon had worn a thin yellow dress that made Henry think of daffodils. The color was striking in Barbara's dark apartment.

Barbara's bookshelves had spread since Henry had been there last, encrusting the last remaining wall space in the living room, and now much of the dining room. Their conversation had been quiet, muffled further by the books. Sharon had spoken of first meeting Jim when she was still a student at Boston University and had gone across the river to Harvard to apply for a job as a research assistant to earn a little extra money. The affair, which had started then, had evolved to their living together the year after she graduated. It had been Sharon who had first suggested that the professor of ancient history turn to writing historical novels to increase his income and as a way of exploring some of his ideas about the odd chances of history. The interest from Little, Brown had come then, at just the right moment. James Frankowski's first novel had been accepted for publication almost immediately.

It was then that the light in the fixture above them at the table had gone out, darkening the room. Barbara had wanted to light candles. Henry had objected. He had long since learned to be wary of women lighting candles. Afterwards, Henry wondered if the warnings of Sharon's temper had been exaggerated.

By chance, he had glimpsed Sharon's face as he fell. Barbara had just moved a dish of grated cheese so that he could put one foot out to balance himself at the center of the table, while he replaced the light bulb in the high old fixture close to the ceiling. He had been turned away from Barbara and remembered thinking he was glad he had not been facing her as the table collapsed.

Sharon first put a hand to her mouth in surprise. By the time his back had found the floor, the plates, catapulted from the end of the table where they had been moved for safety, had found him. Sharon had begun to laugh. It had been Sharon's laughter that he remembered afterward.

Sharon had said, almost immediately, "Don't move. It hasn't touched the floor. We can eat it right off the top of you if you stay still."

He smiled at the thought now, and looked back to Sharon on the couch. Had she moved closer to him again?

He said, "It's too bad the first book didn't sell a little better. Everything would have been different."

Her eyes widened again. "It was such a good book. Epaminondas is such a wonderful character. Did you ever read it? You'd like it. Jim started the story after the great victory at Leuctra and the successful campaigns for the Arcadian league in the Peloponnesus. It begins as Epaminondas has been broken by political adversaries and has taken refuge under an assumed name as a common soldier with an army in Thessaly. He witnesses the very same pettiness in the ranks there that kept the Greeks forever at war with themselves. He realized then that there was no escaping human frailty or responsibility. Jim recreated the second act of Epaminondas' life, the triumph over politics and armies, right to his death at Mantinea, predicting what would happen with the eventual rise of Philip and Alexander. It was a fine book. But no one could pronounce the name. Epaminondas. The publisher called us and said booksellers were afraid of mispronouncing the name and avoided saying it out loud—everyone is so afraid of appearing foolish—so they just avoided it all together."

"Hannibal rolls off the tongue a bit easier."

"But you see, it's the same story. Epaminondas turned away from the corruption of power as well. He might have been ruler of Thebes when Philip made his move. He would have stopped the Macedonians. There never would have been an Alexander. Turning away from power can be as deadly as taking it on."

An idle thought occurred. "Did James know that *Epaminondas* was not selling well when he started writing *Hannibal's Dance?*"

The robin's egg eyes stared blankly at him again a moment too long before answering. What was she thinking?

"He couldn't have. He saw it all as one work, really—one theme. I remember him talking about the second book before he had even finished the first. But he rewrote so much. I'm sure the failure of the first book influenced the way he decided to tell the story in the second. It must have. But he never let me read chapters until he was done with them. He did not appreciate my comments on his style."

"I'll read it sometime. I have a buddy who loves the Greeks and Romans. It'll give us something to argue about. But then, everybody loves the Greeks and hates the Romans."

She smiled. "They love gladiators. Not the robes. They like the swords, but they don't want to think about the ideas. I think everyone in the publishing business wanted their Roman history to have gladiators a few years ago. That's the way it goes. Hannibal wasn't hot enough by himself."

Henry wished he had a cigarette. But then, Sharon did not smoke, and it would have been impolite in any case.

"And you are positive there is no letter from Tremont Press in a drawer somewhere?"

"No. I told you, Jim threw stuff like that away. He didn't like negative reminders."

"Or a name? If you only had a name of anyone else he may have sent the manuscript to…"

"No one I've been able to find…. Would you like another beer?"

She had offered him wine, which he had avoided. The only beer she had was a light brand. He had never been fond of what he called nearly beer.

"No thanks."

"I think I'll have some more wine." she said. She moved by him where he sat on the couch so that her leg touched his. She was wearing a beige dress which acquired a flesh tone in the lower light. It rode a little high, he thought, and made the most of her legs.

He asked, "Do you have a copy of the letter from Mr. Boyle?"

She did not answer. She appeared to be thinking about something else as she poured wine at the counter between the living room and the kitchen. When she returned, her leg seemed to pause by his again, and then she sat down. She was closer now than she had been before. Henry realized her counter-assault had begun.

"I need help through this," she said. Her voice had gone down to just above a whisper. "I need some support…I've been through a great deal of strain over the past few years. Even before Jim died, we had problems. Things were not…as we wanted them to be. He was unhappy. I was unhappy. I think it was buying this condo that was the last straw. Keeping up with the payments. Then the rejections. Then his death. It's been very difficult. Men don't realize—especially these days, with women's liberation and everything. Women still need to feel protected. It goes back to the beginning of time. Politics doesn't change who we are. A woman needs a man to shield her, to take care of her…"

The perfume mixed in the air with the smell of the wine. Her hand was suddenly on his knee. Her lips were less than six inches from his.

The phone rang. In that instant, as it rang the second time, he saw in Sharon's eyes the anger he had not seen before. The pale blue darkened. Her lips closed tight again. She rose and brushed by him roughly this time and grabbed the receiver from the counter.

It was immediately clear that it was Barbara. It was eight o'clock. She had closed the store for the night and was calling to find out if they could use her help.

Chapter Eleven

Albert was half asleep. He kept repeating that he had been up since five that morning. Henry responded that it was still early—not even midnight yet—he could sleep later.

Albert stopped his truck directly behind Tremont Press, blocking the alley and shadowing the dumpster to the building. The heat had them both sweating into already dampened shirts.

Henry climbed out of the cab alone this time. Albert whined again about the time, but it was drowned in the low grumble of the motor. Albert's trash pickups for Ready Rubbish Removal began at six in the morning. Henry had not gotten out of bed until noon.

Albert said, "Don't take all day."

This was the second week in a row. Their first foray had been a mess. They had removed all the bags from the dumpster and brought them out to the field house of Albert's athletic club in Dorchester at midnight. Coffee grounds had gotten into the cracks of the floorboards of the basketball court. Half-finished orange juice and diet cola had spread over hundreds of loose sheets of paper, the liquid multiplying in volume as they rummaged for some unknown scrap of information. A never identified oily substance crept mysteriously from beneath the bags.

The athletic club had charged Albert to have a special cleaning crew come by and take care of the smell, which would not go away. Henry had already given Albert the eighty-five dollars to cover that.

But they did learn something. They had learned that Tremont Press used grey plastic bags, while the charitable fund used black and the lawyers' trash bags were white. The Tremont Press garbage bags had contained mostly packing material, along with hundreds of old publishers' catalogues. They figured the color-coding of the bags was for the janitor, but it made the work the second time around far easier.

Rats scurried from spaces beneath as he opened the top of the dumpster. Henry guessed they were the same ones which had stopped his breath the week before.

Holding a small flashlight in his teeth, he started removing only the grey trash bags, creating a low mound outside the dumpster. He had attributed the fruit juice of the previous week to the charitable fund, and the coffee grounds and the oily substance to the law firm. The fetid air inside the dumpster made him want to gag. Through the metallic drum of his movements against the steel sides of the dumpster, he heard Albert announce the time again.

When Henry opened the gate on the back of the truck to load, a burst of blinding light enveloped him. Albert opened his door with an animal groan from the cab of the truck that startled Henry almost as much as the light. Two policemen left the doors to their car open as they walked up on either side of the truck. Henry kept his mouth shut, having little to say.

"What's up?" One policeman said to Albert.

Henry squinted against the light and Albert shielded his eyes with one hand and closed his cab door to point at his company name with the other.

"I'm sorry, officer. I'm late. I know. I got a call earlier to pick up overflow garbage from number ninety-seven. The job before this one at a house over in Cambridge took all day. We had to get some dinner…. You know. Now, I know it's late, but

I figured we could just get the crap and get out of here without a peep…You know."

The closest policeman kicked one of the plastic bags and then looked back at Henry. There was a moment's hesitation. Looking into the light, the only discernable feature of the cop's darkened face that offered some clue to his thoughts was the sheen of sweat on one cheek. Then he waved the hand which had rested at his belt.

"Hurry it up. Just don't do it again. We'll have some old biddy calling in and complaining about the off-hour noise in no time."

Henry answered, "Yes, sir," and started quickly loading the bags into the truck. Albert just nodded wearily, his eyelids returned to half mast, and climbed back in the cab.

Albert did not mind telling the lie. He did that very well. What he minded was telling a lie that could have been found out so easily. If the cop had bothered to open the dumpster and see the bags that Henry had left behind, there would have been more questions and a lot more trouble. Albert grumbled continuously now as they drove back to Cambridge.

"If it wasn't for the stink he would have looked in that dumpster and known I was shoveling a load of bullshit."

"The part about the house in Cambridge is partly true."

Albert shook his head, clearly at a loss as to why that part of the story mattered.

"This is it. If I'm not doing this stuff on the side even when I get paid, I ain't goin' to do it anymore when I'm not. I could lose my license doing something like this. It's not a joke."

Henry slumped back in his seat, discouraged.

"There's no book on this. I don't know what I'm doing. I'm no detective. Barbara is asking for too goddamned much."

Albert grunted something as he changed gears.

Henry asked, "What?"

"You don't know how to let go any more than she does." He said it louder the second time.

"That's a load of bullshit. I'm the one who walked out of that."

"Yeah, right. Like I'm the one who will choose to sleep on the couch tonight because I didn't come home for dinner."

Henry thought this over a little more seriously. He had refused Barbara's money. But he was helping her anyway. Why? He pushed the thought away. She was a friend. A friend had asked for help. That was simple.

"She's a friend…"

Albert grunted.

"What?"

"You have too many friends. Especially female friends."

Henry thought this over for half a second.

"You're jealous."

"Damn right."

Henry unloaded the plastic bags himself, letting Albert get along home, and brought them up to his apartment two at a time. Mrs. Murray's lights were off, and he hoped she was asleep. He was not sure how he would explain this.

Moving his box fan from his living room to get the full effect, he began to open the bags one by one on the kitchen floor. He calculated that the sound would less likely reach from there to Mrs. Murray's bedroom below.

He found something interesting almost immediately. There were notes in the piles of loose paper from George Duggan. From the scribbling on others he quickly identified the hand-writing of Nora Lynch. The notes were apparently just between those two. There seemed to be no one else working at Tremont Press. Printers' quotes and binding problems filled dozens of loose sheets. A handwritten schedule of publication dates projected six titles over the next three months. Several photocopied manuscripts bore the editorial marks of Nora Lynch.

Over two dozen manuscripts, opened, but still in their original manila envelopes, were marked "No return postage." Dozens of letters from various publishers in New York requested various kinds of information on the two or three authors who had found some audience over the past year. It seemed to be Tremont Press' policy to release authors to larger publishers if they were willing to pay the price. Henry assumed the letters he found were poor offers which had been rejected.

There was a gentle knock on the door.

The way Mrs. Murray stood in the light of the hall, Henry could see the outline of her body through the shear of her dressing gown. She was wearing nothing underneath.

"You are very busy tonight, aren't you?"

"I'm sorry. It's a project I have to finish."

"Trash?" Her eyes darted by him to the scene in the kitchen.

"I'm looking for something that was thrown away. Something important."

"It looks like you have your work cut out for you. Is it going to take all night?"

"I hope not."

She hesitated, took a breath. "Can I help? I haven't been able to sleep with the heat…and all the noise."

He did not hesitate. If she was not going to object, he was already ahead of the game.

"Sure."

And he was sorry for his answer as soon as he spoke. She smiled at him now the way she had the other day.

"What are we looking for?"

"Evidence…"

She frowned. His mother used to frown at him like that.

He began again. "Information—about Tremont Press. It's a small outfit in town. I'm just working off a hunch…. Someone named Nora Lynch works there. She's the editor, and I guess she is the chief window cleaner and bottle washer too. But the whole thing is financed by George Duggan…You know—" Mrs. Murray nodded as Henry spoke, the frown gone, her lips pursed with consideration of what he was trying to say. It was difficult to keep the story brief. "And he plagiarized…Well, he might have plagiarized a work by a guy named James Frankowski. One thing I'm looking for is anything relating to that—"

"Is it legal for you to have this?" She waved her hand over the piled bags on the kitchen floor.

He did not know how long his hesitation lasted before he got the answer out, but he knew he was feeling like a kid in school again. He was a little old for that.

"I'm not sure…I don't think it is, but I haven't got any better ideas."

She stood at the entrance to the kitchen as he explained again the situation with Sharon and Barbara and her request and the lack of response from the publisher when they had pointed out the coincidence of plot and their fear of lawyers. He had actually told her some of the story one afternoon as she weeded in the yard. She seemed to want to hear it all again.

As he finished, she appeared to hesitate only a brief moment before taking a deep breath.

"So, now, what are we looking for?" she said, the smile returned. He set a second chair at the other side of the mound of bags. Mrs. Murray's forehead had sprouted tiny beads of sweat, and the moisture had begun to attach parts of her dressing gown like a second skin.

"I don't know." He had no real idea.

"Then let's get at it...You need some organization here, I see." She pulled the bags he had already opened toward the door. He could not help but notice that her rear-end had not yet begun to sag.

She did not return immediately, but stood in the living room for several minutes.

He leaned out the doorway from his chair. She was looking at the framed photograph of Sasha.

"Have you been seeing Sasha lately?" she finally said.

"Not since the day she came back without her key. She gave the photograph to me because it was taken by her ex-boyfriend. She wanted to throw it away.... I thought it was too beautiful."

"It is," Mrs. Murray spoke, as she returned. "Very beautiful."

They continued to sort through the bags, with Mrs. Murray putting aside anything that might be of interest and re-bagging catalogs, old packing material, and anything obviously useless. Henry tried not to peek up as she leaned forward to remove each handful. Her breasts hung forward then beneath the fabric in a way that made him want to reach out to catch them.

He found it hard to concentrate.

She said, "Here," and reached out a bare arm, her hand holding a small thin pile of sticky desk notes. He peeled through them. Most were unimportant. One was from George Duggan.

"'Finished the new book this afternoon. I'll be in Boston next Thursday. See you at the Colonnade at four,'" Henry read aloud.

The date at the top of the note was July 10th. The next Thursday was July 17th, tomorrow—today—this afternoon.

But Henry had another appointment on the 17th. In the morning, on Louisburg Square. Mrs. Murray spoke before he had finished his thoughts.

"Why don't you go see him? Talk to him. It can't hurt. Get a feel for the man and see if he's really trying to rip somebody off. You know, people like that get accusations of plagiarism all the time. They must have to ignore it or else they'd be constantly fighting battles. They usually have a lawyer—"

Henry was still examining the desk note. At the top of the small sheet was a printed name: Red Hill Camp, Maine. Henry interrupted, looking up.

"Mr. Boyle. Sharon has heard from him. He sent a one-paragraph letter to her which said that any attempt to harass Mr. Duggan would result in legal action with severe penalties, or some such."

Mrs. Murray stood and straightened her back with her hands on her hips. Henry straightened up in his chair and tried to avoid looking at the outline of her body. He had to change the subject clouding his mind.

"I was thinking of something else…I was thinking of submitting Eddy Perry's manuscript to them."

She frowned. It took him another ten minutes then to explain his involvement with Eddy Perry. She sat down again as he finished. Her mood had clearly changed.

"Busy, busy, busy. Do you take any time out to sell your books? How can you afford to pay the rent?"

She was frowning and smiling at the same time. He had seldom seen this done and assumed it was a talent acquired in the classroom as a teacher.

"It'll be okay. I've been lucky just lately. But I want to do something about Eddy's manuscript. And Tremont is really the right publisher for it anyway. They're small. They'd be able to get it out to the audience that would most appreciate it."

The smile decreased and the frown dominated.

"Is there no conflict of interest there? Are you thinking he would publish Mr. Perry's work as a favor after you accused him of plagiarism?"

Henry suddenly felt too tired to attempt an explanation of something he was so unsure of to begin with.

"I didn't accuse him of anything. I don't know what's going on. But both Barbara and Sharon want me to help. I haven't got any idea what to do. I'm not at all sure that what has happened is any kind of plagiarism. The only people who know are not likely to talk to me about it."

The smile came back. Henry felt a wave of tension he knew only one meaning for. She tilted her head.

"There are two bags left. Let's get them done...I need a shower." Her voice had softened now to something he could not imagine she ever used in a classroom.

She leaned low and pulled the tie loose on a bag as if she were opening her gown, and began sorting.

He ripped open the top of the other bag a bit too fiercely, took a breath, and began to pile up discarded manuscripts.

Mrs. Murray was unfolding crumpled wads of correspondence and laying them neatly flat, one after the other, before putting them aside.... He felt the sweat trickle down the side of his cheek to his chin. There was little of interest in the bag he was working on to keep his mind focused. Suddenly he was aware of her simply looking at him.

"You know, I have a bigger shower downstairs," she said. "You are welcome to use it."

He pulled a crumpled sheet of paper from his own bag. It was the second page of a letter from Nora Lynch that Duggan had obviously returned to her with a handwritten note at the bottom. There was no sign of the first page.

Henry clenched his teeth and tried to concentrate.

It was clear Nora Lynch was explaining what she remembered about a manuscript. And it was obviously the James Frankowski book she was speaking of. Henry started reading out loud.

"…in Italy. Hannibal was approaching Rome. I can't say if I read further. It wasn't bad. It was just a little boring. I couldn't have read every word. There are so many manuscripts, I'm going crazy. As I said before to Mr. Boyle, I don't remember the writer's name. Just something about Hannibal."

The note from Duggan across the bottom was more cryptic, and the handwriting made it difficult. Henry had to read it through twice.

"'You did say something. Remember the day at the lake? You spoke of Hannibal under house arrest at Bithynia just before he was executed and wondered what he was thinking after all he had lived through. I'm sure of that much. Did reading the other manuscript get you to thinking about that, or was it from talking to me? It would be good to resolve this. In any case, the new book is almost done. I need a rest.'"

The additional note was signed, "Love, D."

Henry looked up. Mrs. Murray's eyebrows were raised.

"That tells you everything, wouldn't you say?"

Henry searched the sapphire blue in her eyes for an answer. There was some clear authority in those eyes.

"Not exactly. But even if they borrowed the idea unwittingly, do they still owe Frankowski anything?"

One of Mrs. Murray's eyebrows raised. He realized she could raise either one at will, and it made him smile.

There was a knock at the door. He remembered the sound of that immediately.

111

Sasha stood there, barefoot, a thin kimono wrapped around her body, her black hair, longer than Henry had realized, caught in a single comb by her shoulder.

"I can't sleep. It's too hot. And I heard your voices from the window.... Do you have anything cold in your refrigerator that I can drink?"

Chapter Twelve

Henry's affair with Morgan Johnson seemed distant at that moment. He had awakened with thoughts of her many times since her death, but not recently. Recently, he had not thought of her at all. Was that a sign of callousness? Was he that shallow a fellow? It wasn't as if he took advantage of every willing woman he met. The fact was, he did not feel like he was taking any advantages at all. He had trouble enough.

And Della had warned him. In fact, she had warned him repeatedly since he had met her, about almost every girl he came in contact with. She had even warned him about Mrs. Murray.

"You are at that age."

"What age?"

"The age when women can expect that you've fooled around enough and you know what you want in life."

A pigeon landed on the walk in front of them. Della threw a piece of crust from her sandwich at it.

He said, "I knew what I wanted when I was twenty." He thought his delivery was unconvincing.

She threw another piece of sandwich down for the three birds which had just arrived. Henry looked up into the trees around them to see if there were more.

She was not buying his statement. "I don't think so. You're so slow you probably didn't even get started until you were twenty…and, as I said, women can expect it. I didn't say it was true."

He said. "I think women expect way too much of men," and stretched one foot out from the bench toward the pigeons to ward them off.

Della tossed her next piece with dramatic disgust. "It's the only reason men bother to do anything. If women didn't expect anything, men would sit around and drink beer and watch television."

"I don't have a television."

She ignored his defense. "So what *did* you want to do when you were twenty?"

"Sell books."

"That's not very ambitious."

"I'm told that. I'm told that I'm not a very ambitious person."

Della rolled her eyes. "A woman probably told you that, and she was right."

"Barbara," he countered.

"She was half right.... You ought to be doing something that makes you sweat a little more."

Henry thought about his rummaging through a dumpster at night. He was used to her sarcasm. He offered his own.

"I don't think you appreciate me."

"You're probably right. But I would appreciate you more if you would keep naked women out of your apartment."

"Does that include—"

"Except me."

"And why should I be so particular when you can't stay away from Bob?"

"Bob has not touched me in months."

"I thought you said—"

"He tried to. I didn't let him. That's why he's going crazy."

"Have you always had this idea that you drive men crazy?"

"Some men, but not you. You are always surprised. You never see it coming. You're like a teenage kid who wants it all the time but hasn't a clue how to go about it."

Henry smiled. "Thanks."

"It's true, but it's part of your charm. Most guys your age assume they know so much. They're too eager to show their skills."

Henry lost his smile. "And you talk like you know way too much about such things."

Her back straightened with the reproach. She flipped another bit of crust into the wad of moving feathers in front of them.

"My mother warned me. I listened to my mother."

"Why does she know so much?"

"She's been married five times, for Christ's sake. If Oscar dies she'll make it six. She's still a good-looking women at sixty. You should take that into account. I've got good genes."

Morgan had been about that old. He had figured Mrs. Murray to be about fifty-five. He could easily imagine Della at sixty.

"I'll write that down."

"You ought to. You ought to write a book. You do the most interesting things I've ever heard of."

This was a different tack on her part.

"Like play in other people's garbage."

"Like go into the homes of wealthy people to look at their collections."

The memory of that morning's disaster came back to him.

"Well, this time it was a bust. I can't go back there. That woman is crazy."

Della rolled her eyes at his hopelessness.

"She's just heading for forty and making a last-ditch effort to find a mate."

He had told her about his appointment at ten o'clock on Louisburg Square. Henry had gone to look at the books of a divorcée who had cornered him in an alcove against leather-bound sets of Honoré de Balzac and Anthony Trollope.

Henry had actually met the woman before, at an auction. She had taken his card when he explained his business to her. Then, she had talked to him nonstop while he had tried to sort through a box of ephemera. This morning she had been on her roof deck when he arrived, and answered the doorbell breathing heavily from the stairs, wearing a very pink terrycloth bikini. Again she had offered him a running commentary as she led him from room to room, each decorated by a perfectly positioned bookcase of leather-bound volumes. The problem, besides learning more than he wanted to know about her personal life, was that the terrycloth, which had began to roll down at the upper edges, almost came off by itself as she reached from a small oak stepladder toward volumes of "her favorite" red-leather edition of Voltaire.

Henry had described this to Della with some thought of the humor in it, at first. With her sandwich greatly reduced in size, Della tore smaller pieces of bread, and the puddle of flying beggars continued to spread at their feet.

"That kind of thing happens," she said. "I know. I was greeted at the door once by a male friend who was stark naked, dripping wet, and talking on the phone. Totally oblivious."

Henry straightened himself on the bench as a gesture of defense, against her implication as much as the pigeons. "That was an accident. My mind was on something else."

Della raised her arms. Pigeons fluttered backward.

"That's why I think you ought to write a book. You will forget all of that stuff. You're already as absent-minded as a writer. It's in your personality."

Henry was confused. "I thought you said I should think about doing something else—like getting a real job."

"Maybe I'm wrong about that. I'm not sure you're employable. You've been working for yourself too long."

Henry nodded. "I'm glad you came to that realization."

She shook off his small victory.

"But you could change."

With that he stood again. He had wasted enough time.

The puddle of pigeons parted.

He left her on Commonwealth Avenue with four thousand birds swarming around her feet, all looking for bits of the sandwich she had completely discarded in her campaign to lose weight. She had insisted that men really did not like women who were fat. He had tried to tell her that it depended on the woman.

He arrived at the Colonnade Hotel at two o'clock. He was taking a chance. It might be too early. Duggan might not have arrived yet. But if Henry waited too long, he had a greater chance of running into Nora Lynch.

When he told the clerk he had an appointment with George Duggan, he was told Mr. Duggan was still in the dining room eating lunch. Henry had not waited for an escort.

The great man was sitting alone in the far corner by a window wearing a flannel shirt and blue jeans, and squinted slightly as he watched Henry approach across the dining room floor. He was thinner than Henry remembered, and taller. His hair was cut short to a graying stubble.

"Mr. Duggan?" Henry had not intended the question, but it came out that way.

"Yes."

"I'm a bookseller. My name is Henry Sullivan. Could I interrupt you for just a moment?"

Duggan's eyes looked toward the entrance, "I suppose…" probably wondering why the management had let Henry in. He looked up at Henry again. "Do you want me to sign something?"

Henry shook his head and stood at the far side of the table. "No, sir."

Duggan squinted up at him. There was some other thought on the author's mind now. "Sullivan. Like the architect?"

Henry nodded. "Without the 'Louis.'"

"Where is your shop?"

Henry hesitated a brief moment over this. It might sound odd for him not to have a shop.

"I'm a scout. I just have a website."

"Kind of a book-hound then."

"Yes, in fact. That's what I call myself."

"Then you could find me a book if I asked you to."

"Yes sir."

"Good. Do you write?"

Henry hesitated again, even though he knew that there was no way Della could have spoken to Duggan in the short time since he had left her.

"No. I just sell the books. I'll leave the writing to you."

Duggan gestured toward him.

"I just noticed the envelope you were carrying. If it's not something to sign, it's something to read."

Duggan smiled, pulled a cigarette out of a small leather case, and lit it from an old Zippo with the nickel worn through to the gold of the brass at the corners.

"Well, you're right, but—"

"Every bookseller I've ever met wants to write. Funniest thing. You'd think with all the crap they see piled around them—all the books they have to move around and sticker and alphabetize and ship back and all the rest, that they would know enough not to add to the sheer mass of it. But booksellers are the most intrinsically optimistic people in the world. Aren't they? With all that failure stacked around them, they are always looking for Melville—" He paused and blew smoke toward the window. "I like that. *Looking for Melville.* Has a nice ring to it, doesn't it? Maybe I'll remember it again at the right moment— unless you use it first."

"But, I don't write."

"Well, then, what can I do for you?"

"I'm trying to help someone."

"By which you mean to say you're doing something without recompense, for someone else."

The critical note in his voice was hard to miss.

"Yes."

"All right. And…?"

The words Henry had rehearsed quickly fell apart in his mind. For some unknown reason he suddenly felt the edge of exhaustion against his spine. He had been awake for over twenty-four hours.

Henry had wanted to sell Eddy's story to this man. He wanted to sell this book to him the way Barbara could hand-sell a title in her shop if she loved it. But suddenly he did not think it was going to work. Della was right. Again. He was not a salesman. That was just another reason he had left Alcott & Poe. And that was why he conducted his business the way he did now.

Henry started, "It concerns Eddy Perry."

Duggan shook his head. "I don't know him."

"He was a bookseller. He's dead. And he wrote a book."

Duggan nodded. "Just what I was saying…"

"And I was wondering if you could read it. It's pretty good, I think. I'm not a critic, just a reader."

Duggan blew his smoke in a longer plume. "And a seller. That's important. You have a sense of what might sell."

"Well, as a matter of fact, I'm not sure this will sell. It's awfully dark. I just think it's very good. It should be published…"

"I see…Maybe better than very good?" Duggan's words were illustrated by the smoke of his cigarette on his breath.

"Yes. Maybe. And I was over at Tremont Press. I was speaking with Nora—"

Duggan's eyebrows went up.

"She sent you here?"

"No. Actually, she was upset with me for barging in without an appointment. She tried to get me to leave it there. But she looked swamped. And I know you're the person behind that outfit."

Duggan sat back."How do you know that?"

"Somehow. Something I found out."

Henry backed off a bit. It was important not to be too pushy here.

"If Nora heard you say that, she'd be very displeased. She's the boss at Tremont. And she has quite a temper."

Henry took a long breath. He needed more oxygen to fight his exhaustion.

"I know that much. I encountered that. That's why I thought…. She's buried in work. It's piled all around her. This is such a different kind of story, she might be put off by it."

Duggan's hand went out toward the package.

"She gets volunteers from the colleges. They help. But the schools don't teach them how to be critical anymore. 'Judgmental' they call it. In fact, most of them have no sense of judgment at all. Poor Nora can't handle it…."

Henry handed the manuscript to him and thought immediately of turning to escape. If he just left it with the man, wouldn't he read a couple of pages just to see? That's all it would take. Henry was sure of that.

Henry said, "Thanks."

"You can't go yet. I need a little more information than that."

Henry pulled another breath. "It's all in the envelope…I didn't want to waste your time."

Duggan waved his hand as if telling him to sit.

"You drink?"

"Beer."

"Have a beer with me. I'm done for the day. I wrote all morning. I get up early. And I like talking to booksellers. Please, stay a little bit. If you don't, some well-rounded vixen will spot me and I might get myself into trouble again."

Henry sat then—happy at least to be sitting down.

Mrs. Murray's door on the first floor was partially open when he came in. The voice he heard was Della's. He was exhausted. Drinking beer with Duggan and the heat of the day had transformed his body into dead weight. Lack of sleep did not help. And he had to pee. Badly. He thought he was delirious and stopped short to listen in the hope that he was mistaken.

"Is that you, Henry?"

Mrs. Murray's voice sounded cheerful.

"Yes, ma'am," he answered, taking the newel post in his hand to escape up the stairs.

He could hear her move across her floor. The door opened wide. The smile on her face seemed patient—if smiles could be patient.

She said, "Sarah. I would so much prefer it if you would call me Sarah…. Your friend is here."

Over Mrs. Murray's shoulder he could see Della sitting in an armchair by the small fireplace. She smiled at him, like a cat, he thought.

Della said, "Hi."

Henry closed his eyes at them. "Hi. I've got to get upstairs. I'm beat."

Della sprang to her feet. "Oh no, no, you've got to tell us. We've been going over the whole situation while we were waiting. You've got to tell us what happened."

It was a trap. Henry felt like the mouse.

"You'll have to wait a minute. I have to pee."

He ran up the stairs for his door.

Behind him, he could hear Della's voice.

"He can be a little crude."

"Like a little boy," Mrs. Murray answered.

When he returned a few minutes later, they were both seated again.

He had not actually been inside Mrs. Murray's apartment before. It was bright with greens and yellows. She had decorated with English prints of Italian scenes. A picture of her late husband Sam stared off the fireplace mantel at him—unhappily, he thought—nestled amongst an odd collection of objects that might have been picked up on various trips. She had once told him she had traveled all over the world during her summers while she was a teacher.

"Bric-a-brac," she said, rising from the couch as she followed his eyes. "My weakness. I love bric-a-brac. That one there is a volcanic stone from Vesuvius."

"Henry collects girlfriends," Della said cheerfully.

He was not sure he could bear up to Della's wit just now.

"I thought you were talking about the George Duggan thing. If you're just talking about me, I might as well go to bed.

It's a boring subject. I'm beat. And I already know more about me than I want to."

"If only that were true," Mrs. Murray said.

She smiled a little too much like his mother, Henry decided. That must account for the patience.

Della asked, "What happened? Tell us what happened."

He sat down on the couch across from her. It was a small couch, and when Mrs. Murray sat down beside him, he could smell honeysuckle. He was going to be more careful of couches in the future.

He decided to get it over with quickly. "Well, I talked to him. We actually talked a lot. We ended up in the lounge because Nora Lynch did not show."

"And? What about?" Della pushed.

He shrugged. "Plagiarism."

Their eyes widened. Della's mouth opened and shut without speaking.

"And?" Mrs. Murray sat out at the edge of the couch to face him.

"Well, he asked me pretty quickly if I knew a bookseller by the name of Barbara Kraus. I told him I did, and he asked me what I knew about her…."

Both women stared at him, mouths slightly open. Henry had to stop at the sight. He had never had the attention of two women quite so thoroughly in his life. Della was the first to speak.

"And? What did you say?"

Henry took a breath to begin again. "I told him. Just about everything. Even about going through the Tremont trash. I told him that when he asked how I had tracked him down at the hotel."

Della interrupted, "He must have liked that."

"Actually, he laughed and said Nora is still too young to realize the importance of trash. I told him he ought to talk to Albert about that."

Mrs. Murray frowned. "He must have assumed you were using Eddy's manuscript as a way to meet him."

Henry shrugged again. "Well, yes. I was. He does. I told him that much. I explained the whole thing to him. He's that kind of guy. He seems pretty straight to me. We talked about pretty much everything."

Mrs. Murray spread her hands at the air between them. "But you don't have the manuscript with you. You left it with him anyway?"

"Yes. He said he would read it."

Mrs. Murray face was blank. "Extraordinary!"

Henry said, "He was obviously concerned that Sharon and Barbara were trying to rip him off. We talked about that. When I left him—Well, just an hour ago he said he'd call them himself and see what he could work out. I think he understands their position. And he doesn't know how he came by the idea for the novel. Once he picks up on something that interests him, he just keeps following the string until it runs out. He thought it could have occurred to him one day after batting ideas around with Nora. He thinks she might have unconsciously remembered something she had read—probably from Frankowski's manuscript. He doesn't think what he did is plagiarism, but he does think he must owe something to James Frankowski. He admitted that he has always worried about plagiarism. He reads a great deal, but never when he's writing, just because of that.... He said John Boyle is going to be unhappy with him, but he would rather it all be settled peaceably."

There was a silence filled only by the sound of the fan in the window. Then Mrs. Murray sat back.

"I told you so. Mr. Duggan is a professional. He'll work it out. You did very well, Henry. But I would like to know about this John Boyle."

"He's a lawyer."

"I gather that. But is he the same John Boyle who went to Boston Latin?"

"I don't know. I could ask him. Or I could ask Albert."

She blew a bit of air out as if to whistle.

"No. You probably don't want to mention John Boyle to Albert Hamilton."

She explained that the two of them had engaged once in a brawl which had brought the police to the school and put them both in detention for more than a week. Albert was not the type to hold grudges, Henry told her. Mrs. Murray's thought, that they might still bear ill will after more than twenty years, did not seem likely.

"Can I go now?" He seemed to remember using such words in grade school.

"Where?" Della said.

"To bed."

"But you haven't told us all the details."

"Tomorrow.... Good night."

He left them sitting across from each other in silence. He was too tired to guess what was in their minds.

It all seemed like more than he was ready to deal with as he sat in his chair to take off his shoes.

What would it matter that he had not told them the truth? Not all of it. Could he have helped reacting to Della's comment? She had meant it as a joke. But she had meant it as well. He had never collected girlfriends. But that was the way it might appear. His irritation at her for seeing Bob was really the joke. Bob was not the problem. The problem was himself.

He had always had difficulty dealing with girls. Since high school. They clouded his thinking. How would he have explained Morgan Johnson to the two of them—with them staring at him? Not after that remark. They would not have understood.

It had been Duggan who had brought Morgan up, almost immediately after he sat down. Duggan had frowned as Henry began to say something about Eddy Perry.

"Sorry to interrupt, but I can't help thinking we've met before. Could that be?"

It had caught Henry off guard.

"Yes. Almost. Once. In passing…About a year ago."

Duggan pointed a finger at him. "At the church. At Morgan Johnson's funeral service."

"Yes." Henry had not expected to be remembered.

"You are the fellow she—Well, you know, I feel pretty stupid about forgetting. We all loved Morgan. She was the woman of our dreams. I might have asked her to marry me a dozen times. Even when Heber was alive. I have no class when it comes to things like that. But you were the one."

Henry was astonished now. What were the words for this? What was he to say? The words he found were not the right ones.

"How do you know this?"

Duggan grimaced and shook his head. "She told me. We were great friends, after all. After Heber died, I asked her to marry me again. I drove down to her house on the Cape and presented myself. God forbid Nora should ever find this out. We were already seeing each other then…But, I had been in love with Morgan for twenty years. I know she knew it. I only hope Heber never did. If he did, he hid it well. He was always the best agent a writer could have, even when he was sick.

"But after he died, I went out there and asked her again.… Nora is a lovely girl—but Morgan. You knew Morgan. She was very kind. She told me about you then. She called you her book-hound. I have to admit it caused me quite a bit of pain. I'm used to getting things I want now. It's just part of being rich and famous." Duggan raised his eyebrows at himself. "And she knew that as well. She was always too honest for her own good. Heber had been a good husband. But she felt guilty about her relationship with you. She was depressed. And there I was, defending the situation all of a sudden. Heber had been sick for so many years. I told her she was foolish to blame herself. I think I also told her that she was foolish to have fallen for a kid like you instead of the great me.... But that was it. You will never know how miserable you made me...and probably many others."

Henry was not sure if he had spoken even then. Yes, he had. He had mumbled something foolish. "I don't think that I was really worthy of it. She seemed to see more in me than I saw myself."

Duggan had lit another cigarette and let a moment pass over that appraisal.

"She was a good judge of human beings. She certainly saw through me. I'd say you can't be too bad a fellow or Morgan would not have had anything to do with you."

He had never felt worthy of it. Morgan was uncommon and very foolish, right to the end. Her trust in others was her flaw. He could not say that to George Duggan. Henry had found Morgan at the wrong time—too late, or too soon. He said nothing more about it then. But this was a bond with George Duggan he could not ignore.

Later, when the phone rang, he was disoriented. He was sure he had only just fallen asleep. Sunlight glazed the window.

He said, "Hello," with his eyes closed.

There was a silence on the line before a voice spoke.

"Mr. Sullivan?"

"Yes."

"My name is John Boyle. I'm an attorney. I work for George Duggan."

"Yes, sir."

"I was wondering if you could come down to my office for a chat."

Henry had been dreaming. He had been dreaming about a summer visit to Cape Cod when he was perhaps ten or eleven. His sister had been teasing him. She called him Pokey because she could outrun him so easily, and he had called her Gumby. One of the great summers of his life—mostly because his mother had been there as well. He could still hear his sister's voice as his head cleared.

Henry had always considered his father a simple fellow. He made simple rules. He liked beer on tap, the Red Sox, and Ella Fitzgerald—his favorite Irish singer, he called her. His father had told him once, shortly after Henry went into business for himself, "Never go to a lawyer's office unless he's working for you. And then only do it to cut time off his clock." Henry heard the words plainly in his head as well.

"I'm pretty busy right now. What is it you need?"

"I wanted to talk over this problem George Duggan is having. Is there a time that would be more convenient?"

"Sure. I go to the Blue Thorn in Inman Square quite a lot. You want to come by and talk to me there?"

This was greeted with the same dead silence he had heard before. Henry wondered if he was on some kind of speaker phone and others might be listening.

Finally, Mr. Boyle's voice returned. "It would be more convenient if you could come into the office."

"Convenient for whom?"

The silence returned briefly.

"Will you be at the Blue Thorn tonight?"

Tonight seemed rushed to Henry.

"Tomorrow. I'm meeting a friend there tomorrow at three."

"Tomorrow then, at three."

The line went dead.

Henry drifted back to sleep.

Chapter Thirteen

The phone rang. Albert started speaking before Henry had the receiver to his ear.

"Wake up, Romeo. I don't want to meet the beast by myself."

Henry focused his eyes on the ceiling. "What time is it?"

"Two-thirty. I thought you were going to be here early."

"I'm coming."

Henry dropped his clothes on the floor as he made his way to the shower, ignoring the ringing of the phone the second time. Turning the water to cold, he danced against the chill.

He chose a freshly washed pair of jeans for the occasion.

The phone rang again as he dressed. It was Barbara.

"Do you want me to be there?"

A mental picture of Barbara telling the lawyer he was a cretinous moron flashed through Henry's mind. "No. Albert's going to be there. He'll protect me. I'm fine."

He told her he had to go.

She hesitated. "Good luck.... Thanks."

He tried to remember when the last time was that she had said thanks to him. He could not remember her ever saying it to him before, and now she had said it twice within weeks.

When he walked in the door of the Blue Thorn, Albert was already at the largest table beneath the overhead fan. Two other men sat with him, both beefy. Their suit jackets were off, showing wide suspenders over ironed and perfectly white shirts, their ties loose. They were all laughing. The loudest laugh, Henry guessed correctly, was coming from John Boyle. It looked like a gathering for a poker match.

Boyle rose from the table and shook Henry's hand. He was at least three inches taller than Henry, and perhaps as imposing as Albert—broad-shouldered and muscular. His head was shaved to a well-tanned dome. His hand was warm and dry.

The other fellow was Ted Schultz, a specialist in copyright law, he was told. Schultz's hand was wet from his beer glass, and he gripped too hard trying to make an impression. "How did you get stuck with this?" Boyle asked as they sat.

"Doing a friend a favor. Barbara asked me. She was my boss once." Something in Boyle's squint implied that he knew there was more to it than friendship.

Boyle went for the meat immediately. "What is it you think that Sharon Greene wants?" He was not going to waste any time. The voice was calm. It reminded Henry of his Uncle Jack. It was a professional gambler's voice. Cold.

Henry put his finger up for Tim to see, and then answered. "Just compensation, I think they call it…. She's lost Jim. She doesn't want his work to be lost. She was his researcher. And she is the beneficiary of James Frankowski's estate. She has a substantial stake in it."

There was the slightest change in Boyle's face, perhaps a loosening in the squint. Henry wondered if he had inadvertently revealed something in his answer.

"And what do you think Barbara Kraus wants?"

The very asking of Boyle's question made Henry think there was more to it than the obvious. He would have to be careful. Boyle tilted his head and made marks with one finger in the condensation on his own glass of beer. A moment extra of thought was gained when Tim showed up with Henry's usual pint.

Henry sipped a mouthful off the top and swallowed slowly enough to savor the taste and irritate anyone who might be impatient. "Well, I'd say all Barbara wants is for Sharon to be compensated as well."

"Compensated? For what?" Boyle's voice had not raised, but the question had the quality of a slap. Henry looked over at Ted Schultz. Schultz's eyes were on the bubbles in his beer. Henry gave Albert a glance. Albert's face was blank—just like it always was when he was in the middle of a major move as they played chess. Boyle's eyes were on Henry's.

Henry took another long cool sip before speaking.

"George Duggan has made a great deal of money from sales and rights to *Dreams of Bithynia*. The story was clearly taken from a work by James Frankowski. Sharon Greene would like financial compensation from George Duggan for that fact."

Henry was unhappy with the mechanical quality of his own delivery.

Boyle moved his beer aside and set his elbow on the table, with his thick forearm filling the white sleeve and his starched cuff like a collar below his upright fist, a gold cuff link gleaming above the softer glow of a gold watch band.

Boyle's hand opened, fingers wide in the air. He turned the fingers down one by one. "Fact: Sharon Greene was not married to James Frankowski. "Fact: there is no evidence to show when the manuscript for *Hannibal's Dance* was written. Fact: James Frankowski's mother, his rightful heir, is very upset at this whole thing and is worried that her son's good name may be damaged." Henry noted that there was no depth to Boyle's eyes—only the surface glaze of light, as if there were a second reptilian eyelid that was closed. The threat was completely contained in the single gesture of his forearm. Boyle's voice was still cool. "But more importantly to me, is the fact that George Duggan's name is in danger of being damaged. That damage could be worth a great deal of compensation."

Henry focused on the watch. It was an antique, rectangular. He had always liked the look of old watches. The hair on the back of Boyle's hand extended onto each finger. He had not used his thumb in his demonstration.

Henry set his own elbow on the table and held up his own hand, which he worried might appear slight by comparison, and then raised his thumb alone as if he were hitching a ride.

"You forgot the fact that a wrong has been done here, and there should be some fair compensation for that."

He lowered his thumb and grabbed his beer, drinking several mouthfuls before putting it down. Albert was smiling. Boyle's face was blank.

For reasons Henry was not sure of, they all left the Blue Thorn at the same time after Boyle had dropped a twenty dollar bill on the table, as if they had been in a conference room at a hotel and he were tipping the clean up crew.

"I like the picture." Albert said later, looking at the large photograph of Sasha on Henry's living room wall.

Henry asked, "So tell me what you were laughing about when I came in to the Blue Thorn?"

Albert smiled. "A joke. Boyle told a joke. It was a lawyer joke.… Do I know that girl?" Albert looked harder at the picture. He sat forward. The couch frame groaned.

"Yeah. You met her when I moved in last summer. She was the one who helped." Henry unconsciously patted the pocket of his shirt for his cigarettes before remembering he had none.

"Holy moly. That little thing…" Albert squinted. "I guess so. I wouldn't have recognized her. But I ought to remind you, I know Boyle."

Albert looked out the window now as if he had said nothing at all.

"How well?" Henry asked, just remembering Mrs. Murray words.

"Like I said before. Just from high school at Boston Latin. But he's a real shit. Don't trust him. He was a shit then and he's a shit now…. We both had Mrs. Murray for English in our junior year."

Henry considered this a moment as he leaned forward and picked up his bottle of beer from the floor.

"What do you think he meant by what he said at the end?"

Albert's eyes had returned to the picture on the wall.

"Are you seeing this girl? I thought you were seeing Della." Albert used his half-empty bottle to point.

"I am seeing Della…when she's not seeing Bob. Do you think it was a threat?"

"This girl looks like a one-man woman. I'd try to get something going with this girl if I were you, and let Della chase after Bob. Boyle is just testing the temperature of the water. You did good. There are no threats. The water's just a little warm."

From Henry's angle in the chair, the glass of the photograph captured the reflection of the window. Sasha's head was obscured by a bright rectangle of modernist anonymity. "Della's not chasing Bob right now. I guess she's chasing me. I think Sasha is still in love with the guy she broke up with…. So, why did he say he was advising Duggan to seek compensation for the damage to his good name? Isn't that a threat?"

Albert rested back on the couch, his eyes surveying the room. "That's really the best time to get something going with a girl—after they've just broken off with someone they thought they loved. You step right in. You show them what real love is. You get everything the other guy got and more…. He didn't say they were going to do it. He said he was giving that advice. It's a potential threat. Sharon Greene hasn't done anything yet. She's still in the clear."

Henry shook his head dramatically.

"You know nothing about this. You married your first wife when you were still in diapers. Alice picked you up on waivers because she needed a new pitcher for the stretch. Am I wrong to say you have only slept with two women in your whole life?"

"Technically—"

"Technically you're not qualified—"

"Technically, it's not due to lack of opportunity. It's because I'm happy with what I've got, and because Alice would kill me if I wasn't."

"She who must be obeyed." Henry shook his head and returned to the subject at hand. "So what should Sharon do?" He was feeling impatient.

"I'd say…if Sharon doesn't hear them making nicer noises, I think she ought to get the story in the newspapers. The papers will try the whole case out of court and then she'll get her deal. So what about Barbara?"

There was a danger with the newspapers, Henry thought. They protected their friends. Duggan was well liked. "What about Barbara? And why wouldn't the newspapers simply come to Duggan's defense? He's the hometown boy who has done all those good deeds."

Going to the press was a whole new thought. Henry had not considered that. Albert was a move ahead on him. Albert shook his head at Henry for being naïve.

"He's big. Reporters hate the big guy. He's a guy, she's a girl—no brainer. He's rich. Reporters hate rich people."

This did not work for Henry. He paused to consider this with another sip of beer. In the silence he became aware of a moan. It repeated. He looked at Albert. Albert looked side to side. The sound repeated, precisely. It was not a woman in ecstasy. It was a violin. He had never heard Sasha practice such a sound. It repeated again.

Henry shook his head in protest. "I don't trust reporters. They don't get the facts straight. They take sides. They never bother to know the facts behind what you're talking about, so they never ask the right questions.... But why did you ask about Barbara?"

Albert sat back on the couch and gave Henry one large eye.

"She's still stuck on you. Your helping her out on this is going to cause you some problems."

The moan became louder, and faster.

Henry defended himself. "She's a friend. She asked for help. I just wish she had some friends in the publishing business. She's never cultivated that side of the business. Most of the reps just push the titles the publisher has bet on. Barbara really needs to get help from someone inside. It's all procedure now. What she wants are some records. When was the manuscript submitted and to whom. I can't believe with all the queries and all the hoops they make writers jump through to get their work read, they keep such lousy records."

Albert looked at his own beer bottle and judged what remained. "I think the problem is her friend Sharon. She's the one kept lousy records."

The moan now ended in a short squeal. Albert's eyes rolled.

Henry took a breath. "If Frankowski had used an agent like everybody else, none of this would have happened. But because Little, Brown came to him for the first book, he didn't understand the whole publishing racket. He really was just a professor who wrote books on the side.... Besides, Sharon had a reason for dumping her records. Going on to someone's computer is like talking to them. It's raw. She didn't know there was going to be a problem. Sharon doesn't seem to have a lot of friends. And even after fifteen years, she and Barbara are not really that close. And Barbara is pretty much alone now, herself. And you don't know the half of it—"

The violin stopped. The sudden silence made them both look to the ceiling.

"Which half?" Albert finished his beer with a single swallow.

Henry told him about Sharon's advances. Albert listened without saying anything. At the end he winced and grunted as if to say this was all Henry's fault. Then Albert complained, "I wish you had a TV. The game is on."

"Turn on the radio." Henry pointed.

Albert reached for the brown Bakelite radio beside the couch, pulled the loose cord free with a little irritation and set it in his lap as he tuned the dial. It began to hum.

"This is the twenty-first century, Henry. You should get a digital. One button does it…. By the way. Did you find a replacement radio for your little truck?"

The sound of the Red Sox announcer broke clear of the hum and Albert set the radio back.

"Benny did. Found a junker in a lot somewhere and bought the radio along with some leaf springs and a couple of other parts. Good deal. It's like new. I came by to give you a ride, but you weren't home."

Albert stretched his legs and grunted. "You owe me more than a ride."

Albert's face was dramatically sullen. The Red Sox announcer was saying, "Way back, Way back… Foul ball!"

Henry said. "What? What did I do?"

"Remember, it was my money bought that truck."

"It was mine. The part I borrowed, I paid you back."

"But you tricked me. If I had known you were going to use it to bid on that truck, I would have bid myself."

"You dropped out."

"'Cause I knew I didn't have any money left. You had borrowed it."

"No. You dropped out cause you thought the rich-looking guy in the blue jacket was going to stay in the bidding. You dropped out."

Briefly, Albert considered this.

"I want interest," Albert finally answered.

Henry sat up. Tim Wakefield struck the batter out.

"Like what?"

"I want to borrow it to take Junior up to Lake Richardson to fish. Those old car radios get reception up there the new ones don't. I can listen to the ballgame while I'm fishing."

Henry sat back. Fishing was a sport he did not understand. He could listen to the ballgame in the comfort of his own home.

Chapter Fourteen

Mrs. Murray was sitting on the steps to the porch. She had a collection of weeds in one gloved hand and seemed to be taking a breather. More weeds were lying wilted in the shadows on the short walk. The sun had set, and only the glow of the sky illuminated the narrow yard. The still air was pungent with the smell of the tomato plants at the side of the house. Her pruning had produced a small pile of dark-colored fruit in a wide wicker basket beside her.

Henry paused at the metal gate. To him, she appeared to be very sad at that moment. He was not sure if it was only the cast of light on her face, or something real.

"How's it goin'?" was all he could think of to say.

"Pretty well.... It's a nice evening, don't you think?"

Her voice was uncertain. He suspected she had been thinking on things past, more than the present.

He opened the gate and walked to the bottom of the steps as he answered, "Pretty fine. Makes you want to run around in a field and catch lightning bugs."

It was what he did every midsummer night when he was a kid.

Her eyes widened. "Yes! Exactly.... Where are the fireflies? There used to be so many fireflies."

"I guess there aren't enough fields in Cambridge."

"No. No, you're right. You need fields. I remember when I was in college at Bennington, I took a summer session because I'd been sick the winter before.... There was a wide-open grassy field there. They've built something on it since then. One night we had the most amazing time. There was no moon. It was terribly hot, and we were all outside for what little air there was and the stars were brilliant in the sky—and the fireflies came and it was as if the stars had dropped right down out of the sky, onto the field; and one by one we began to run about in them, until there were dozens of us, all twirling and circling in the starlight, and…well, we weren't wearing all that much any-way in the heat, and people just started shedding their clothes rather naturally. It was an all girl's school then, remember. The sweat was so heavy you could see the reflection of the fireflies on our bodies as we danced. There was no music. Some gig-gling. Some laughing. Breathless words…. There we were, all madly running around on the wide-open grass, chasing madly through the stars as they winked. We all had long hair in those days, and some girls had the poor bugs tangled in their hair…I think we were all in a dream. You should have seen it."

It was a nice thought.

"All girls," he repeated

"Yes…then."

Henry's imagination of hundreds of naked young women running in the half-light of an open field beneath the stars actu-ally stopped his breath. He could easily imagine Mrs. Murray running naked in the grass with lightning bugs winking in the loose flag of her black hair.

Her face had changed. The sadness was gone.

He wondered, "Were you a hippie then?"

"Oh, gracious no. There were very few real hippies. Most of us just dressed the part when it suited us. I was very middle-class…well, perhaps not typical. My family have always been teachers. Both my parents were. And my grandparents. Except Grandpa Huffy. He was a farmer. But Grandma Lu—she was a teacher. In Greenfield."

"Huffy and Lu?"

"Humphrey and Luella."

"They don't make names like that anymore."

"No, they don't."

"People don't run naked in the fields anymore, either."

"No, they don't…"

"It's too bad…"

"Yes…"

Henry climbed the steps past where she sat.

"Take some tomatoes," she said. "I can't eat them all."

He thanked her and took two.

"A woman was here to see you earlier," she said, half turning to look up at him on the porch.

"Who?"

"She wouldn't leave her name. I asked. Thin. Fairly tall. Very blonde. Blue eyes. Very nicely dressed."

"Sounds like Sharon. The woman whose husband wrote *Hannibal's Dance.*"

"Yes! It was her, I'll bet it was. Yes."

It was odd that she should come here, Henry thought.

"Thanks." He started to move again.

"And your phone has been ringing all afternoon."

That could be Della, of course, but a lot of people were getting his number these days. He was going to have to change the number soon.

"And there's a letter. On the table in the hall…. You get so few letters. Almost no junk mail. Why is that?"

"It all goes to the post office box. No one has my home address." Almost no one, he had thought.

She shook her head and squinted at him, as if studying something mysterious.

"You know, you are very old-fashioned. You have a computer, but, beyond that, you seem to live in another age…. It's the books, isn't it? The books. They're part of an age gone by, now."

"I guess so. Probably so."

He picked up the letter before the screen door had struck, and read it as he held the tomatoes beneath his nose, enjoying the smell. The letter was from the Law Offices of Boyle & Doyle, a request for him to make an appointment for a deposition.

Upstairs, he fingered through the phonograph records on the floor before he sat down. It troubled him that he had not yet found a good case to hold the records. He worried that they might warp in the heat. It was something else he had better deal with sooner than later.

Pulling a Copland from one stack, he slipped it on the turntable before sinking into his Morris chair. It concerned him as well that he was tired again. He was going to have to get his schedule back. He definitely felt like he had less energy than he used to. Was he getting old?

Tomato juice sprang from his mouth and dropped to his shirt as he took his first bite. He was dribbling on himself like an old man.

By the time the second part of "Our Town" had begun, he had drifted toward sleep. The knock at the door that opened his eyes was unfamiliar.

She was wearing one of the peasant dresses she liked to make herself from odd fabrics she found. He had always liked them better than her usual jeans.

"Barbara…" The surprise must have shown on his face, and she half-smiled in response. She looked around the room a moment before speaking, her eyes stopping on Sasha's picture.

"I need to talk to you. I hope you aren't in the middle of something…I tried calling. I know you just don't answer the phone sometimes."

He turned down the music, offered her a beer—which she took, to his surprise, given that she had always preferred wine—and they sat again in the living room.

"What's up?" His attempt to put on a cheerful face seemed to have an opposite effect on her.

She crossed her legs. He had always liked her legs.

"I am in more trouble than you want to know about. And you know I wouldn't ask if I could avoid it."

He was confused. He thought he was already helping her.

"Just tell me what you need."

"Well, more than anything, I need more money. You know I borrowed money from Sharon—well, borrowed is not technically correct. She owns a third of the store now...." He did not know that exactly. He had assumed there was an arrangement. Barbara looked down with some inner shame. "But the losses keep mounting. The sales in the store have continued to drop. They are down by at least a third of what we were doing as recently as 1999. And the rent—you know about the rent. I dropped my health insurance. That was almost four hundred dollars a month. We are way behind on all our bills, and I've stopped buying almost anything new. Trade credit is still bringing in quite a lot of used stock, but it's not really enough. People who actually read are happy to get credit when they bring in books, but the occasional readers and the collectors dumping things don't want credit, they want cash. I haven't been to an auction in over a year."

"I noticed..."

She shrugged. "I mean, what are my options? We had such an enormous overstock in the basement that we haven't been hurting that much for titles yet, but you know how it is. You get a new lot in and it's like spore in the air to the book hounds."

He said, "I know."

She smiled weakly. "We are behind on our rent. The landlord has an offer for the space from someone else. If we move...well, you know. It'll cost a fortune. We can have a sale, but moving will still cost too much. And then we'll have all the new cost of establishing ourselves in another location. You went through some of that with me back in the eighties.... Besides, you know having a sale is only good for short-term gains. The week after it's over, some cheapskate is asking when the next sale is going to be. We built that store on having good stock, not cheap stock. We built a reputation...."

The tone of her voice was not convincing. She knew who she was talking to. It was just an incantation now.

"It doesn't matter, Barbara. That age is over. There aren't ten people in ten thousand who pass your store every day who know who Edna O'Brien is, or Henry Green, or Anthony Powell, or Jean Rhys, or Compton Mackenzie, or—"

"Quit! Stop. Right—I know. You know..."

She was pained. This was the voice he had begun to hear too often many years ago, before he had finally left Alcott & Poe—but then it was about other matters.

He sat forward to speak, lowering his voice. "Okay. Look. The point is that you're selling to a smaller audience. Fewer and fewer people out there are truly literate. More and more people think they're literate, but don't think enough to want anything more than a television set and the latest George Duggan novel. And you want an answer. You want a solution...I don't have one."

She offered a wan smile in return. "You did. You went off and started your own book business. You saw it coming. You told me it was coming. You were right."

This was unfair. He had only seen the obvious. He had left for other reasons, but he still admired Barbara for holding on to the old ideal. When he had left, the monthly costs for the store had been almost thirty-thousand dollars. It must be a great deal more now.

He suddenly felt guilty. This was his own shame, after all. "It's no comfort to me. I can't afford much more than a fifty-year-old truck, and when my friends come to me for help, I don't have diddlysquat to give them. I have my precious freedom. My independence. And I might have two thousand in the bank right now. But that's about all. And if you want it, it's yours."

Her eyes changed. They glistened in the light of the lamp. She was crying. He had only seen that once before.

Her voice was husky. "You know that's not enough…but that's really the point, isn't it? You can't really help. I'm just hurting you by coming here and putting an edge on it." She took a few short breaths. "You know…when my father died a few years ago——"

He nodded. He remembered her telling him. Henry had met her father only once. The old man, at least a foot shorter than Henry and still a bantam of muscle, had taken Henry's arm in a vise grip and pulled him to the side. "She's yours, you know. You'll never do better. Let her think she's the boss, and she'll never say no. Just like her mother."

Henry could remember the light in the old man's eyes.

Barbara shook her head to hold in the tears. "He was broke. He had gambled every last dime away. Horses. Poker. He loved the risk. That was the way he always ran his business. You know about all that, but the money he put aside for Mom—that disappeared too. She had made investments, but the taxman came after he died. Dad hadn't paid some tax or another when he sold his company. The IRS came after their property. She never told me. She just paid for it all. And in the

145

end, there was nothing…I've been helping her since then, of course—but she's feeble now. She has dementia. Now—" she took another gulp of air. "And now I can't help anymore. It's as if now, I'm feeble too…."

He moved over to the couch and held her as she shook with short breaths and tears.

This was a different Barbara than he had ever known. If she had needed him a little more once upon a time, things might have been different. As she calmed, he wondered if he had changed as much. He knew if he spoke, she would focus on what he said, and regain some measure of the self-control she cherished. And he had in inkling of a new idea taking shape.

"You have a few more cards to play—a few more options. Your hand isn't all that bad. Downsize. Have a real sale. Fifty percent on everything. Then move to a smaller space. Pick the parts you like the best, and get rid of the rest."

She began to interrupt. "But we've worked so hard…" Her voice was trapped in her throat.

What was he going to say to that? She had worked more than twenty years away.

Oddly, his only thought was from a favorite book that he had just read again that summer. "You're a rancher. There's a drought. You do what you have to do, so that when it rains again, you'll still be there to feel it on your face."

Those were not exactly the right words for it.

She hit him with a blank stare of skepticism. Her hands mashed the tears on her cheeks. She sniffed. "What do you know about ranching, city boy?"

"I was reading a book. Elmer Kelton. *The Time It Never Rained.* It's Albert's favorite Western. Read it. It'll buck you up."

A brief smile crossed her face. He realized how warm she felt.

She broke away from him, pulled tissues from her pocket, and blew her nose.

"You can't get everything out of a book."

"No, you can't. But I'm just telling you to change a little. You've already changed. You took Sharon in as a partner. I would never have believed that. But you're going to have to take a few more steps. You can't run a museum for the public to come and see what an old bookstore used to look like. You have to make yourself new again. Reinvent yourself."

She blew her nose again and tilted her head at him.

"Henry. Twenty-three years! In October it will be that long since you came in the door, skinny as a wet dog, and asked for a job. You haven't changed one damn bit. Why do you think I can?"

He had the best answer to that.

"Because I *know* you can. You can do anything you want. You always could."

She wiped her nose a last time.

"Right!" She gave that a single affirmative nod. "But I need some help. Not just with money. With Sharon. It's a miserable partnership. We don't argue that much, really. We just don't speak most of the time. I already told her we might have to move the business. She became irate. She wants me to find some additional capital so we can hang on until this slowdown is over. She thinks she can build enough internet sales to make a difference. She thinks moving will be a disaster. And she wants to sell CDs, for God's sake…and I'm not so sure she's wrong. But she's not the same as she was. She's very protective of her territory. Before she became a partner, she was easy to deal with. She was precise. Orderly. But since then, she's the one who's really changed. She doesn't get to work on time. The cataloged books are a mess. I think it's psychological. Her life was overturned when Jim died. I suppose he was more responsible for keeping her life together than I realized."

Henry hesitated with his thoughts. "What can I do?"

"You can talk to Sharon for me."

He sat back and blew air. "I think I should keep my distance from Sharon. She seems to be in heat. You don't need me involved in that. All you need is a little money and some reasonable advice."

That made Barbara smile broadly. The smile was a little lopsided. Her teeth were slightly crooked because her father had refused to keep paying the orthodontist after the first year. It was the smile Henry had once succumbed to after resisting for too long. Not at all perfect. If he had given in to it sooner— if they had married long ago, what might have happened?

She took his hand and squeezed it. Her hands had always been warm.

"It's all right…I was just hoping your grumpy old Uncle Jack had finally died and left you his rare collection of early-twentieth-century bottlecaps or something."

She still remembered his tales of Uncle Jack, the default cause of all family problems when he was growing up.

"My dad has dibs on those. He swears he going to outlive Jack to get them. He always thought they were his anyway."

"I remember."

Henry sat forward. He really had only one offer to make.

"But I do have an idea. Tell me what you think of this—you know my client list? That's all I have, really. It's up to about seven hundred and thirty-five dealers now. I can select things out of your online catalog and put them into mine. I won't even have to redo the listing. Sharon has done all the hard work already. I'll just remove the price. You'll have to let them go for a lot less than you have them listed for now, because I'll be selling to other dealers, but they'll bring in some quick cash. I'll sell them for you, and you won't have to have a general sale right away. You can plan your next move."

She stared at him a moment, her face slack.

"But what about the long term?"

"In the long term, we are all dead. The economy has been down since at least September eleventh and all that. It's coming back. It has to. I agree with Sharon about that. Business will get better as people feel looser with their pocket money. It will give you more time to think. But it will never be what it was. And if it's time to fold the tent—you've had a good run. If there aren't enough people out there who can read outside the box of the bestseller list, then maybe you can downsize, maybe you can find a size that suits the few people who do...."

Her eyes were fixed on his in a way that hurt.

"That's so sad, Henry. That's what we were trying to stop from happening at the very beginning. It's what you could see coming years ago. That was what we used to talk about late at night."

"We did....And you did it. You made things happen the old way for a while. But I think all of that may be over now."

Chapter Fifteen

Henry was discouraged. He had chosen fifty books listed at the Alcott & Poe website to put up for bids on his own, and Sharon had been unable to find eleven of them in the shelves of the office where the rare and delicate books were kept. He already knew that the business problems of the last few years had forced Barbara to cut the staff. Two student part-timers were not enough support. This, coupled with Sharon's other difficulties, left little time for housekeeping.

He had remained too long in the upstairs office, trying to help. Finding piles of regular overstock mixed with cataloged books, he had separated them. Double-stacked shelves rose well beyond his own reach and required the constant shifting of a ladder. Books which had been recently pulled out to show potential customers had not been put back correctly. Odd volumes missing their mates were shuffled in with broken bindings needing repair. The eccentric sizes of older books created space problems on shelves designed for the usual octavo and quarto dimensions of modern volumes. His interaction with Sharon had disintegrated into bickering.

"That shouldn't be there!" Following him from shelf to shelf, Sharon restacked what he had moved. "Why did you put that there?"

"It was already there. I just put it back where it was before."

"It couldn't have been. It belongs with the biographies."

The edge in her voice was sharpened by the quickness of her response.

In the narrow spaces, the pale blue of her eyes caught little light from the fluorescent fixture above. There was no room for the two of them to pass each other without being much too close.

It was for that reason he had finally retreated down the stairs to sit with Barbara at the front desk, leaving his list with Sharon to search alone. She would be able to spot the titles faster in any case, having handled them before.

"She's angry," he said to Barbara from where he sat on a stool at the far end of the counter to watch the daily passage of humanity while he waited. Barbara sat behind the cash register, pricing a small stack of newer titles. She seemed uncomfortable with him there. If he remembered correctly, he had not been behind this counter since the day he had left his old job at Alcott & Poe.

A Mozart violin concerto on the radio was too loud for the quiet of the store. The store cat, a short-haired orange tabby named Homer, tried to climb Henry's leg. Henry brushed him off, and the cat jumped into Barbara's lap instead.

Barbara answered without looking at Henry.

"She is. We surprised her with this idea. She doesn't like it."

"I felt like I was a hunter in a mother bear's den."

There were *two* mother bears in this den, he thought.

Barbara worked her fingertips around the cat's ears, to the animal's obvious pleasure. "I suppose things look worse than they really are. Sharon usually finds any title we need in a few minutes. It's just the problem of managing all those books in too little space. Especially the pamphlets. I hate the ephemera. Some of those are only a few pages long. They disappear in the cracks. Maybe that's why I like the modern first editions. They're easier to deal with—easier to find, easier to describe, easier to ship."

They could both hear the sounds of shifting and moving from the office above.

151

"But everybody has those," he said. "I was picking out the other stuff, because they're titles you don't see as often. And for price. They'll bring higher prices. I picked out over fifty titles that are worth over two hundred dollars each at retail. And there's more. You can't have stock like that sitting upstairs for years when you're in a financial crisis. There might be half a million dollars of retail stock in that room alone."

Barbara knew this, of course. And she understood that she was going to get far less for these books as Henry sold them off. She must have been torn by the ambivalence, but she was settled on the idea now.

Barbara greeted the few customers coming in and asked if they needed assistance.

One young woman stopped and stared about herself, mouth open, then spoke out loud to no one in particular.

"Is this a library?"

Barbara smiled but did not answer. It was better to pretend the question was a joke than to accept the fact that so may people on the street had no idea what a bookshop once looked like before the age of chain stores and plastic shelving.

The register remained quiet.

Henry looked back down an almost empty aisle at one of the part-timers as she put stock up on a high shelf. Was that girl really so young, or was he getting so old? He hooked his thumb toward her and turned back to Barbara.

"Sharon has to find more time to keep things in order. Couldn't some of the students help her?" This question sounded rhetorical even to him.

Barbara's tone of studied patience made it obvious.

"No. She won't let them. They really don't know enough about it all. And besides, Sharon actually does put in a lot of time. She catalogues at least twenty books a day. She's not punctual anymore, but she stays late. And I don't think she sleeps well. She always seems tired to me."

It was Barbara who looked tired to Henry, more than just a slump to her shoulders. The cat looked back at Henry, unconcerned by their worries.

Henry said, "Tell her to take a break. Take a vacation. It's summer. Things are slower now, right?"

"She took a vacation, in the spring, but it didn't seem to help. She came back looking as tired as when she left."

He could not help but think that it was Barbara who needed the vacation. "Is it the store that has her worried? Or the book?"

It was probably just the money, Henry thought—almost always it was money that worried people. He was happy to be out of that loop.

Barbara's sigh harmonized with the purring of the cat. "I'm not sure…I told you she's changed since Jim died. She doesn't talk to me like she used to. For years, I felt like her older sister—the way she used to come to me all the time with her little problems."

Henry began, "It's still only a couple of years since Jim—"

Barbara interrupted, "Psychologizing is easy, of course. But I'm beginning to think she's getting worse, not better. I suppose she really was dependent on Jim, and of course he took advantage of that. He was a difficult guy."

Barbara would have her own definition of difficult.

Henry asked the obvious. "Did he fool around?"

She gave a short laugh. "Only with his students."

"How do you know?"

Barbara shrugged. "That's how he got Sharon. Isn't it?"

"But she stayed with him."

"She couldn't let him go."

"And now she's dependent on you."

"I suppose.… When things started getting pretty slim around here, I suggested she might want to keep her eye out for other opportunities, because we might not make it. That's when she came back with the offer of a loan."

"But that was a good thing wasn't it? Would you have been able to hang on over the last two years without it?"

"No. But now she has what's left of the money from Jim's insurance tied up here, and things have only gotten worse."

He wondered how it was so damned easy for money to get in the way of friendship. "So, she's under a new strain and there's no place to turn, with Jim gone. You don't think she can handle it. But you've been in that position for years, Barbara. You've been carrying this load by yourself from the very beginning."

Barbara ignored this. "But, that's not the point—"

"No. That's just you," Henry answered.

A woman approached and stood, book in hand, waiting for help, as if unsure how the process worked.

Barbara shook off her thoughts and smiled.

"Can I help you with anything?"

The woman tapped the cover of her book with an index finger.

"I was wondering if your prices are fixed. This one seems a little steep to me." There was a whine to the woman's voice.

She put the book up on the counter and Barbara opened the cover. It was a recent copy of a bestseller, in fine condition, already marked down.

"It seems about right. It's half price." Barbara watched the woman's eyes. The customer pulled the book away again and opened the cover herself, flipping pages carelessly, as if they had little value.

"Barnes & Noble has the same title brand new for one third off. Shouldn't it be at least half of that?"

"But this isn't Barnes & Noble."

"I know where it is." The woman answered quickly.

Barbara's voice changed. Henry knew she was not in the mood for this kind of exchange.

"Then you know we can't price our books like Barnes & Noble either."

"Maybe if you made them cheaper, you'd sell more."

"You mean, lose a little bit on every sale, but make it up on volume?"

The woman offered a blank stare to the common joke.

"So, can you go down on this a little?"

Barbara's smile froze in place. Henry did not know where she found the reserve.

"Maybe it would be better to pick out something less expensive. We have a great many paperbacks."

The woman slapped the cover shut and threw it back on the counter.

"I don't need some smart-ass clerk telling me what to buy."

She left. Barbara shook her head and put the book aside. Henry rose from the stool.

"It takes all of ten minutes behind the desk here to remember just why I left in the first place. I guess I'd better be going now. Tell Sharon I'll come by tomorrow for the books."

Barbara smiled weakly and looked away, as if looking for something to do. The cat had disappeared.

Outside, Newbury Street was filled with young women intent on buying shoes, and panhandlers leaning themselves at the young women. Street musicians who had never learned more than the effect of percussion on plastic and metal buckets overwhelmed other street noises. In the ten or fifteen minutes he had been behind the counter, no one had bought a single book from Alcott & Poe. Across the street, a steady stream of kids left a more fashionable store with small plastic bags stuffed with CDs and DVDs. It was not a picture Henry liked.

The bright orange of a parking ticket glared in the sun from his windshield at the meter. He had stayed a little too long.

He grabbed the ticket, read the fine, and then had the odd thought that orange might look good in a pinstripe against the green up the side of the truck. He would have to think about that.

Traffic had slowed on Massachusetts Avenue, narrowed by construction. Henry shifted down to second gear and rode the clutch. The engine muttered but offered no objection. He liked the sound, and fed the engine just enough gas to keep it going. Muttering. That was something funny, after all. It was his grandfather MacNeill, who had once owned a truck just like this one, and so often muttered to himself. Mac, it was said, was an unhappy man who lived twenty years after his wife passed, and never saw a happy day without her. In the picture of Henry's mother when she was a girl hanging from the side of the truck, Grandpa Mac was staring forward, but Henry always imagined his muttering. Henry's mother had escaped into her books from an early age after her own mother had died. She was always happiest with a book in her hands. Now the irony was that his own father lived on, alone, as his grandfather had. But then, Henry's father never muttered. He seldom even spoke. His lips went flat and his face whitened, and anyone seeing him knew he wanted to speak. It was not the words he lacked, or the thought. It was purpose, as if it were no use to speak because nothing would be changed by it. The words would trap in his throat, cutting off his breath. Henry had seen it so many times.

The day Benny had finished with the truck, Henry had driven it over to Brookline for a visit. His father had looked at it long and hard. There was no irritation, only bemusement. Then he had criticized it for being a toy. He had said, "Your mother would get a kick out of it, though. She always loved that old truck of Mac's."

Henry parked the truck at the garage with Benny and went home. There were book orders waiting, and he answered some email. The afternoon heat had softened him, and he had begun to feel sleepy.

When Sasha knocked lightly on the door, it startled him. She appeared wide-eyed and worried.

"Hello…" She took a deep breath, as if trying to calm herself. "Can you help me, please? I'm sorry. I should call the police. But I don't want to if I don't have to."

Henry motioned for her to come in, but she remained at the door. He asked her what the problem was.

"Frank, my ex-boyfriend, is stalking me."

Henry shook his head to sober himself. "Where? When did it happen?"

Her eyes widened further to the whites all around. "Last week. Yesterday—there's someone outside now. He's watching. I can feel it."

"Frank?"

"Or someone else. He has friends. He's angry I left him. He's afraid I'll start seeing someone else. He is very jealous."

Henry imagined a jealous Frank barging into his apartment and finding the picture on the wall.

"But you said now. Is he watching you now?"

There was still sunlight mixing into the leaves of the trees beyond the window. It seemed an unlikely time for stalking.

She nodded.

Henry went down the steps as quickly as he could, barely getting the latch on the screen door open before he burst through. The street was as empty as it had been when he came home. Most people were still at work or on summer vacation.

He walked around the corner and then back through the gate and around the house. The mother of one of the kids he had once waged an hour-long snowball fight with during the winter was pinning laundry up on the line on her back porch.

"Excuse me, have you seen anyone hanging around?"

"Just you."

"Thanks."

He turned to go.

"And the guy in the big blue car. He sat over there near the corner for at least an hour. He's gone now."

"What'd he look like?"

"Like a guy in a car."

"Thanks."

Henry asked Sasha what color car her ex-boyfriend had. She told him it was blue. He told her to call Frank and tell him to stop or she would call the police. She promised she would after protesting that she never wanted to speak to him again.

With that interruption over, Henry spent the next hour researching some titles he had noticed at Alcott & Poe. At least one was a nice item—signed by the author. It had seemed under-priced, and there was no entry for it on the store website.

Another knock on his door was quick, almost sharp. Unfamiliar. He wondered who it was and had already decided it was Sharon before he saw her standing there with a oversized box in her arms.

Her lips parted and bowed, as if unsure of her words, before she spoke.

"There are two more in the car. Can you get them?"

Her earlier scowl was gone. Henry reached for the first box, which appeared much too heavy for her, but she walked past him instead, and Henry went down the stairs. When he returned she was standing in front of Sasha's picture.

"Do you know her?"

Henry stacked all three boxes by his desk.

"Neighbor."

"Oh."

The sound of the "oh" carried something more in content.

"Just a friend," he added.

"Oh." She said it again, and sighed as if tired from her effort, but there was no sign of sweat.

"Would you like something to drink? I've got—orange juice. Beer. Milk...." His mind ran over the short list of things again, looking for something he had forgotten.

"Thank you. Water would be good." Her lips parted in a half smile.

He put ice in a glass and ran it from the tap.

When he returned, she was fingering the odds and ends he had collected on the windowsill near his chair.

"What are these?"

Henry picked one up. "Chestnuts. They lose their shine when they dry out."

"What are they good for?"

He put it back with the others. "Memory."

"Do you grind them up?"

"No. I mean, they're just there to remind me of something."

"A girl?"

"...Yes."

She smiled and sniffed. "Men are sentimental over the oddest things."

Only when she sat down on the couch did he realize he had forgotten to ask her to sit. Henry sat in the relative safety of the Morris chair. What he had immediately noticed was that the top of her dress was barely supported by the slight rise of her breasts. She was not wearing a bra. He was sure she had been wearing one at the store. Perhaps the heat had its effect.

He said, "Thanks for bringing the books over. You didn't have to. I told Barbara I'd come back tomorrow."

She laughed at his words as if he'd made a joke. "I wanted to do it. I felt bad about this morning. I growled at you when you were trying to find the books. I know you were just trying to help. I've been a little too touchy. I'm sorry."

He said, "It's okay." But he was not sure of that.

She smiled now as if slightly ashamed and adjusted herself on the couch, shifting in his direction. He noticed her lips again. Why did they appear to be so soft? The color had changed. And he could smell perfume he had not noticed in the office at the bookstore—something French, he guessed—not at all flowery. She looked down at her glass of water, giving him free rein to see what he wished.

She said, "We haven't had a chance to talk more about James' book. I wondered what you might have found out."

As she spoke, she shifted again, but this time she had reached the end of the couch, in the full light of the window. She did not look like she had recently come from a room full of dust and leather rot. She might have just dropped by from a shopping trip to Bloomingdale's.

He said, "Not a lot. Nothing new. I've written several people in New York. Emailed them, actually—editors who may have seen the work. No one seems to keep reading lists more than a few months at most. No one has any correspondence with James that they can locate. I contacted the people on the list you gave me, using my own company name, to see if I might get more of a response from them than you got. Nothing—actually, a couple of people are annoyed that we've contacted them more than once."

She responded quickly to that. "That's just too bad…" then her eyes raised toward the ceiling as the sound of Sasha's violin edged the silence with a squeal of bowing.

"Sasha." His eyes went to the picture.

"Oh," she said.

Sharon crossed her legs. As thin as she was, her legs were her best asset after her face, and he could see most of them now. He cleared his throat. He was annoyed with himself for feeling so tense. His voice was a little too loud for the distance between them.

"I've spoken twice with Boyle. He's getting more and more protective of Mr. Duggan. I think he figures we want to wear them down. He wants to put an end to it sooner than later. He's pushing for depositions."

"I received one of those letters," she said.

"But without an actual legal proceeding pending, there's no reason to go along with that."

She shook her head. Her short hair flared in the light. "I told him no."

"Good." Henry said. He was not sure the word actually made it beyond his throat.

"I am very appreciative of the help you've been giving me." Her voice had changed now, lowering so that he expected her to reveal something he must keep to himself. The violin picked up its tempo, repeating the same notes over and again. "I know you're taking the books on to be helpful…I really am grateful."

It was the pitch of her voice which had changed, like the low notes on the violin.

Henry worked at keeping his focus. "I'm planning to talk to Duggan soon. I'm going to try to see him without Boyle. I think Boyle is holding things up. Duggan would just as soon make some kind of offer and have it over with."

"You've given this a lot of your time."

She sat forward on the couch, her bare leg close enough to his now for him to feel the warmth, even on this hot afternoon. Her blouse gaped.

He was sure he could see the tip of her tongue at the edge of her teeth. He said, "It hasn't been a problem. Business has been a little slow for me as well." He knew for certain he was under attack again. And an odd thought made him smile. He thought of reading the Hornblower novels when he was younger, and the Patrick O'Brian books just a few years ago. He was thinking about how they brought the ships in close for battle, fired a broadside and then closed enough to board the other.

The pale blue of her eyes was unreadable as she answered. "Anyway. I apologize for the way I acted today," she said.

She touched his hand where it folded over the end of the armrest.

Henry looked for something to say. "Things don't seem to be getting any easier with time." He was unsure of exactly what he meant.

Sharon shifted forward just a bit more. "No. I'm wearing a little thin. I need your support. I need someone to help…I don't know how Barbara puts up with me."

Barbara! The safety of a reachable shore presented itself. He said, "She's a rock."

Sharon offered a hint of pity in her voice. "She is, but even she's starting to show signs of wear."

Henry answered with a little more confidence. "She'll handle it."

Sharon sat back just an inch or two. The delicate blond hairs of her eyebrows arched. "Why are you so sure?"

"Positive. I know her pretty well." Henry felt his footing.

Sharon shrugged. "People change."

Henry started a laugh. It sounded like a nervous laugh to him, and he swallowed it.

"That's exactly what Barbara and I were talking about. But, maybe, change is too strong a word. People grow. Most people grow," he said. "I'm not so sure about myself." He head shook once as if to deny his comment.

"And you're not worried about Barbara?"

"No."

The bow was drawn slowly over the strings of the violin in one small moan.

Sharon moved away just a bit more. "She has made remarks lately…It's difficult in my position to be as sympathetic as I want to be. Everything I have is in her hands."

Henry straightened himself with the opportunity. "Good hands. She'll pull it out. She might have to recreate the store a little—"

Sharon shook her head at him. "You mean move it." Her voice had risen with the violin to the middle strings.

"Yes—"

"It would cost too much." The note was flat. She straightened now.

He tried to sound reassuring. "Not if it's planned well."

She sat back again as if the thought exhausted her. "It would be a disaster. It would break us."

He was curious at her certainty. "What would you do instead?"

Her answer was ready, as if already spoken many times.

"Change the mix. Add remainders. Get rid of all the older novels that no one reads anymore. Put in some sidelines. We're on Newbury Street, for heaven's sake. Everyone has side-lines. More cards. T-shirts, CDs, DVDs."

Her lips had thinned and pressed together. Henry let a second of silence pass as he studied her face.

"Barbara is a bookseller. She can't do that very well if she's ordering games and posters."

"It's what people want."

"She's not interested in giving people what they want. She wants to offer them the best she can. She wants them to discover something better. If they don't buy it, so be it. She'd rather fail at doing what she thinks is right."

"That's foolish. We could lose everything!"

The top strings of Sasha's violin could be heard, played softly, as if at a great distance.

Henry sat forward now. "It's idealistic. But it's worked for her in the past. It's what she knows. What she loves. And she wants to find a way to keep doing it. That's the only future she wants."

Sharon shook her head only once, but without doubt. "It won't work. It's a slow suicide."

Henry answered. "Barbara will work it out. She's a survivor."

The violin suddenly screamed. It sounded like a cry from the street.

Chapter Sixteen

He was hungry.

He had hit several of his favorite book haunts and found nothing. With most of the students gone for the summer, fewer books were showing up. No book auctions. No calls to look at an estate in more than a week.

And now Della was not answering her phone. He had left a message. He was in the mood for a hot pastrami at Michael's Delicatessen, but it was a long trek to Brookline by himself. It would be a lot more fun if Della wanted to go to the Coolidge for a movie, so they could grab some food at Michael's on the way. He wanted a hot pastrami. He did not care what the temperature was in the sun. And he wanted to see Della. And keep it simple.

Henry turned toward Harvard Square. There was always Ellen. He could stop by and see Ellen at the Widener Library about de-acquisitions. He had been meaning to do that for weeks. They were always disposing of something they should be keeping. The rumors of rare volumes and alumni gifts buried in warehouses for years only to end up in auctions to raise more money for some new expansion were a reality he had often benefited from. Public announcements were often limited. The auction listings seldom gave the source in cases like that, lest it raise a protest from an alumni family. They always assumed their gifts would be kept. Year after year.

He usually did better at those sales, because he was not always going against collectors with deep pockets. His inside source was Ellen. Ellen was a sweetheart. It was too bad she was married.

Vincent McCaffrey

The wall surrounding Harvard Yard shut out the noise of traffic as suddenly as the old trees cooled the air. As much as he would always be just a visitor to those precincts, he liked them. It was the one area of Harvard University that still carried the ghost of a past devoted to books, and perhaps some remnant of a present devotion to learning. The Widener, a great granite twentieth century mausoleum amidst the quaint brick buildings of the eighteenth and nineteenth centuries, was even yet, at least for the most part, a library, and a home for books, and a place for study.

He was stopped at the desk and then directed to a phone. The old days of making his own way downstairs to Ellen's office were over. Just another change since September 11th. On the phone a recording told him she was on vacation.

The feeling of being at loose ends was suddenly overwhelming. Maybe he would stop at Bartley's instead and get a burger. Della could be anywhere. She could even be out somewhere with Bob. There was no use in starving to death. He was not anxious to be home by himself, and this thought upset him as well. He usually enjoyed being by himself.

Remainders displayed in the window of the Harvard Bookstore were the same as the week before. He walked on, his irritation filling his stomach.

A small gathering of tattooed self-mutilators and lost souls clung to the shade at the edge of the brick-lined pit near the subway entrance. One passed a small joint to a friend, the smell of the grass reaching beyond the haze around them. In the quiet of the heat, no cops were within sight. Henry's mood worsened.

At the corner Japanese tourists holding maps pointed to the brick wall of Harvard Yard and asked him to take their picture. Traffic was light. The air had taken on the baked smell of an oven, the sky was a soiled blue of haze.

And now he was thirsty as well. But he wouldn't be going to the Blue Thorne today. Albert had called to say that his old boss Myron had passed. Albert would be busy for a couple of days. There would be no fun in drinking beer alone. And Tim might take the chance to tell Henry some other tale of woe. There was always some other tale of woe to tell. Henry had had enough woe.

He dropped down the steps to grab a program at the Brattle Theatre, and then kept walking as he read through a disappointing line-up of shows repeated once too often over the years. The last fragments of the happy disposition he had begun the day with crumbled. At an empty intersection, he looked with sour impatience at a red light, waiting for the change instead of taking advantage of the lack of traffic because it used just a little more time. Perhaps Della would be back from where she had gone by the time he got home.

Still a block from the apartment, his eyes picked up on the dark blue of a car just beyond the turn to his own street, parked in the shade. He did not recognize it as belonging to one of the neighbors. A Ford Crown Victoria. He walked on as casually as he could, his eyes scanning the area for Sasha's boyfriend. He wondered what her Frank would look like.

Henry could see little in the car itself because of the reflection of light and leaves in the broad windshield. He was almost beside the car before he saw that there was a man inside apparently reading a newspaper, but looking away toward the house. The side window was open for air and Henry leaned down.

"Frank?"

The man was startled. He had clearly been focused on the other direction. He was middle-aged, overweight, clean-shaven. He did not seem to match any mental picture Henry had of Frank, the master photographer, and stalker. He seemed familiar, but Henry did not think he knew him. The man's reaction was sudden.

"I'm not Frank. So who the hell are you?"

Henry said, "Bugs Bunny." He was not sure why he said it. It just seemed appropriate.

"Don't get funny, asshole."

Henry made the obvious guess.

"Why are you watching that house?"

"None of your fuckin' business."

"It's my house. It's my business."

"Fuck off."

"Do you think the police would have any interest in your hanging around watching people's houses?"

"Run it up your ass, junkie."

The man had turned the key in the ignition and now he pulled away in one motion. Ford Crown Victorias were a favorite with the police. Henry wrote the license plate number down.

When he reported the incident to Sasha, she was confused. She described Frank as only slightly taller than herself, thirty years old, bearded, and soft-spoken. She turned suddenly and went to the phone, punching numbers angrily, leaving Henry to stand at her door.

She did not say hello when someone answered.

"A man is watching my house. Do you know why a man is watching my house?"

In the silence, as she listened to the answer, Henry noticed that the spot on the wall which had once been occupied by the picture that was now in his apartment had been filled by another—almost exactly the same, but in this one, Sasha was dressed in a dancer's black leotard. He figured that the two pictures had been taken at the same time.

She was speaking into the receiver but holding it away from her head as if afraid to allow the phone to touch her ear. "Why should I believe you?…It's not true…. You don't care." The replacement picture was nearly as beautiful as the other. Henry studied the picture as she continued to speak. "This scares me.… My neighbor Henry caught him watching. I think he's a stalker."

Henry's eyes scanned the room for books. A stack of magazines sat against one wall. There were no books. Sasha was not a reader. Her violin and bow lay across the pillow at the center of the room.

She spoke again. "He's gone now. But I think he's been here before."

From below, Henry could hear Mrs. Murray open her door, and then the front door. He went out on the landing and leaned over the rail.

"Sarah…"

Her face filled the narrow space between the banisters below. "Hi."

"Hi. Sarah…there was a man sitting in a big dark blue Ford Crown Vic across the street there just beyond the corner. Middle-aged guy. Clean-shaven, hair thinning and dyed an orangy-brown. He's evidently been watching the house. You wouldn't have any idea why, would you?"

She looked away and then up again. She looked more than just surprised. She looked disturbed. "No…But it sounds like a cop."

"It does, doesn't it…."

Henry wondered if Mr. Boyle might be involved.

Sasha stood at the door again.

"Thank you, Henry…I don't think the stalker is Frank. Frank was very surprised. I think Frank is worried about me now."

She smiled. Her smiles always disconcerted him.

Henry went back to his apartment and called the number on the letter from Boyle.

A secretary said she would take a message. He left his name. Twenty minutes later, as Henry finished brewing tea to put it in the refrigerator, the phone rang.

"Boyle. What can I do for you?"

"I'm not sure. I heard that you come from a family of cops."

"Three generations."

Henry described the situation. Boyle listened.

"So what does this have to do with me?"

"Just me. I'm wondering if you can do something I can't. I have no connections at the police department. I've never even been arrested. Is there any way you can find out why this guy is watching my house?"

Silence. Then a grunt. Henry thought of Albert. Then Boyle let a long breath out. "You want me to do you a favor?"

"Yeah, as a friend of George Duggan...and Albert Hamilton."

Another breath passed the receiver, this one blown a bit harder.

"I'll get back to ya."

After Boyle hung up, Henry wondered where he had learned how to press people like that. It wasn't his usual style. The only example that came to mind was Barbara, back in the old days, talking book publishers into giving her credit when times were slow.

The phone rang again. It was Della. She sounded cheerful. He asked her about going over to Coolidge Corner.

"I like the part about Michael's. But let's not go to the movies. Why don't we visit your dad instead?"

Henry countered, "I saw him a couple weeks ago."

"I'd like to meet him. We could take him out for a little pastrami."

Henry felt like he had been ensnared by something he could not see.

"Why? He's just an old grumpy guy. He fixes old radios and then sits and listens to them for hours."

"Maybe its because he doesn't have anybody else to talk to."

"He's got his buddies. He still works."

"Have you shown your father the truck yet?"

"Yes."

"What does he think?"

"He thinks it's silly. It's a toy, he says. I said yeah, it's a toy. He said I was getting too old for toys. I said that I was not looking forward to being too old for toys. He said I did n't spend enough time looking forward at all. You know how those conversations go. You lose, lose."

"I'd like to meet him."

"You wouldn't."

"I would. I'm curious what you'll be like in twenty years. Come on."

"I'll be sixty. He'll be seventy in November. But I'll still be old and wrinkled. You won't like the picture."

"Why don't you let me be the judge of that?"

Chapter Seventeen

Junior sat in the middle. He had grown by several inches since the previous Tuesday, when Henry had last seen him. But then, he had been growing that way for years. He was going to be bigger than his father, and was not far from it now. The bench seat was thigh to thigh across, with Junior twisting his left leg over to avoid the stick shift. Henry avoided shifting gears as often as possible.

"Did you remember the coffee?" Albert said.

Junior let out a little air between his teeth before he answered.

"Yes sir."

The sun had tilted off behind them now and the clean trough of road took them forward as if it were all downhill, even on the upgrades. Henry tried to keep his mind on the driving, as much as his thoughts wanted to slip off onto a dozen side roads of problems he was not making good sense of.

"If you take the truck we're going to miss the Sox game tonight. Junior's radio hisses as bad as he does."

"I don't want to be up here all week, Albert. I'll get the bus from Rangeley as soon as I'm done. Maybe tonight. There's a seven o'clock bus to Boston."

"You won't make it tonight. You don't understand distances up here. Miles are longer. You are going to end up sleeping in the truck, so you want to bring a blanket. I'll pack a couple of things when we unload. I'll put 'em in a blanket, and you can carry 'em with you just in case you have to leave the truck."

"The road goes all the way."

"Those are dotted lines. That DeLorme map is a fine piece of work. This is a fine truck with a nice low gear, but you may not be able to take this all the way in there. This truck wasn't made for rougher trails."

It made no sense for Henry to argue. He had no idea. He had never been a boy scout, but it was better to be prepared. That made sense.

Junior nodded forward, his eyes closed by the monotony of the passing trees.

"Kids," Albert said, nudging his son awake with his shoulder. "All your brother Danny does anymore is sleep. I won't take him fishing anymore."

Junior hissed.

Henry rethought his plans. It really was just one plan. He had no back up.

He was going to drive up to Duggan's camp—he liked the sound of that, Red Hill Camp, like something from olden times—and apologize for being such an uncivilized bit of human crud for barging in, and beg his pardon and tell him within the first couple of sentences that it was a matter of life and death or he wouldn't be there, and hope that George Duggan was really the same guy he drank beers with a couple of weeks ago.

John Boyle was doing his job. That was clear. But that did not mean that Henry could not go around him.

"Turn at that patch of grass."

Ahead, the grass strip beside the road widened and the gravel spread from the shoulder into a parting of the trees.

"I don't see any lake." Henry wondered.

"It's over there. A mile."

Albert had offered to go with him to Duggan's camp. Henry had rejected the idea of three big men driving up on Duggan in the middle of the woods.

Henry slowed, his fist on the knob of the stick shifting against Junior's leg as his boot worked the clutch.

Junior said, "Just be careful, Mr. Sullivan, that you don't grab the wrong one."

Albert pushed his son with his shoulder. "Shut up, Junior. We don't need any high-school humor right now. Take the way to the right, Henry…I know it doesn't look like a road, but it is."

A shelf of rock protruded from beneath the roots of stunted pine, offering a ramp to the wheel ruts that separated the grass and disappeared into the grey fingers of dead undergrowth. The truck took the shelf in stride and passed over the tall center grass with the sound of a continuous brush on the underside.

Albert said, "This is marvelous." A grin fixed his face.

"Dad's big ol' truck got stuck there last year. The trees have grown in on the trail and he won't cut 'em back"

Albert shouldered his son again. "You don't have to tell the whole world…. They don't make trucks that ride high like this anymore. My truck is so long it catches the rock right at the middle. That's all."

Junior pushed back at his father.

"I had to carry most of the supplies from here to the camp last year. Dad said his ankle was bothering him."

Grasshoppers flew before them. The sun swatted at them through the shadows. The road dipped, climbed, and at last the trees parted onto the slate blue surface of a lake that must have been miles across, pushed by a steady wind that wrinkled the surface of the water like old skin.

Junior let out a whoop. He was on the heels of his father out the door, and as quickly into the back of the truck and unloading the inflatable boat.

"Camp supplies first, Junior. Mind your business."

Albert pulled a blanket from a duffel and tossed an assortment of small supplies into the middle, rolled it and tied it at both ends with a short rope so that Henry could sling it over his shoulder.

"You want to take my cell phone?" Albert offered.

"You know I don't like cell phones."

"Just this once. You're going to be out in the woods, by yourself."

"I'll be fine," Henry said.

Within fifteen minutes, Henry had waved goodbye to the closing curtain of undergrowth beneath the pines as he made his way back out. The map was open on the seat beside him.

Using his thumb against the scale, he calculated again the distance to Red Hill, north through Rangeley and southeast through Madrid, then northeast. Perhaps sixty miles at most. Keeping an average speed of forty-five miles an hour, he should be there in an hour and a half—by two o'clock in any case.

He was pleased with himself. With Albert and Junior gone he felt more like he was off on an adventure. He whistled "Appalachian Spring" over the hum of the truck engine and stopped for a quick cup of coffee in Rangeley when it looked like he was ahead of time. The road through Madrid and north again lengthened in an elastic snake of curves and halts for summer traffic.

He reached the small building beside the road that called itself the Red Hill General Store and Post Office just after three o'clock. Four SUVs filled the graveled space at the front.

A heavy man in a soiled fisherman's vest leaned behind the counter, keeping an eye on half a dozen teenagers, both boys and girls, who pored over the cassettes of adult videos at the back of the small room.

"Can I do for ya?" The man spoke without actually looking away from the kids.

"I'm looking for Red Hill Camp." Henry said.

The man snuck a look at him now, and then refocused on the teenagers.

The man asked, "Where is that?"

Henry thought twice. "Mr. Duggan told me that if I got lost, I should ask the man at the general store. Is there someone else around here that might know?"

The man raised an eyebrow.

"When did he tell you that?"

"When he was in Boston two weeks ago."

The man considered this a few seconds while snatching looks toward the kids.

"Mr. Duggan yelled at me the last time I sent somebody up to his place."

Henry pulled the notepaper with the Red Hill Camp name printed on the top from his shirt pocket and unfolded it, reading it so that the heading might be recognized from a short distance, but no more.

"It's okay. I think I just turned at the wrong place. I'll figure it out." Henry started to leave.

The heavy man held up his hand. "Just a minute…" then moved toward the crowd at the back.

"All right, Fran, Tom, out of here. You're just sixteen. The rest of you, I want to see your driver's licenses before you get another idea."

There were moans and other sounds and the group filed out en masse. The girls giggled. One rolled her eyes as she passed Henry.

The heavy man returned to his post and pulled an old bill from a pile of paper, turned it over to the blank side, and started to draw with a stubby pencil.

"Looky here. This is the way…"

As the man spoke, Henry could hear the roar of the SUVs and the spit of gravel from beneath the tires hitting the side of his own truck.

He was on a small gravel and grass road within a few minutes, rising onto the side of a ridge, presented with a view of a few small lakes below and three scattered mountains. After dropping, crossing a creek, and rising again, the road divided at the top of the next ridge. The trees were thick at both sides. There was no fork on the penciled map drawn by the store-keeper. Perhaps he thought it would be obvious at this point.

Henry studied the road itself. Isn't that how they did it in Western movies? The road to the left was the better traveled. What did that mean? Would there be a lot of traffic to Duggan's camp? But that way seemed to turn back away from the general direction of the camp. Henry took the road to the right. Within ten minutes, his left rear wheel spun in a void left by the run of water against the gravel.

He jockeyed the truck, making matters worse, and filling the quiet air beneath the pines with the grey smoke of burned rubber.

According to the map, he had to be close. He got out of the truck and began to kick rocks free from the soil and pile them into the void. This had little effect as they spun out with the turn of the wheel.

He found a dead branch and used it to work a larger rock free from the moss which fastened the slabs like mortar. Mosquitoes buzzed at his ears and he raised his collar and swatted with whatever hand was free.

The tire grabbed his carefully constructed platform and tossed it away.

He rebuilt the support with a broader base of fallen branches and braced it across the gully that he figured had been made by the snow melt. When the woods lost their depth and most of their color to shadow, and the sky above him was no longer framed by the sunlight on the uppermost leaves, he turned on the Red Sox game and listened as he worked.

In the fifth inning he kicked at his construction and it did not move. He shifted into low gear and the truck crawled forward. As the wheel left his platform, the earth at the edge of the road gave way. The truck tilted and settled. The wheel spun. Jason Varitek hit a home run.

He thought briefly of sleeping in the open back, then opted for closing the windows tight against the mosquitoes and propping his feet against the door on the down side.

The smell of the truck was a perfume of motor oil and rubber and the materials once used to trim old cars. He wondered why such smells could not be bottled and used to replace the synthetic odor of recent models. He fell asleep shortly after the Red Sox bullpen had lost the game and he switched the radio off. The radio light had been comforting. Now, through the windshield, stars swayed in the river of sky above the road—if a road was what it was.

He awoke with his neck stiff where it had rested against the metal of the doorframe. A cloud had settled down in the woods around him. The yellow of sun infused the mist just above the treetops and cast an amber glow onto the forest floor.

Stepping out into the air was like entering a pool of water. He pulled a moment against the stiffness in his back, and then surveyed his work. If anything, he calculated, he was worse off than before. And he was very thirsty. His stomach growled.

Standing in the quiet of the road, he listened.... Somewhere there was the sound of a voice. Perhaps voices. Someone was talking. The road ahead fell downward through ferns into a small valley nearly dark with thick growth.

The voices came through the trees, from up the hill. He calculated that they were roughly in the direction of the other road he had not taken, in any case. At the very last moment, Henry grabbed at the blanket roll Albert had made for him. The map had fallen to the floor in the night, unseen.

The ground was clear on the rise, well carpeted with pine needles, and he began his climb with increasing strides, covering ground quickly. It felt good to be moving. In ten minutes he was on a ridge with the pines spaced almost evenly apart. The ground falling away from him appeared to be even more clear of undergrowth as far as the eye could travel. The pines there stood taller, the trunks considerably wider. Above him the clouds had broken in tatters against a hard blue. There was no sign of the other road. The sound of voices ahead had quieted.

At first he tried to stay near the top of the ridge he had crossed. This played out and reformed and rose to some point higher in the trees repeatedly, until he was too tired to follow. When the trees cleared unexpectedly, he found himself on a low cliff, looking across the tops of oak and maple toward the side of another rise. Directly below him, the face of rock was streaked green by seepage, drawing his eyes into a dark crevice with no visible bottom. His balance wavered, and he drew back. He had never been good with heights. He looked out again, over the trees, trying to ignore the void beneath him. When his head began to feel light, he turned back.

There was still no sign of the other branch of the road, so he tried at least to stay on the same level, avoiding going up or down. The voices he had heard before returned, and became stronger again, closer, as if they were traveling in the same direction. He repeatedly stopped to listen. Still no words could be understood.

When once he was sure the voices had changed direction, coming now from below, he let gravity take his feet downward through the open space between the sap-streaked trunks. He reached a small river of rock, with no sign of water. The woods were denser here, and because the rocks were larger and made walking more difficult, he climbed back toward the ridge and the clear spaces below the pine.

Sounds reached him occasionally from other directions— knocks and cracks he figured to be from the trees. Once he caught the sound of a small plane which he followed with his ears. It was not circling. It was not for him. It was headed straight on for something, perhaps north to Moosehead Lake. That might have given him a sense of direction if he had the map. He had already cursed into the quiet air for forgetting that.

As he stepped across another ridge of rock, the voices, louder now, were somewhere below him again.

He let his weight carry him through the open space as he had done before. Moving quickly again made him feel briefly better—at least until his body jerked forward suddenly, his knee buckled with a step across the pale green lichen on a rock, and he collapsed, tumbling to a stop against a large tree. Sap came off on his hands as he pushed himself up.

There was no pain. Nothing broken. Nothing even sprained. But the voice was clearer here. It was then he saw that it was not a voice at all. It was the babble of running water—and he was thirsty.

A clear dark flow filled the space between shattered grey rock. He knelt to it and watched small insects swarm inches from his head. The water was as cold as ice melt and numbed his tongue.

Henry unrolled his blanket on a flat bench of rock to see what he had. There were matches in a plastic bag, insect repellent, a pack of Fig Newtons, several rolls of heavy cord, a flash-light, a knife. One larger packet unfolded into two thin plastic sheets—silvered on one side—each of which he figured to be about six feet square. There was a small wad of toilet paper inside a sealable plastic bag like the ones Albert used to pack his fish in his basement freezer. This afforded Henry what he thought momentarily was a humorous view of Albert's mind. He laughed. He did not like the sound of it as it echoed in the trees. Albert was too often right. Henry took the toilet paper out and kept it aside, but reused the bag to carry water.

The shadows had gone from green to blue. He knew he should be headed back to the truck at this point, but he just as surely knew, as he stared up the slope he had just come down, that he could not retrace his steps. He was the fool. He was lost. Another mosquito found him with that thought still fresh.

At a place where the earth briefly flattened, he could see the way ahead was not as clear as it had been, and that it was not undergrowth he was seeing, but the grey of darkness.

He tied a cord between the two smallest trees close by and made a lean-to of sorts from one of the sheets. The other he placed on the ground beneath. He walked far enough away and dug a hole and used a bit of the paper Albert had so thoughtfully provided. Then he covered his exposed body with the insect repellent. After gathering a small nest of firewood, he made a teepee of sticks as he had seen in camping books through the years, and lit a fire. Instead of illuminating the woods around, the shadows that guarded him disappeared suddenly into darkness. He created a hearth of small rocks, watched sparks drift upward into the branches overhead and worried about causing a forest fire, then let the fire die down to smaller flames and began to eat his Fig Newtons. Once begun, he could not stop himself. The package was empty in minutes. He put the blanket down on the plastic and laid down on that, pulling half the blanket over himself, and fell asleep.

Henry awoke to a smell he knew, even in Brookline. A skunk had found him.

The darkness beneath the pines was dense and the fire was dead. He was not sure he should use the flashlight, if it might frighten the skunk.

He thought twice.

As he did, there was the sound of someone walking close by. The sound stopped. He stopped his own movement to listen. The pumping of blood in his ears roared. The walking began again.

Henry slipped his hand down by his body, encountered the flashlight where he had placed it, slowly pulled it out from beneath the blanket, pointed it and pushed the button. Four, six, eight pairs of eyes stared back at him. The deer did not move for most of a minute before elevating in the air, like a ballet troupe, and bouncing away into the pine, flashing their tails at him handkerchief-like as they did. The skunk waddled after them. The blue light of morning was announced with the knocking of a woodpecker and a loose chorus of birds at a distance. Henry calculated the direction of the birds as he opened his eyes and before he actually moved. The air was crisply cool. He had slept very well and was happy with himself. To his memory, this was the first night he had ever spent alone in the woods, and it had been a success.

Then it began to rain.

He rolled up his blanket quickly, with the contents he wanted dry and then turned the blanket into one of the plastic sheets, tied it at the ends and began to walk in the direction of the birds, with the other sheet over his head and held by his free hand. He imagined himself looking like an odd grandmother figure, huddled beneath the plastic as he walked.

Shortly he was at the bottom of the fold of the hill. The direction of the birds, which were silent now, took him upward again. In the rain, there was no direction to the light. In any case, he had walked less than an hour when he found the marks of someone else who had been by recently through the pine needles. He followed this trail for less than half an hour before he recognized one particularly ugly mushroom at the base of a fallen tree and knew that the trail was his own. He was going in circles.

Below him was the camp he had made the night before. He found it fairly easily. He knew what lay in the direction of the birds, and this time set out simply downward, toward the lowest point he could find. In less than an hour he had reached a lake.

Swamp, marked by a disorderly fence of dead pines, played out to the right of him. To the left, a small ridge rose from the water and headed back in the direction from which he had come. Following the shore to the left, he soon found the creek again. After drinking with his face submerged in the water, he sat there on what appeared to be the most comfortable of a bad selection of rocks larger than himself, and thought about his situation. It was not long then before he heard a voice again. He ignored it, until it spoke his name. And spoke it again. Not so much spoken, as sung.

"Henry, oh Henry, where are you my Henry / Oh Henry, oh Henry, where have you gone."

The song had something of the lilt of an Irish folk melody, but the voice belonged to Della Toth.

And she was alone.

Her white knees flashed between the trunks of the trees. She screamed when she saw him. He had never heard her scream before. And then she collapsed on the ground, as if in a faint.

He stumbled, running to her, scraping his hand. She was laughing when he reached her.

"What's up, doc?" She said, looking up at him from the ground.

He could not speak. He sat down beside her.

"Well, I don't know about you," she said. "but I'm lost.… Do you have any Fig Newtons left? I'm hungry. And I'm thirsty."

Clouds had divided in the open space above the lake, and the gray had gone to blue. As she spoke to him, lying there on the pine needles, exhausted, she told him what she had done. She pulled the wadded Fig Newton wrapper from her back pocket and presented it to him when he admitted to her that he had eaten them all.

She said, "You shouldn't litter."

Finished with her account she announced she was thirsty again. The sun had bloomed above the water, and in the near distance they could see a mountain. He had no idea what mountain it was.

It all seemed incomprehensible to Henry. Della had asked Bob to drive her to Maine. And Bob had done it. Henry could not imagine why she would ask Bob, or why Bob would agree.

"I didn't ask. He volunteered. He loves me…" she said.

"But to take you all the way to Maine to find me. Me!"

"He was there when Barbara called."

"Where? In my apartment?"

"Yes. I came looking for you. You didn't tell me you were going to Maine."

"How did you get in? Mrs. Murray?"

"No. She came up later, after Bob came looking for me. No, it was Sasha who let me in." She looked at him critically. He did not understand.

"How did Sasha get in?"

"Down the fire escape. She said she always did it that way.… I wondered what she meant."

"She only meant—"

"Then Barbara called. She had something to tell you. I told her you weren't there and she told me to call Albert, which I did. It was then that Alice told me what you were doing, which sounded pretty adventurous for a guy like you. Then I told Alice that I wanted to go to Maine, and she told me—"

"What do you mean, 'A guy like me'?"

"Well, you don't hear the words 'bold' and 'bookseller' used together very often, do you?"

Alice had given Albert's cell phone number to Della. Albert had directed them straight to Red Hill, worried that no one had heard from Henry the evening before, and maybe concerned about Mr. Duggan's reception. Bob had volunteered to pick her up before dawn, and they had arrived at Red Hill by 8:30. Della figured she had been lost since about nine o'clock. She had forgotten her watch.

Henry wondered, "Did the guy at the store direct you up the road?" He must think there is a convention at the camp.

"No…Do you think Bob would ask directions? Noooo. He's got some kind of satellite connection in his Jeep, a GPS, and he coordinated it with an old map he found somewhere. A gas station map. Bob collects old gas station maps. Did you know that? You ought to talk with him about that. You might be able to sell him something. And Red Hill Camp used to be a real camp. A boys' camp."

Henry did not interrupt her to say that he knew nothing about old gas station maps. Perhaps because the idea intrigued him. But she had last seen Bob as she called Henry's name and wandered off up the hill following the sound of voices, away from where Bob's Jeep was stopped behind Henry's truck on that narrow bit of road.

"I tried to get back, but when I did it was all gone, like the road had disappeared."

"You were on the wrong side of the ridge. I did that too."

They decided not to move. If she had found him, someone else could as well.

Then she began to remove her clothes.

The sun fell directly on the water where she waded in. Henry took a deep breath and followed her example.

Chapter Eighteen

Henry was surprised that her nose should be cold, or even wet. Her naked body was close behind his, beneath the blanket, and felt warm. The work of woodpeckers sounded across the lake. An owl hooted forlornly in the blue light beneath the pines. He opened his eyes on the red and gold sun trapped in the rock faces of the mountain across the lake.

A cold nose touched his ear. His hand went up to wipe it away, and found the soft warm muzzle of a dog.

"Here, Matty," came a voice.

Henry knew the voice. Della's head was already turned as Henry looked back through the woods beneath the back opening of their lean-to. It was George Duggan.

The dog was an English foxhound. White and brown and black. Large and slightly stocky. Its ears flapped loosely as it turned its head at Duggan's command. When Henry was a kid, in Brookline, their neighbor had kept one like it, along with an Irish terrier. It was the kind of humor their neighbor was given to.

Duggan turned his back as they dressed. The dog watched.

"I made your friend Bob stay at the camp. He seemed a little flustered. Worried about losing Miss Toth—"

"Della," she said, hopping on one foot as she wiped the pine needles from the other.

"He showed up at three in the morning with that Jeep of his blazing. He was just likely to get lost again. These woods are great for that.... Matty is the hound to find anybody though. He was on your trail in half a minute."

The dog stood still at the sound of his name and looked up at George Duggan for instructions. Duggan bent and scratched him behind the ears

"I used to get lost here on purpose back when I was a boy. Used to come to the camp every summer then. When they closed it and the lumber company bought it, I got upset about all these old trees being cut down. So when I could, I bought it back from the lumber company. Twenty-four hundred acres. And I've bought the lumber rights on four thousand more.... That's a nice lake. I swim there most mornings over from the far side.... But this is pretty nice right here, now that I think about it."

Henry had certainly taken the wrong fork. He had figured that already. He was thankful Bob had turned back on the right one. It seemed he had coasted slowly along the road through the woods, honking his horn, with all his lights on or flashing. Henry and Della had heard nothing.

Duggan led them on a path made invisible by low ferns around the edge of the lake, and in half an hour found Red Hill Camp scattered in small green shuttered buildings beneath enormous pines. The largest building, a log cabin of two floors with shelter overhangs displaying the beams of the roof was like something in a postcard from long ago. This structure was closest to the lake and attached to the short body of a pier being suckled by canoes.

Duggan started cooking them breakfast immediately, assuming a position behind a broad stainless-steel stove. In shorts and a T-shirt it was obvious he was a very fit man. He might be pushing sixty, but his hair was cut short enough to hide his balding. He was at least Albert's height, less a few pounds.

Bob had already eaten with Nora, and had previously paddled with her to the center of the lake where the view was best, with the thought of spotting them. She now sat in a corner of the cabin by the window which faced the lake and shuffled paper in folders while making phone calls. Henry felt as if she were ignoring them all.

Bob was effusive. The white of his skin was mottled in red at his cheeks.

"This is great! This is the way to live!"

"When I was a kid," Duggan interrupted, "it took two hundred and fifty dollars to stay the summer. Now I get offers of ten million just for the lake from outfits that want to subdivide it into fifty lots and sell each parcel for a million. Sadly, everything costs too much."

Duggan blew a great plume of cigar smoke toward the beams above.

Bob offered, "I'd buy one, if I had the dough."

"That's the problem, isn't it though? There are so many people who would. I don't know what's happening to the world…" Bob's face fell. Duggan finished, "It's not your fault. I'm not blaming you. If I was in your position, I guess I would too."

It was Duggan who suggested that they stay the day and spend the night, even before they had pulled the truck from its trap on the road. Henry called Albert and was told everything was fine. Bob was less sure. He looked toward the window, where the mountain had gone from gold and red to grey and silver in the sun. Nora sat there with her back to them, speaking to someone about paper sizes, and it was as if the red of the mountain had settled in her hair.

"I've got to go…I better go…" Bob said. "Business…someone's computer has crashed somewhere in the universe, and I'm the only one who can save it."

Henry sympathized with the predicament. Bob was the fifth wheel.

He turned to Della and told her he would be seeing her soon. He said goodbye to Nora, and she waved while talking into the phone. He did not look happy to leave, but Henry was glad to see him going.

When she finished with what work she was doing, Nora remained aloof. It was nothing she actually said, but in her tone and the contrast with George Duggan's friendliness. She did not ask about Sharon or Barbara. Her questions about internet sales and the current used book market were only polite.

To Henry's tale of complaints, she said, "Publishers can play that game as well, of course. They can sell directly to the public. It's the bookshops which are on the short end of this revolution."

But Henry was not finished.

"But it's the sense of place that's lost with that. A bookshop is a place of books. Browsing in books is a matter of smell, and texture, and time. It's having all those strange new worlds within reach. It's the conversation…." He stumbled on the memory of the cheapskate woman in Alcott & Poe. He was not happy with his inability to find the right words.

He looked toward Della, who was chatting about Hungarian food with Duggan. Nora smiled patiently at him after he stopped.

"We don't get to smell the sweet perfume of horse manure on the streets any longer, either," she added.

Nora seemed very much in the thrall of the new day of the internet. After lunch she went out on the lake again alone. They could see that she had her cell phone with her and spent much of the time talking.

Duggan asked for help with the two-handled bucksaw and they cut a hip-high pile of logs for the fireplace within an hour.

Afterward they sat on the porch and wallowed in a warm breeze that pushed into the shade of the pines from off the lake.

Duggan had sprawled in a heavy board Adirondack-style chair. They had started to speak about *Penny Candy*.

"Mr. Perry was unusual…But, you know that."

"I didn't know—not until I read the book," Henry answered.

The big man got up then and sat on the hand rail with his back against a post, his voice lowering in a way Henry remembered from the memorial service for Morgan Johnson.

"His talent was unusual, of course, but I meant something else…. It's odd to say this now, after his death, but he was a survivor. You actually see a lot of them in history, because the survivors are the ones who make it and are written about. But they are actually not so common as they appear. The hardships of history are Darwinian to the extreme. I have come to believe that the importance of chance is far smaller than most Modernists assert. If chance were to predominate, mankind would still be scratching two-dimensional figures on the walls of caves. In the short term, chance may play a larger roll, but in the long term it is the inexorable force of the human spirit which succeeds…. Think of it religiously if you wish, but I see it as the spread of life. Here's this fellow, Eddy Perry, who might have given up a thousand times, but had that bit of sinew in his heart that made him try again, and again. If anyone deserved to win, it was Eddy Perry. With all his faults. He had earned it."

Henry had thought the same thing. "Chance turned against him in the end, though. His last bit of luck was bad."

Duggan shook his head. "Luck? I'm not sure…Perhaps. There is such a thing as luck, I suppose. But all I'm saying is this: that luck has less to do with things than most people think."

"You found us in the woods," Della said.

"That was Matty." Matty's ears went up.

"Della found me." Henry said.

"She knows you. She guessed your direction with a pretty good sense of who you are, and then she found your trail. That was plain as can be."

Henry took a leap. "You found Nora."

"Nora...No, Nora found me. I'm just an old reprobate who couldn't take his eyes off her. She gets that every day. She came up and talked to me one day after I gave a speech at Boston University. She volunteered to help with a project I had started there. Later on, when she was working with the fellow I hired to get Tremont Press going, she understood what I wanted and made things happen there better than he did. We had some common interests. It's what civilizations are build on, common interests."

Della looked at Henry.

"Common interest. See?"

"Hot pastrami." Henry answered.

Nora's canoe drifted in low silhouette against the sheen of the sun on the surface of the lake.

"Does she like Eddy's book?" Henry asked.

Duggan looked behind himself to the small figure.

"Yes...You'll be hearing from her about that. She wants to know who owns the rights."

Henry shrugged. He had not given that much thought.

"I'm not sure. Legally. You know from the book that he has no relatives left. I thought—in the introduction he says that the book was written for Janet Fowler, as a gift, he says. Isn't that as good as a will? He gave it to her."

Duggan wiped his face with his hand.

"I'll talk to Boyle. He has a guy—you met him, I believe— Ted Schultz. He can figure it out. I think that would be a fine idea."

Henry settled back with the idea in his head. It sounded right to him. The other canoes bobbed against the pier, knocking gently. To one side, the quiet of the shuttered cabins seemed to want the sound of kids running wild.

"This must have been a great camp."

"It was the best."

"How long has it been closed?"

Duggan surveyed the structures with his eyes.

"Twenty-something years. In the late seventies. The recession then killed it."

"No chance of opening it up again?"

Duggan looked at him with a squint.

"Yeah...we had a writer's conference up here last year.... My kids spend their summers here."

"How many children do you have?"

"Three."

"Three's a good number." Della said, pressing at Henry's arm.

Duggan said, "It turned out to be a lot more than I bargained for."

Della's asked, "Where are they now?"

"With their respective mothers. I have three fabulous children, two by my first wife and one by my second. They spend a lot of time with me up here. They have the run of the place for now...but kids are as selfish as writers are. They need their own time. They possess it. My first wife did not understand that. She wanted to share the time I needed to write. It didn't work. My second wife is my agent now. I sometimes think it was Heber's little joke. He was the one who recommended her to me before he died. But at least she understood my need for time, and everything was cool until she got pregnant.... That's when I got a vasectomy. I'm way too selfish a man to have all those children. But as undeserving as I am, they've given me a lot more in return than I have ever been able to give to them. Nora and I agreed at the start not to get married. I guess I don't want to take a third swing and strike out. But she's like you," he turned to Della. "She wants to have kids someday."

Duggan rose then with his own thoughts and took one of the canoes and paddled to the center of the lake where Nora floated. She was still lying on her back, sunglasses pointed at the sky and her elbow sharpened, to hold her cell phone at her ear.

It occurred to Henry later, as he listened to a loon in the evening light across the shadowed lake and the mountain had once again caught the red of the sun, that he had never once, since he had left home at seventeen, taken a vacation. He said this aloud to Della as she closed her eyes to the sun. Henry had experienced days without work. He had gone to New York many times, but always because he had books to buy or sell, and not just to eat pastrami sandwiches. He had spent a day at the beach, but not a whole week, as he had when he was a kid.

His father had sold the little beach house long ago, when the property values went crazy on the Cape. No—probably just because his mother was no longer there. But even so, it seemed a distant memory.... He had driven by the little place one time. Someone had torn it down and put up a big grey-shingled box. He pushed the memory away. In any case, he could not remember once going away on vacation to relax or escape. He admitted this now to Della. He had liked being in the woods, being away with her. She grunted, or the dog did, as she moved her chair closer to his on the porch. He was not sure she understood.

Matty sprawled beneath them on the deck.

"Remember the loon last night? I had never heard a loon before," he said. "I thought it was a human cry. It sounded like someone moaning."

"That was me." She put her cheek against his arm.

"No…"

He was cornered. On one side, the whole world was laid out before him, and on the other, she held his hand to her breast.

"Did you hear what George said about Eddy Perry's book?"

"Yes. That was pretty good." Her eyes were closed.

Henry said, "It's worth the trip."

Della squeezed his hand. "Did you talk about the other thing?"

"No…Not yet. Maybe. I'm not sure I want to."

She did not ask why. He hoped it was because she was thinking the way he was about it. She sat up to pull the blanket they had used the night before from off the rail where it had been left to dry, and spread it over their legs to cut the chill.

"Nora says that loons mate for life."

"I wonder if that has anything to do with why they're called loons."

She hit him beneath the blanket.

They used the blanket again on the way back in the truck to cut the wind as they sat facing backwards in the open bed, the inflatable boat folded beneath them for a seat. Albert had refused to sit back there alone and opted to drive. Junior had thought it better to sit in the cab than with Henry. Della said she had not ridden in the open since she had dated a guy with a Harley in college.

Della huddled close beneath the blanket and held his hand against her knee.

She said, "And how about George Duggan?"

He was not thinking about George Duggan at that moment.

"Right. How about him?"

"You like Duggan." She said it, more than asked.

"I do," Henry answered.

"He gives them what they want—"

"True…But he tries to pull Barbara's little trick. He slips in a little something extra. He puts in fresh carrots. He uses a little different sauce. He writes thrillers and slips in a bit of history for seasoning. I guess for my taste, it's still too processed. Even if it makes him feel better about what he's done. I preferred the Frankowski book, after all."

"Don't you think it's better that people read a Duggan novel than watch TV?"

He jerked at his hand but she held on.

"Relativism! That's exactly what makes it all wrong."

She was not going to make it simple. "You have something against relatives?"

"Moral relativism!"

"He's just trying to entertain people."

"He's part of the system."

"But you said you liked him."

"I do."

The large cooler near their feet leaked water from the melting ice, and the smell of fish wafted in the boil of air around them. Albert had done well. Junior had done better. Henry was looking forward to an invitation to eat some of Alice's famous fried fish.

"Is that going to make it hard to help Sharon?"

He did not answer that. He was not sure what he could do now to help Sharon.

Della persisted. "How about Barbara?"

And he thought differently about that, now.

"I'm not sure she can save the store. With all the changes. The number of people who can read goes up, and the number of people who want to read goes down. The ones that do, all read the same stuff. Any chain store can supply that crap

cheaper than she can. Barbara's whole thing was to keep all
those authors alive who wrote so well but got passed by in the
bestseller parade. But that takes too much space for a real estate
market that measures inches."

Della looked directly at him. "Could she move it to the
country?"

What was working in her mind?

"But that defeats the purpose, doesn't it—if she takes it out
where most people can't get to it, just because the overhead
is cheaper. The only ones who would come are people who
already know what they're looking for. The idea of the bookstore in the city is that more potential readers can find you. You
don't run away from the challenge, just because it's difficult....
Well. Anyway. She needs to find a space she can afford. I think
she is going to have to move."

Della looked at him long enough to make him uncomfortable. The swirl of the wind wrapped her hair in a veil across
her face, her eyes glistening between the blond strands. She had
been letting it grow.

"Do you feel like you ran away, by doing your business the
way you do?"

He was surprised that she should think of that. Of course
he had considered that a few thousand times.

"No. You still don't believe me when I say I don't like the
human race. People can be okay, but the race is lost. Working in
a store like that, a person has to put up with the worst of it. For
me, there is just too little of the best. Barbara can keep going all
day because she sold one Angela Thirkell or one Nevil Shute.
I get hammered into the ground after I've sold the third copy
of Danielle Steele or Anne Rice. I don't have the guts Barbara
has, or I'm just too much of a snob."

"You're a snob," Della agreed, and looked away.

"Sure. You give people a choice. You put two meals out in front of them. One is fresh and prepared with a little creativity, and the other is processed junk food. Nine times out of ten they will pick up the processed junk food. Why? Because they're familiar with it already. They saw the ad on TV. Why bother selling books to people if that's the way they think? Let Barnes & Noble do it!"

"That's not the way your dad thinks."

Henry looked into the brown of her eyes. Chestnut brown, he thought. She blinked innocently at him.

"You've only met him once."

"That was enough. He's right up front. No pretense. You know what he thinks. He doesn't look down on other people."

"He's a worse snob than I am…I don't look down. I'm a realist. It's the way people are that I don't like. They are so seldom better than they have to be. Besides, it's a rhetorical question. Just because the world is full of maroons, doesn't mean you have to act like one yourself. We can go to Michael's Deli instead of McDonald's. I can sell the books I like to people who like the books I sell. I can be happy. The world is still a glorious place in spite of the human race."

She did not answer right away, looking back over the traffic that followed them.

"Your dad seems lonely."

" 'Cause he is."

"Why don't you live at that house with him?"

" 'Cause then he'd be lonely, and I'd be miserable. It's not me he needs."

"He seemed pretty happy to see you."

"You missed the part about the haircut."

"He's right, you need a haircut. And I like his stories. He was very sweet."

"That's because he likes you. I could see it. The stories are all lies."

Della frowned at him. "You're just saying that."

Henry adjusted his position so that he could look her in the eye.

"He has been telling the story about how he met my mother as long as I can remember. Mom said he was telling it before he even met her."

"She didn't steal his clothes when he was skinny dipping?"

"No. He read it in a book we used to have. H. E. Bates, I think. He liked it. It's the kind of story he likes. They actually met at church."

"You weren't born on the seat of a truck?"

"No. I might have been conceived there. I was born at Boston Lying-In."

"Did he know President Kennedy?"

"Dad used to go to St. Aidan's because he didn't like the priest at St. Mary's. The Kennedys did too, once upon a time. Only God knows if they were ever in the same building at the same time."

She seemed to consider this for a moment.

"I still think he's sweet."

"He's a curmudgeon—a disappointed man—a cynic. I may think the human race is hopeless, but I still go about my business in the hope that I'm wrong. Dad has no doubts. He's playing the cards that were dealt him, and not asking for more.... That's the thing. After my mother died, he stopped taking chances."

"He didn't seem depressed to me."

"Never. Getting depressed is my father's idea of a capital crime. It's giving in. It's letting the bastards know they have you. Never. He laughs. He laughs at God. You'll hear him say it. 'God can have me and do what he wants with me any time he wishes. While I'm waiting, I'll have a beer, please.'"

"And if your mother had lived…how would things be different?"

"He used to just laugh…. His stories, they were mostly the stories his father had told him…. Everything was a story. But his own stories were the best."

"Tell me one."

Henry knew the one he liked the most.

"He rewired a big Victorian house on Commonwealth Avenue the year after I was born, one of those really big ones out toward Newton. It took quite a few weeks. The old ball and wire had to be replaced. But then, after it was done, the fellow, a man named Crimmins, went bankrupt before he could pay the bill. My dad—" Henry shook his head. "My dad understands things like that. He'd been through it before. He shook the man's hand and wished him luck and then, as he was leaving, he looked again at a picture in the hall that he had admired several times as he came and went doing the job. It was a small watercolor of a little shack on a dune in Eastham on the Cape. Crimmins took the picture off the wall and handed it to him. 'It's not much, but you can take this before my other creditors do,' he said. My dad thanked him, said he'd hang it by his writing desk, and was about to turn and go when Crimmins said, 'But you won't be able to use it until August this year, because it's rented through July.' And that was how we got our little beach house."

She gaped, the wind wrapping the hair into her mouth.

"Is it true?"

"Sure. It's where I spent every summer of my childhood."

"But how do you know the story is true? That it's not like the others your father told?"

Henry thought about that a moment.

"Because he told it in front of my mother."

"So? Would she have called him a liar?"

"She would have winked."

"Did she wink?"

"Not that time."

Della brushed the hair from her lips. "You've never told me a story before…"

"I guess I didn't have any to tell."

"Or is it you never gave the story a chance? Your dad has his story. What's yours?"

Henry could not help but think of Eddy Perry then. Eddy had found his story in the midst of everything.

"I don't know."

"Sure you do. You're in the middle of it, aren't you? It's all around you, isn't it? Isn't it just a matter of whether or not you think it's worth the telling? And whether you have someone to tell it to? Your dad told the stories he wanted to tell, and he told them to me because I listened."

Henry had no answer for that. It sounded true enough.

Behind them now was a barely wavering chain of cars, as far as he could see, holding steady in the road as the world rushed away. It felt just like that. Such a familiar sensation, sitting there in the back of the truck looking at a world that passed away as he sat still and watched.

Chapter Nineteen

Her father owned a clothing store in White Plains. I guess he lost it to the discounters. I'm not sure. But I know they didn't have any money."

Barbara consumed one end of a burrito. Henry sat back in his chair, his eyes looking over the line of people waiting to pick up their orders on the other side of the small room. The tables between were filled with students. The clatter of talk was mixed with the tinny sound of Spanish guitar from small speakers high in the corner and dampened by the metallic hum of the air conditioner. The standing line was mostly middle-aged men looking sullen and impatient, perhaps anxious to get back to a pre-season football game on the television, their eyes fixed on the people in the open kitchen behind the counter, as if staring would make them work faster.

"You knew her at Boston University?" Henry asked.

"No. I was graduated before she came. But Alcott & Poe was on a list of job possibilities at the university employment office. They're always sending me people—or at least they were when I could afford to be hiring. I think she found me that way."

"She must have been pretty smart if she got some kind of scholarship. Boston University isn't cheap."

Barbara shrugged. "She's smart, but that's not how she made it. Her husband paid for it."

"I thought they weren't married."

Barbara shook her head. "Not Jim. Before Jim. She was married right out of high school. Some old guy I never met and she never talked about. It came up once. She didn't discuss it. One of his kids showed up at the store to talk to her. He had passed away and he had grown kids from his previous marriage. She was upset afterward and told me a little more than I think she wanted. But they were long divorced at that point. I don't think he left her anything. He did pay for her college, though. I know that."

"What was her married name?"

"Weiss. And she called herself Sherry then. They called her Sherry when she was a kid. She had dropped the 'Sherry' by the time she first applied for work at the store. Sharon is her real name."

The burrito was gone. Barbara's ability to inhale food had not changed. Henry worked again at his own meal as Barbara watched him.

Her face changed with another thought. "She's really a self-made woman, you know. I've seen a picture. She was cute in a girlish kind of way. A little chubby. Her hair was dark brown then, and she had braces all the way through college. I guess the old guy paid for that too."

"Do you think she married him for his money? Or does that seem too mercenary?"

Barbara shrugged again. There was a flicker to her eyebrows. It was clear to Henry that such thoughts had long been buried in Barbara's mind.

"No. I think she made her way the best she could. It's pretty hard to judge people at a distance. And everybody makes mistakes. But she's always been square with me."

Henry was not satisfied.

"People who do things like that don't suddenly become dishonest. They have done things before."

Uncertainty came back to Barbara's face. She was not ready to believe him.

"It just never occurred to me. Why would she lie about something like that? Just for the money? What if she were caught? It's so much effort for so little. If she wrote the book herself, why say Jim did it?"

He had imagined a dozen reasons. But it mattered what the real reason might be. "It's a guess. I don't know. You say she has never stolen from you. But I know the way you deal with money. I'll bet you don't really know.... The money—hell! A typical author might get a ten- or twenty-thousand-dollar advance, if they're lucky. If the book doesn't make it, that's it. Nine out of ten books don't make it. Right? Jim Frankowski's previous book is a good example. But Duggan is going to make millions on that one book alone. He could give her just ten percent—less than he gives his agent—and he would still be in the millions, and she would end up with at least a hundred thousand dollars.... Yes. The money."

The sound of Barbara's protest weakened. "But if she has the talent to write, wouldn't she want to write for herself?"

Henry held his burrito in both hands to keep it together. "She might. But then again, she sees all of those other good writers who can barely make a living. Why struggle?"

Barbara protested again. "Personal pride."

Henry had an idea about that. "She may have sacrificed that long ago."

"But she has it. I see it every day. Look at her. She's worked hard. And why put so much into the store, if all she wants is money? There's no money in selling books. It doesn't make sense."

Henry stated his case again. "It doesn't make sense to me that Duggan stole another man's story."

Barbara studied the distance between them rather than meet his eyes. "Sharon and I are so different. It would be so easy to be at odds over everything. Remember how you and I used to argue? But she makes the effort to get along—even more than I do. And I've let her know a dozen times how grateful I am that she decided to invest her money in the store. I told her then that it wasn't her wisest move. I warned her of the risk. I made her think about it for two weeks before she did it."

Henry nodded. "Maybe that's where her pride is, then? She's worked at the store for almost fifteen years. Maybe she did it to save the store?"

In the half hour since they had met for dinner, Barbara's face had gone from happy—simply that he wanted to have dinner with her—to stunned, and wishing she did not believe what Henry had suggested.

She said, "I'm not going to be able to sleep tonight. You've put something into my head that I'm going to have to deal with."

He had worried over this for two days before asking her to have dinner with him.

"I had to tell you. What else could I do? I'm sorry.... But you can't just confront her with all this. You have to have something more than my dark thoughts. If I'm wrong, you'll be hurting someone you owe a great deal to. She'd quit. If she demanded that you liquidate stock to pay her back, it would be all over for Alcott & Poe. I think you should wait. I told you at the start that what I was going to say was just between us for now. I just want you to be aware...I want you to be careful."

Barbara turned her head and watched the men working in the open kitchen. "I think she loves the store. I think you're right about that. She's always spent extra time getting the entries right and straightening shelves and doing the little things. Maybe she's not doing as well since she lost Jim, but that will pass, I think. She was awfully good before that.... But this thing with Jim's book is too much to believe."

"I'm sorry. Should I have kept it to myself?"

"No…" She reached a hand out over the table and put it on his. "Thank you."

He leaned back, looking for the safety of a little more distance over their small table.

"What will you do?"

She smiled, obviously unsure. "I'll keep it to myself. And if it turns out you were wrong, I'll still keep it to myself. I won't remind you every now and again that you were wrong. Not often, anyway."

His own attempt to smile failed. "Some things pass. Some things work out. Some things go in cycles, and other things just flatten out and end…. You'll work it out. You have enough to worry about just to save the store. But I'm not sure the book business is going to come back. Not the way we knew it, anyway."

Barbara shook her head, as if to clear it. "What's next? What's coming?"

"A different world. It's a new century. A new millennium. At least as different from the one we knew, as the twentieth century was from the nineteenth," Henry leaned forward so that he could speak more softly. "You know, there were people around town, when I was growing up, who remembered horse trolleys in Brookline Village. My dad used to say I was blessed because I didn't have to carry ice up three flights of stairs, and he still called the refrigerator an icebox."

Barbara huffed at the thought. "I suppose. But the future looks pretty bleak just now. I wish I could have the first ten years of the store back. I loved that time. I never seriously thought then that it would ever end."

Henry smiled. "It was pretty good,"

Her eyes were on his now. "It never occurred to me then that you would leave."

How was he going to answer that? She knew why he had left. She was looking for support at a bad time and he was not the person who could give her what she needed. He nodded toward the young faces at the tables around them to avoid her eyes.

"I don't think any of them look very far into the future. We were younger then. You deal with things as they come at that age. Someday they'll be standing in line to get the takeout."

She was still looking at him. Her hands were folded together on the edge of the table. "Do you remember the day you first took me to the Gardner Museum? You couldn't find a parking space and it was raining so hard I didn't want to get out of the van and walk. I asked you why you wanted to go to an old museum, anyway. You described how it looked inside, with all that medieval stuff, and then you said you loved it because it was a piece of the past that hadn't changed. It was something permanent.... I thought my little store was something permanent."

"You didn't have Isabella Stewart Gardner's money.... But if you had, would you have spent it on a little old bookstore?" He saw her face go blank. He had stepped in the wrong direction, and tried to salvage the idle thought. "—Well, you might have. You are the type. Most people would have spent their money on a big piece of crap in the suburbs and snorted the rest away in technology stocks."

She smiled at that. "No. Don't forget, when I opened the store, all we had were the new books. You were the one who started going to the library sales to find the out-of-print titles people kept asking for."

"You encouraged me."

"You were incorrigible. I learned that much from you."

"I was just learning as I went along." He did not add that he still felt that way.

She was pinning him to the wall with those eyes. She said, "It worked then. What happened?"

He said, "The world changed." His voice weakened with the thought.

Her smile was gone again, with the sudden sadness darkening the lines of her face. He wished he could hold her just awhile, with no consequences. She clasped her own hands together for support.

"I wish I could stop time, like in a book. I wish I lived in a museum." The way she said it startled him. It was what he heard in the tone of her voice. He knew those words.

"My mother used to say that.... You know, she was the one who used to walk me over to the Gardner on rainy days when I was a kid."

"You told me that, the first time we went. That's how I knew you were serious. You told me it was your mother's favorite place."

"I guess I did."

"It's a beguiling thought. But if we did live in a museum like your Mrs. Jack Gardner did, it would mean someone else would have to take care of us. There has to be a Mr. Jack. There's always a dark side to it."

He tried to shrug the idea off. "It's just a daydream. We can't preserve the past." He knew he was lying. He did not believe his own words. And she knew it too. She forgave him for it.

"Is that all we're doing then? Should I give it up? Should I let the store go?"

He had always liked her eyes. He did not avoid them now. He had always liked to look into her eyes before.

"No. The past isn't finished with us yet. Not yet. I think it's the past that preserves us."

Chapter Twenty

Henry parked the truck in the shade of a tree cut short to make way for electric lines and grown thick with smaller branches. Dover, New Hampshire, seemed like that kind of town to him, cut oddly by road and river, but thick with houses in the spaces between.

The house he wanted was a small white box opened at the top by the flaps of dormers, wedged beside an overgrown cedar never trimmed and now twice the height of the roof.

A little girl, perhaps four or five, dressed only in OshKosh overalls, dug with a spoon at the dirt beside the short walk. Beside her was a plastic cup with a cut flower from a hydrangea bush bursting from the top.

Henry watched her work for a moment, holding his brown paper package with both hands in front of him, until she took the time to look up.

"Is this where Janet Fowler lives?"

The girl ignored him to dig a moment more, before finally speaking. "Do you think the ants will eat it?"

Henry considered this before answering.

"It looks so much like a pile of ice cream. They might make a mistake. But I don't think so…I think they will know."

She nodded. "My mother is in the kitchen." Her diction was precise.

Henry rang the doorbell. The door was open to the screen and he saw her in the half-light walk forward from the back of the house. She did not open the screen door.

She had the look of someone he already knew. This was the woman at the beach from the picture in the plastic frame. She was about the same height as Eddy Perry had been. Not as thin. Her hair was cut too short. She was wrapped in an over-size apron which hung oddly like a dress, with her legs exposed below and her feet in cheap rubber sandals. She seemed tired.

She nodded when he said her name.

"I'm sorry to trouble you. I wondered if you had a moment to talk.... I knew Eddy Perry."

She still had said nothing, but looked at him from head to foot, her eyes stopping at the package in his hands, then at the little girl, and then across the street at his truck.

She spoke up for the girl to hear. "My daddy had a truck like that. See that, Honey? That truck looks just like the one your grandfather had once when I was your age."

The girl stood and looked at it, resting the back of one hand on her hip with the spoon dangling from the other.

Henry said, "I'm not sure I can say what I wanted to in front of your daughter."

The woman nodded, and pushed the door open.

"Come sit in the kitchen.... Honey, you stay in the yard."

The girl sat down to her work, and Henry followed the mother to the narrow room at the back where a table, folded down to half its size, was covered with cut vegetables.

Glass jars were lined up on the counter. Two pots steamed on the stove. The kitchen heat was only slightly relieved by a fan in the window over the sink.

She spoke to him without looking, and adjusted the heat on the stove. "Just bought some fresh tomatoes and green beans. I like to put them up for winter." She waved him to a chair away from the stove, by the back door.

Henry had never seen home canning before, and he watched as they spoke.

210

"You know Eddy has died?" He felt awkward beginning like that. The thought had only just occurred to him she might not know.

She did not look at him to answer. She ladled loose lumps of tomato from one of the pots into mason jars set in a tight cluster on the counter.

"You mean killed.... Someone killed him. That much I know. I read it in the paper. My mother brought it to me one day.... She had held it aside for a week before showing it to me."

Henry wiped the sweat from his face with his hand and then wiped his hand on his pants.

"Yes. Well, it's not a long story, but it's difficult to explain.... In any case, I knew him, and I came by some of the contents of his apartment."

"He didn't have much. I know that."

"Not a lot, by most standards, but he did have this."

Henry handed her the package.

She wiped her hands on her apron and ripped it open from one end until the top half was exposed, then put it down on top of a stool.

"Is that the thing he always talked about writing?"

"Yes."

She turned the flame down on another pot and shook her head.

"I guess he did that much. He made a lot of promises he couldn't keep. I guess that's one he made good on."

There was a matter-of-factness to what she said that made it sound bitter.

Henry answered, "Better than made good. It's a fine book. He wrote something extraordinary."

This made her turn to look at him again. She studied his face until he was uncomfortable, and then tapped the manuscript with a long spoon.

"He couldn't have written this if he was doing dope."

"No. He was off drugs…for quite a while, evidently."

She studied Henry for another uncomfortable moment before she spoke again.

"You came up here to give this to me? Is that all?"

"Yes…mainly."

He had intended to say as little as possible, mostly because he did not think he had it in him to say much more, but now he had become curious.

She wiped the sweat from her cheeks, and then tilted her head to the side.

"I don't have any money…"

She might have hoped for something more than a pack of paper, he thought. He had no idea how desperate she might be. Henry had sold the Tom Clancy book and used the money to pay his last month's rent. He wished he had set some of it aside.

He said, "I'm sorry. I guess I can give you a little. I don't really have a whole lot myself.…"

Henry dug in his pocket and pulled out the four twenties he had stuffed there for getting gas or books he might stumble across on his way.

"No!" She let out a single bark of laughter. "I'm not asking for money. I just don't have any. I thought you were looking for some kind of reward."

He was embarrassed for his own stupidity.

"No. I'm sorry. I was just trying to do a favor for someone. Someone past forgetting, as they say. No.… I'm a bookseller. Like Eddy. More like Eddy, I think, than I would like to admit."

She smiled wryly. "You're all a bunch of odd ducks. And I know about ducks."

Henry stuffed the money back in his pocket. "Right. Well. Eddy set some standards in that regard. And I never really knew him well. But I was the one who bought the book from him—the one who gave him the money that he was probably killed for."

She put the back of one hand on her hip just like her daughter had, and smiled again, this time more broadly.

"Guilt. You're on a guilt trip."

"I guess, quite literally."

He smiled back. It was true. He was not sure what all he was guilty of, but certainly something worth this small trip to New Hampshire. Her tone went to mock exasperation.

"Jesus! Eddy was going to end up dead sooner than later. His drugs would have killed him."

Henry realized she had not yet understood.

"He had really quit. He was trying to get things in order."

Her smile faded. "You don't know. You didn't know him like I did. I tried. I tried and tried. He would quit for a short time, but he always fell back."

Henry looked her in the eye to make his point. "He didn't this time.... He quit and he wrote his book."

She stood by the stool, with the spoon raised, and looked down at the package, suspiciously. Finally she picked it up again, removing the rest of the brown paper wrapper, the spoon wagging from the loose grip of one hand. Henry had gotten the copy spiral-bound, and she opened the manuscript to a page at the center and read it.

A drop of sweat darkened the page before she closed it. "It reads well…I'll read it as soon as—" Her tone changed. "Why did you bring this up here to me? Why did you think I would want to see it? Had he told you about me?"

Henry was a stranger, shown up at her door out of nowhere. How could she understand that?

"No. It actually took some doing to figure out where you were. But I brought it to you because it's yours. It's his story and he wrote it for you. He left it for you…"

Her spoon hit the floor, as if it had slipped away. The metal rang like a small bell in the air. Her face seemed suddenly impassive. Henry picked the spoon up and offered it to her, but she did not react. She was still holding the closed manuscript in both hands. He knew there was more than sweat on her cheeks now.

"It was the first thing he ever promised me, you know. Even before he quit the drugs the first time…"

The silence, with her words halted as she looked blindly through tears at a spice rack on the wall, made him speak.

"How did you meet him?"

She sniffed. "I was a social worker for the city of Cambridge…Eddy was just one of about thirty or so addicts I was supposed to check on regularly. It was a light load. I couldn't find most of them, most of the time. So I used to talk with Eddy longer than I should…. He was a smart guy. A nice guy. And he knew about things. He was a treasure of information about almost anything, really. And I just talk too much…and Eddy ended up listening to me. He listened to me. You know how it is—I mean, why does someone go into social work? Because they need help themselves. Right? Eddy had me talking so much I couldn't shut up. He never really talked about himself. Ever." She looked at the manuscript again. "He had no self esteem. He thought just about anyone was better than he was. But he was different…. And I fell in love with him."

Henry could see her eyes then. The tears released in a solid trail through the sweat and fell to the floor from her chin.

"I'm sorry." Henry said.

"You're sorry? I—He was a sweet guy. I wouldn't have left him, except…" Her head tilted sideways again, as if bearing the weight of words she could not say.

Henry guessed. "Is that Eddy's daughter?"

She nodded her head and wiped her cheeks with the palm of her hand before saying the word.

"Yes."

"He didn't know, did he?"

"No. I even never told him I was pregnant. I just left when he came floating home one night. I couldn't take it again."

Henry looked up the hall through the screen door toward the small figure still huddled on the walk.

"When I saw her…you know, she has something of Eddy in her looks."

Janet Fowler squinted as if suddenly hurt.

"I never even sent him a letter. I just left, with him laying there on the bed.… I was angry. I was not about to have a child around him.… And I wanted the child."

Henry looked down at the floor to avoid the pain in her eyes.

"He says, somewhere in the book, that he wanted a kid. Isn't that incredible? With all he went through—with all he survived, he still wanted a kid."

Her voiced weakened and broke. "He told me that too…once."

Henry said, "You'll like the book, I think."

She took a short breath. "I want to read it…"

Henry adjusted himself to his prepared speech.

"But there is something else I wanted to talk with you about…I've already spoken to someone about publishing it. It wasn't my place to do it, but I did it before I realized there would be a problem. I just wanted to do Eddy a favor, and make sure the manuscript would not be lost. And they want to publish it. They think the book is a fine piece of work and ought to be published.… But they need your permission."

Her eyes searched his. Her face fell slack, the tinsel line of tears unwiped.

"My permission?…You mean, he actually did give this to me? I didn't know what you meant."

"Yes. Legally. It's a literary property. It has some value. And because Eddy is dead, and he specifically gave it to you, it's yours."

Henry told her to read the dedication. He watched her eyes as she did. The tears held momentarily until she was finished. Finally she looked again at Henry's face.

"Do you think it's the right thing to do?"

It seemed an odd question to him at first.

"Yes. I think it is a fine book and it deserves to be published."

She meant something more. "Will you help me with it? Will you see to it that it's done properly? That it's done well? I don't know about things like that."

Henry had not seen it as a responsibility in that way, only as a matter of fact.

"Sure. I think it'll be fine."

"Then do it. Please, do it."

"But you haven't read it yet."

"That's okay. I'll read it…soon. When I can. I have to get myself prepared a little.… But that's no reason to keep it from being published. I don't want to be the judge. I can't be his judge.… No. I did that once. More than once. I walked out on him. I left him."

"You had a child to think of."

"But he needed someone to take care of him…I've thought this before. A thousand times I have thought this before. He could be here. He could be with me now. He would have followed me if I had asked him to. Maybe he would have quit if I had taken him away. And now it's so clear…how I misjudged him. I was just another unlucky turn in his life. I didn't love him enough. I didn't think he could quit on his own. I didn't believe in him. I misjudged him."

Henry had to stand. He wanted her to read the book. He wanted her to understand now, before she blamed herself for something she did not do wrong.

"Losing you is what did it, though. Losing you is what made him quit. I guess you'll never know what would have happened if you had stayed. But because you left, he quit the drugs, and he wrote his book, after all. You'll see that. Read his book, and you'll see that. And you'll see that he knew it, and that he loved you."

Chapter Twenty-one

Henry was reminded of Albert's observation about the geology of trash as he examined Nora Lynch's desk. The loose pages of letters were overwhelmed by thick veins of manuscript. Yellow stickies grew flower-like from the strata. Padded manila mailers and FedEx boxes leaned against one another at the far side in great tectonic upheavals. He noted that there was no typewriter to be seen, only the over-bright face of the computer screen.

This time she had shown none of the anger she displayed when he first came to the office unannounced—perhaps a slight cold front of annoyance. She buzzed him in quickly after he said his name into the brass device at the door, and was waiting for him at the top of the stairs. She had not offered to shake his hand, but led him to her desk to talk. He apologized for his impatience after calling earlier and getting an answering machine. She had not yet checked her messages. When he tried to make some small talk about his visit to the camp, she cut him off and asked him why he had come by.

He said, "To keep things simple. To get things straight."

She was unsympathetic. "Nothing is ever simple. The only straight line comes before the punch line."

She was not going to make it easy for him.

He told her about his visit to Janet Fowler. This too she interrupted by taking incidental calls on the phone. He had met Nora three times now and had formed the impression that her personality was nearly opposite to her red-hot exterior. When she stood suddenly and left to go to another room, probably to make another phone call, he hoped she was trying to reach Duggan and not Boyle.

Around the corner from her desk, out of direct sight, two student interns worked at opening and sorting incoming mail. The rip of envelopes made Henry think of air escaping a tire. He could tell that they were talking about a recent movie, but their voices were nearly absorbed by partitions and the wall-to-wall carpet.

A cursor blinked at the end of an unfinished sentence on Nora's computer screen. Her letter concerned a writer Henry did not know, and was none of his business, but he read it anyway.

"I have never had the pleasure of working on a scallop boat during the winter, or any other time for that matter, and it is difficult for me to imagine the bitter sting of sea spray when the nets rise from the grey boil of the water, or the numb manipulation of fingers in gloves filmed by frozen slime. I remember such description from another book of a few years ago, and it still comes back to me when I walk beside the ocean in harsh weather. I wish you had offered your own experience of such things to seduce my imagination into believing the plight of David. His story seems to be an interesting one, but I was unable to finish this. I hope you will be able to go back to this manuscript and give it the time it deserves."

Henry had seen rejection letters before. Editors seldom ventured beyond the boilerplate. It was obvious to him why Nora could not keep up with the incoming waves of manuscript. Rejection letters of the kind she wrote must absorb a great deal of time.

He was curious about the correspondence piled in the rise of small mesas near the surface of the geological formation

219

before him. He pulled at a manila folder closer to his chair. It was marked for Boston University. Henry tilted the cover back— resumes for potential student office help—then pushed it back into place. He listened for her return in the near silence and then reached from his chair for a letter on another pile and peeked at it. A writer begged for more time with revisions. Nora's note in the margin gave him until July 4th, already over a month past.

"I've always liked the word 'deadline.'" Nora suddenly stood over him. The carpet had muffled the sound of her approach. He put the letter back as she finished her thought. "It has a ring to it."

She picked the letter up as she sat in her chair, looked at it briefly, and put it back in the stack where Henry had found it.

Henry tried to pick up on the theme. "I'm trying to finish up a few things myself."

Nora waved her hand at the stack. "Eddy Perry made his deadline, and he didn't need an editor to tell him when it was." Her words surprised him a little. Black humored as they were, the words betrayed a sympathy he was not sure she would have had. "I write letters like this every day. Usually to the same writers, again and again. Something happens. Sometimes after we accept a work and ask for corrections, they suddenly decide they have to rewrite the entire thing, they don't like the name of a character, or want to add a chapter to explain some bit of action. But I don't think Eddy Perry would have done that to me. When he was done, he was finished."

Henry wondered out loud, "If he had lived, do you think he would have written more?"

Her face was not impassive as much as unforgiving. "Perhaps…. Some people only have one good book in them. We'll never know. But our problem is this: who owns the rights to *Penny Candy*?"

She tapped a copy of Eddy's manuscript, half buried in a surface layer on the desk.

Henry answered, "Janet Fowler."

"Good enough. I can agree to that—but do you realize that you have a claim?"

"Why?"

"You found it. It was thrown away. We have confirmed that Eddy has no relatives. The courts have held previously in some cases that objects found in the garbage can be claimed. The dedication might be interpreted as just that—a dedication."

"But there is no other claim. I gave the original to Janet Fowler. It's hers."

Nora paused. "You're sure?" The pink of her skin made her appear much younger than she was. She wore no makeup. Her eyes, which had darkened once when speaking to him, were clear water painted with sky.

He said, "Yes." This was the same woman he had watched at a distance not so long ago and speculated about. He had not thought about that since, but Henry had made up his own mind.

The ruddiness at her cheeks appeared to grow. He thought she was blushing and realized it might be because he had given away his thoughts.

Nora looked away. "I spoke to Janet yesterday. She'll be coming down this week to meet with us."

"Did she read it?" Henry asked, wanting to know what she might have said.

"Yes. She told me about your visit. She apologized again for being rude to you. I'm not sure what she did, but she seemed nice enough to me. She said she started to read the book right after you left. She seemed to be a little weepy over it. Of course, I don't know very much about her relationship with Eddy."

"It was difficult."

She looked back at Henry, eyes intent, but still with no readable expression. The blue might even be gaudy set against her skin and the flame of her hair. He thought she might be a difficult opponent in a game of poker, or chess for that matter, if only because he would find it difficult to keep his own concentration.

Nora pulled another sheet of paper from the midst of the pile. "Boyle wants you to sign this."

He admired her sense of organization.

Henry read the three paragraph letter twice without clearly understanding it.

"What does it say?"

Her voice was matter-of-fact. "It is an assignment of any right or claim you have. It recognizes the claim of Janet Fowler to all rights in the manuscript."

Henry pulled a pen from a clutch in a coffee mug at the edge of the desk and signed the paper on the line above his printed name. "I told her I would take care of things. I don't want to be letting her down."

Her voice lowered. "You haven't. We will do our best to see to it."

"Thanks."

Henry put out his hand and Nora took it. He had expected it to be cool, but it was not. Finally she smiled at him.

"George was right. He said you were okay...I was sure you had another motive with all of this. Boyle bet Duggan you wouldn't sign the letter. I'm glad I was wrong."

He admitted his thought. "Not entirely..."

One eyebrow dipped above an intent blue eye.

"What other motive have you kept from us?"

"I'm still trying to help Barbara."

She squinted at him now with both eyes. "Barbara!" Nora swept the air with her hand. "She's the mystery in all this. Why does she keep at it? I've been to her store, you know. She doesn't know me. But I love old bookshops. Really!" Nora tilted her head at him bullishly. "I can see you're not convinced. Lately I've been collecting the early Alfred A. Knopf titles. I found two there the last time. It's wonderful. Very nineteenth century. Very Dickensian. Very romantic. She makes me jealous. She lives in a movie set. A museum. Totally unreal—" Nora mistook the sudden reaction on his face to the coincidence of both women making the same allusion, and changed her direction and tone. "Look. We're in the twenty-first century. Barnes & Noble can have a brand new copy of any out-of-print title reprinted for less than a dollar a copy. They can sell it for less than five dollars and make a profit. How is your Barbara going to sell an original used copy of the same book for ten dollars to a public that wants to consume books like they do with a television show?"

Henry knew she was trying to speak to him on his own terms. There was no time to tell her what he thought. But then, he thought, she should at least understand.

"Why do you publish short runs of new authors that will never turn a profit?"

Both her eyebrows rose. She smiled briefly and stood without answering, waiting for him to stand as well.

"I think you know—because of George Duggan. Because he's as big a nutcase as your Barbara." The beginning of a smile came and disappeared. "You must believe, more than anyone, that I would like to know how James Frankowski and George Duggan came to write so much of the same book. If I'm to blame, it was done unintentionally. Believe that. George has always gotten me to talk. Just because he listens. It's one of his great virtues. But I still can't believe I would have related that much of the story without remembering it.... Anyway, Boyle has instructed me not to talk with you about it. I know I shouldn't. But you have just shown enough faith in us—I know it's George you are trusting more than me, but even so—I just want you to know that I'm not holding anything back."

Henry knew he could say nothing to her of his thoughts concerning Sharon.

"Thanks."

Nora shook her head. "I imagine Sharon Greene must be even more confused by all of this." But her words were flat with her own suspicions.

And then he suddenly knew something more. He watched her eyes as he spoke.

"Do you remember anyone from when you were at school, at B.U., named Weiss?"

"Sherry Weiss…"

"What do you remember?"

"Not much. We were roommates our freshman year. Heavy girl. Lonely…. She wrote a lot. I think she was a lit major. I lost touch with her pretty early on…Why?"

"Did you ever have any kind of run-in with her?"

"No…Well, yes. She would borrow things. We had a row about it…But roommates always do that."

Chapter Twenty-two

Henry the Eighth to six wives was wedded, / One died, one survived, / Two divorced and two beheaded." He had kissed her too soon. He should have waited. But he had been looking forward to kissing her all day, and he had done it on impulse when she appeared unexpectedly an hour early. Her words were nonsensical, some game she was playing. She often said odd things when he surprised her. There was no reason for her to be upset with him.

"Which ones should I behead?"

"Do I get to choose?" She appeared delighted with the thought. She was carrying a small bag of something, about the size of a large purse, but he could not remember her carrying a purse before. He was unsure of what it might be.

"I suppose. I love them all, of course. I would never be able to decide. What's in the bag?"

"Some stuff.… Well, if I get to choose, I would pick Sharon and Barbara to behead. They're causing the most problems. But that would be catty of me, because I know you were once pretty stuck on Barbara, so we can say she will be divorced. We can cut off Nora's head, instead. That leaves Sasha, and Mrs. Murray, and myself. Well, I know I'm going to be the survivor, and Mrs. Murray is too old so she can die, and Sasha can be the second divorce, even if you never really knew her in the biblical sense—did you?"

"You mean, did I 'know' her?"

"You knew her before you knew me."

"But I've never 'known' her."

"Well, perhaps not very well, but you knew her, or else she wouldn't have given you that."

She pointed to the photograph on the wall.

"That was a gift," he said, a little too defensively.

"I'm sure you earned it. But that is done with now. It's time to fish or cut bait."

Certain things people said always irritated him.

"Albert says that all the time."

"Albert is an intelligent and perceptive fellow. And he is correct."

"I don't fish."

"That's okay. I'll do the fishing if you'll cut the bait."

"That sounds interesting, but I thought we were going out to eat and catch a movie first."

She raised her eyebrows,

"We can stay home if you like."

"It's up to you. What's in the bag?"

"Toothbrush. Underwear."

"I see."

"I'll let you see later. Let's go to the movie now."

This would have been fine with him. But he had left the closet door open. He had been answering an email inquiry about one of his books. She walked into the small space with her jaw slack. He could not help but notice the way her hips rounded the thin material of her dress.

She said, "They're so beautiful, lined up like this. Books are naturally beautiful, aren't they?"

Her fingertips lightly brushed the spines of the books on a shelf beside her.

He said, "Yes."

"They make you want to touch them."

"Yes."

"Make you want to know what's inside."

"Yes."

"You're very lucky."

"I am."

She turned to him. "I work in an office all day where every chance I get I look out the window to escape. Some big honcho in personnel sent a memo out last week that said we were spending too much personal time on the internet. They won't fire us, of course. They need us. And we would all quit if they tried to cut us off the internet. We produce more software than they can use. But everyone hates it…and meanwhile, you get to handle books every day."

He said, "You earn three or four times as much as I do."

She said, "But you do what you like."

"Not always."

"Most of the time. But what would you do if you couldn't sell books for a living?"

"I've never thought about it."

"Liar!" She seemed excited by her discovery. "You just never thought about it exactly that way. You've even told me that you think the book business is done for. You're not stupid. You think things through. Now tell me, what would you do?"

Maybe another lie was in order. "I'd go to work for Albert."

"You would not!" Her jaw went square. She was serious and he needed to answer.

"No. I wouldn't. But the business of books won't end that way. It'll end with a whimper. A whole lot of complaining. A good deal of blaming. The people at the funeral will not look at each other, eye to eye, because they are all guilty of neglect. There'll be a few tears. A little bit of 'Do you remember?' And at the wake they'll all drink to the deceased and talk about what a good chap he was. Well liked—but old, and beyond his moment. A decent sort. Had a temper at times. Stumbled on the truth occasionally. Not always faithful. Took the money more than once…But did his best. Wanted to do better. But he couldn't adjust to this brave new world. Very sad. Oh, gee, where's the time gone? I'll have get it on audio so I can listen to it in the car. We must be going."

She smiled in spite of the tone in her voice. "That's very cynical of you."

She gave his words her best stone face. She was not good at that. There was too much light in her eyes. Her hair was bright with it. The yellow in her hair was honeyed by the light from his old floor lamp.

"Sorry. You're right. But I'll be at the wake nonetheless. Even if it's me they're gabbing about."

Now she was suddenly sad. This was something new. This was not the tough girl he was used to.

"Can't you do something? You could find a way?"

"Maybe…Maybe I'll find a way. But I'll tell you what I'd like to do now."

"Go to the movies?"

"No. Not right now."

Chapter Twenty-three

Albert was on the ground, sitting back, his hands braced against the cement of the sidewalk as if sunbathing at a beach, as Henry approached. With the building the Blue Thorn occupied filling all of the corner but the sidewalk, Henry could see little else through the group that clustered around. The strangeness of the sight caught Henry as funny before he reacted to the seriousness of it. Someone else was there, just out of view, their shadow moving in the late sun, which had fallen behind the building and cast a hard yellow light up the side street onto the scene.

As Henry pushed through the small crowd to the open space at the curb, Albert had gained his feet, looking quickly in Henry's direction. Someone in a white shirt came around the corner, dancing forward like a crab on the sand. Albert moved aside. It was John Boyle who turned briefly to look at Henry as he came on.

"Stay out of this!" Boyle's voice was a bark.

Henry moved in closer, but positioned himself between two parked cars, shielding the sun from his eyes with his hand.

Albert's face was blank of expression. Blisters of sweat crowded his forehead. He was breathing through his mouth. Something more than sweat glistened by his nose. He winked at Henry.

Boyle launched himself forward again, half crouched, jabbing low. Albert dodged, but this time came back quickly with a roundhouse punch that landed at the bottom of Boyle's ribs.

Boyle bent sideways with the pain. Albert hit him quickly again in the same place, and then, opening the fist of his left hand, he slapped Boyle's face. The crack of the flesh echoed over the passing traffic on the street.

Albert grinned demonically now. "You aren't going to get any fuckin' dental bills paid out of me, you son of a bitch."

Boyle tried to speak. Albert's right hand was back now, slapping the other side of Boyle's face. Then again with his left hand. The slaps had the snap of a leather belt.

Henry looked around at the assembled. Mostly it was a collection of Blue Thorn regulars. A few passersby held back in a knot safely at the far corner across the street. It was not the sight of two middle-aged men fighting on the sidewalk which brought their attention, Henry thought. This was Cambridge after all, if only Inman Square. What titillated their politically correct senses was the image of a black man and a white man fighting it out in broad daylight.

There was another slap. Albert's arm's brushing aside Boyle's defensive gestures. Albert hit him at will now. Boyle's eyes lost focus. There was blood smeared on the lawyer's face, over red welts, but Henry was sure it was Albert's. Boyle's feet shifted backward, the dance gone, until his body was pinned against a car. His crouch had become a stoop. One side of his suspenders had come loose. The white shirt was showing the grey streaks of sweat and several splotches of red.

Albert swept his foot against Boyle's legs and the man collapsed at the curb, sitting then against the tire of a car.

Albert said, "Where's your damn friend?" scanning the surrounding faces for Ted Schultz. He was at the back of the crowd by the door of the Blue Thorn. Albert waved him forward.

"Your buddy needs your help. Drive him home. I'll pay the bar tab this time."

Albert turned past Schultz and went into the bar. Henry followed.

Henry said, "I missed the fun."

The joke was that it had always been Henry who had gotten into fights through the years, and Albert who had avoided them. Albert was too big a man for most to contend with.

"You didn't miss anything. It didn't last long enough. He's an empty suit."

Henry pulled a chair out from the table decorated with three half-finished pints. "What happened?"

"Tim told us to step outside with it, when we started to argue. The son of a bitch tripped me as I walked out the door, like we were in the friggin' schoolyard again. Nothing changes with some people. Then he hit me as I got up. A real champion shot. Would have broken my nose if I hadn't thought to go down again. Smart ass. Said he'd pay the doctor bill, just for the pleasure of it...Made me mad."

"How did it happen?"

Albert smiled and then winced with some small pain. "That was me. He was already here when I came in. Never knew a lawyer who was early. I think he likes Tim's house ale...But Phil Harrington was here too—he and a couple of his reporter buddies from the *Globe* were taking a late lunch. I think Phil would rather write for the sports pages than the State House crap he does. And he knows us. He was in school with me and Boyle. I went over and talked about baseball for a few minutes. But they were on their way out. They said hello to Boyle as they left."

"What was the problem with that?"

Tim interrupted the tale then with two full glasses and a steaming cloth, which he handed to Albert. Albert wiped the sweat from his neck before he took the remaining smear of blood from his face.

"Phil. Phil made a remark. Like he always does. It's his 'I'm in the know and I'm smarter than you, so don't try to hide anything,' kind of remark. Like reporters do. He stops and says to Boyle, 'Don't take advantage. It wouldn't look good.' That's all he said. Who knows why. Just to be saying something, I guess. Boyle went ballistic. He must have thought I told Phil something. He says to me, 'What did we tell them?' Well, you know I thought you ought to go to the papers with the Frankowski thing anyway, so instead of saying, 'Nothing,' like I should'a done, I got too smart for my own good and said, 'Not much.'"

Henry sipped the light foam off the top of his pint and smiled happily.

Tim had remained for more of the story. He said, "Good show," when Albert paused. From Tim this was high praise. He had seen one too many barroom fights.

Henry said, "So what happened then?"

"Then Boyle says he'd sue us until we were both out picking trash just ahead of the city garbage truck. It was a good image. I told him, I liked his imagery. So he got loud. He said he hoped Barbara Krause liked the image as well. So I told him he hadn't changed much. He had always been the kind of guy who liked to pick on women. It was the only way he could get it up."

Henry laughed. Albert tried to smile and groaned instead. The inside of his lip was split and had started to swell.

Albert heaved a sigh. "Well, in any case, I'm sorry. There goes any chance of help from them."

"Maybe." Henry was not as worried. "That's still up to Duggan."

Boyle had called them to set up the meeting. Henry figured that was Duggan's idea. Whatever they had wanted to talk about was still waiting.

Henry and Albert drank another ale and speculated over what the purpose might have been, before going home.

Albert let him off at the corner. In the dusk, Henry did not notice Bob until he reached the gate. Bob was sitting on the steps with his head in his hands.

For a brief instant, as Bob rose, without speaking, Henry thought it might be his turn for a fight. He imagined a choreographed tumble into Mrs. Murray's tomatoes before he spoke.

Henry said, "Hi," and stood at the gate and waiting for Bob to make his move.

Bob shook himself. "Hi…Sorry to be over here again. Della really gave me an earful the last time. But I was looking for her. She's not home. She wasn't home last night, either. I don't really want to be stupid about this. You know? I just wanted to talk with her."

There was a sound in Bob's voice Henry had never heard before—a pained suffering.

"What's the problem?"

"I guess I've gotten things a little mixed up.…" In the light of the porch, the growing red on Bob's cheeks looked like the splotched rouge on a vaudeville actor instead of the fierce welts he had seen on Boyle. Bob looked away in some embarrassment. "I really do love her. She's a great girl. But I've decided to break it off for good. I just wanted to tell her…myself."

Henry had spoken with Della on the phone earlier. She had known Henry had an appointment that afternoon. He had said he would call her.

"I'll tell her."

"I'll bet.… But it's a little more complicated than that. She's going to find out that I've been seeing someone else, and I wanted to be the one to tell her that."

Henry nodded, "Well, she's seeing someone else too, so everything is just fine."

"Right. But its not the same…I mean, Della's really stuck on me. I've known her a lot longer than you. She's a very sensitive person under all that bluff. And I really do love her. I didn't want to hurt her feelings."

"She'll be fine."

"I probably shouldn't even be telling you this."

"No, you shouldn't. I don't need to know."

"But it's not my fault. Nora is such an extraordinary person."

"Nora?"

"Nora Lynch. I've never met anybody as smart as she is."

Henry struggled to control the expression on his face.

"I think George Duggan would agree with you about that."

Bob straightened himself to full height. "George Duggan is too old for her. He's just a father figure. You know, Nora's father left home when she was just eight years old. She has a thing about older men. She couldn't help herself. But she's broken it off with Duggan."

Henry's breath escaped. "Jeez." He wondered if this was going to be the final insult. Accused of plagiarism, Nora dumps Duggan and Albert slaps his lawyer around. Eddy's book would never be published.

Bob added, "I'm two years older than she is myself…"

Mrs. Murray cleared her throat, her voice coming from the silhouette at the screen of her open window.

"You guys can talk about this stuff some other time, can't you? I'm trying to read…Anyway, I think Sharon What's-her-name ought to pitch her tent up in Maine with old George. She can get some pine tar under those fingernails of hers and then they can settle things between them. But in the meantime…"

Henry told Bob he would tell Della to call him as soon as possible. Bob apologized again and wandered away to his Jeep. Henry had not even noticed it in the twilight of the street. Della did not answer her phone. She had not even left her answering machine on. As Henry changed clothes standing on his mattress, legs spread for balance, he realized he was not balancing very well. Two ales should not have had that much effect, but then, it was three. He had taken Albert's second order when Albert had complained about his lip. And he had not taken time for dinner.

Henry decided to walk.

The walking cleared his head. He was not really worried about Della. She could take care of herself. She could be doing anything. She could be at the supermarket. She could be visiting an old friend. She could be at the movies. But, he just wanted to see her. Little more than a week ago, he would not have done this. If she had not answered her phone, he would have assumed she was fine and he would have called her again in the morning. Now he couldn't wait. Life was changing all of a sudden. He wondered if he was too old for changes like this.

Della's roommates were both students and still gone for the summer. She was the big sister. She did not like being thirty-three. She had said once to him that she wanted to "stay in touch with what was going on." He had warned her it wouldn't work. She would just become a voyeur observing their habits. Della had bragged, "They're the ones who watch me! They don't seem to have any energy."

Henry sympathized with her roommates.

No one answered the doorbell. He stared up the face of the building toward her windows.

"Look under the flowerpot on the right."

The voice from behind startled him, even though he knew it immediately. Bob walked across the street from where his Jeep sat in the open space by a fire hydrant.

"Right." Henry tilted the large pot on edge. It was a foolish place to keep a key. He would have to speak to her about it.

"I was going to wait here, but if you're going to go up.... Well, I guess I'll wait here anyway. I don't want to get towed."

The apartment was dark. Henry guessed she had not been home since that afternoon. It was a messy place. Della was not much of a housekeeper. But he knew that already.

Scotch-taped on the living room wall was a photograph. He had to turn on the light to see that it was a picture of him. She had taken it the day they had gone to Crane's Beach, and it took him a moment to realize it was another of her small jokes—taped up in about the same place on her wall as he had hung the picture of Sasha in his own living room.

Her bed was unmade.

A box of breakfast cereal and a bowl were on the kitchen table. He thought that might be from the previous day because she had eaten at his apartment that morning, but the milk was not dry in the bowl. She was obviously one of those people who ate cereal any time of the day. Another habit he would have to get used to. At least she had been home recently.

He scanned the CDs in the rack by her couch.

What did the two of them have in common? Movies? She liked foreign films. He couldn't stand them. She liked pop singers and he was fond of classical music. Food. They both liked greasy food.

The bookcase by her door was overfilled with paperback bestsellers, mostly Oprah books. She read them on the subway to work and at lunch, and the spines of the books were bowed and creased.

What was going on here? What was wrong with him? Why wasn't he sitting at home reading a book himself?…But then, Bob had used the word. Bob had said it without a thought.

Henry brushed at the dust on the clear plastic cover of the record player. He drew a heart in it. He was in love with Della. Simple enough.

So where was she?

He went down the stairs and out the door, expecting to see Bob there, still waiting. The Jeep was there, the motor running, with Bob inside. Someone else was with him. When Henry looked through the glass, Della did not seem happy to see him. Henry went around and climbed in the back.

"I'm sorry…" She was not given to apologizing. He wondered what she had done. "I wanted to talk to Barbara. I thought I would surprise you. You always say she's the best. And she needs help…I thought I could volunteer. I could do it weekends. And I could learn something about books. I would love to know more about books. We could talk more about books together, and you wouldn't haven't to explain everything to me."

Bob groaned and put his head against the glass of the window on the driver's side.

"That's okay…" Henry started to say.

"Well, it was pretty stupid, really. I didn't call and make an appointment. I didn't want her thinking about it too much. I mean, she still loves you. She might not want me around. But she wasn't there. Nobody was there."

"They close at eight." Henry said. His eyes caught the dashboard clock—8:15.

"This was before. This was about seven-thirty. I went thinking I could ask her to have a cup of coffee with me after she closed. But the place was dark."

That did not make sense.

"The tyranny of the door," Henry said, out loud. "There must be something wrong…"

Bob turned to him.

"Did you say tyranny? What tyranny?"

Henry leaned forward from his seat. "Barbara says it all the time. 'The tyranny of the door.' The door must be opened at a certain time, and closed at another. One of the first laws of retailing. Barbara believes in rules like that. She wouldn't break them. Closing the store early would not be like her."

Bob shrugged, "Maybe she was feeling sick."

"She has people she can call. She could have called me. Anyway, Sharon would have been there."

"Maybe something happened…" Della said

Henry asked, a little too loudly, "Like what?" Why was he overreacting to everything all of a sudden? He touched Bob's shoulder. "Can I use your cell phone?"

Della kept speaking as Henry called the store, and then Barbara's apartment. "I knocked. I knocked, but the lights were out. The street was pretty busy."

Henry asked, "All the lights?" Barbara's phone buzzed repeatedly in his ear.

Della said the words again. "All the lights."

Henry took a larger breath and tried to calm his voice. "She always leaves a few lights on, so people can look through the window at the books."

Bob said, "Maybe there was a power outage…" But the words had no conviction.

"Maybe," Della said, "but the lights were on next door."

Bob offered, "Maybe there was a robbery."

There was a brief silence as Bob's question lingered in the air.

Della's words were not a question. "Bob. Could you please drive us to Alcott & Poe. Please."

It took a very long fifteen minutes to reach Newbury Street. Henry did not speak. There was too much crowding his mind. He was already angry now, for not thinking this all through beforehand. He might have anticipated some of this—perhaps all of it.

Della said, "I guess it's good I went, after all," into the silence.

Bob shook his head as if it were all hopeless. "I can't understand why you would volunteer to work in a bookshop. There's no future in books."

Henry could not wait for the slow crawl of Newbury Street traffic and got out running a block away. He could hear Della behind him.

As she had said, all the lights were out. Both locks on the door were engaged.

"I could kick it down, but it would seem pretty stupid if it's just a blown fuse or something really mundane."

Della said, "Barbara can change a fuse, can't she?"

Henry did not answer. He decided to try the back. He knew, from long ago, that he could reach one of the second-floor windows from the fire escape, and if the catch had not been changed, he could slip it open with his pocketknife. He had actually done it once when he had forgotten his own keys.

The "rat fence" which surrounded the parking area at the rear had been installed to keep the bums from using the space behind the building as a toilet, and only secondarily to stop rats from getting in through the open doors as they loaded or unloaded the store van. The chain link was woven with flat metal slats, which made seeing into the area from street level difficult even in the daylight. It was obvious from the pool of dark as he approached that the floodlights, which were always on for safety, were out as well.

The sound of the engine of the van reached Henry even before he grabbed at the links of the fence. Any hope he had that this was all some kind of mistake was suddenly lost. His fingers ached on the metal. The slats made getting a foothold more difficult, forcing him to pull his weight up and over the top rail.

The van idled in the space in front of the closed loading door, the same boxy old Ford he had driven years before. He had been with Barbara when she bought it, already used. It appeared to have been repainted, and the gold lettering of the Alcott & Poe name caught the ambient light, but he could not see through the windshield. His jeans caught on the cut edge of a link and ripped as he dropped down into the darkened enclosure. He landed clumsily.

He tried the van doors and then shouted, "Do you see a brick?"

Della had just pulled herself to the top of the fence behind him and now looked from her vantage point, before jumping back. At the rear, where the back of the van nearly touched the wall, he found a vacuum cleaner hose curling down from the side vent window. Grey duck tape had been plastered around it to keep it in place. He ripped it free, and exhaust fumed at his face. When he grabbed the open edge of the small window, bracing his weight against the wall, part of the glass broke loose in his hands, but the space it left offered little light on the interior. He had calculated that his body might just fit through, when he heard Della's voice.

"I'm throwing it over. Watch out."

The shadow of the brick arched in the air and landed roughly on the roof of the van. Henry jumped to grab it, stepped up on the front bumper, and then shattered the windshield as Della came over the fence. His body slipped easily on the small bits of glass as he twisted through to the passenger seat headfirst and reached for the van lights before he was completely in. Someone was lying on the open metal floor at the back. The stink was suffocating.

"Move away. Get away," were the only words that came to mind, using what breath he had.

Della jumped for the side.

Henry rolled into the driver's seat, shifted gears, and stepped on the gas. The fence buckled as the bumper struck the closed gate. He backed the van up again until he heard the crunch of metal against the brick of the wall, shifted gears, and stepped on the gas again. The fence gave way, folding the chain link over the shattered window.

Bob had made it to the end of Newbury Street using his horn as well as portions of the sidewalk, and then come around and down the alley from the wrong direction, a police cruiser blaring at him from behind. He arrived at the rear of the store just as the Alcott & Poe van broke through the fence and blocked the way.

Henry jammed the shift into park and slipped through into the back, trying not to stumble now over the body he already recognized. The back doors gave way when he turned the handle. Barbara lay facedown in the dust of the rusted metal floor. He grabbed her hands to pull her free of the fumes. The gloves she was wearing came loose, and he pulled them off. Her hands were warm. He felt suddenly dizzy, but then, he had not taken a breath in what might have been minutes.

Later, he thought it all through repeatedly as he sat in a small waiting area near the emergency room at Boston City Hospital. Bob had taken Della home.

A young woman sat beside him, whimpering. A man with one hand wrapped in bandages sat across the narrow space, his eyes on the woman. They were the only ones left after a rush of late-night emergencies had filled the room earlier. Thankfully, Henry did not have to wait longer. The police had questioned him right there, shortly after he arrived. Another officer spoke with him about an hour later. Someone came through to ask if he knew what kind of insurance Barbara had. He told them he was pretty sure she had none. Then a nurse came through and told him that Barbara was conscious and talking. They would not let him see her, but if she was talking, she was going to be okay.

The old van was rusted out underneath. Barbara's penny-saving had saved her life. The leaks of air from below had forestalled what would have happened given a little more time.

The police told him about a note found on the printer in the office. Henry had not seen it, but he had explained that it was not likely to have been written by her. Barbara had wanted to die, it said. The Barbara he knew would live through anything just to be able to say she had. They suggested she was depressed. He had argued that she was unhappy, but not depressed. She had options. "What are the options?" she would say to almost any problem.

Henry got a cab home. The sky had gone to grey with morning. He was exhausted and fell asleep in his Morris chair.

The knock on the door that awoke him was not the one he might have expected.

Sharon had pinned her hair back carelessly, one blond wisp clung below her chin like a necklace. Her pale skin had darkened beneath her eyes, but her cheeks were reddened, without makeup, in a flush. She brushed the hair back with a finger. It fell again. He noticed two of the nails on her right hand had been cut short. He was sure she had been doing a fair amount of crying.

"I'm sorry to wake you. I'm so sorry. The police came this morning and told me what happened. I just wanted to hear it from you. They wouldn't give me any details."

He felt numb, as if the little sleep he had gotten were worse than staying awake. He did not want to be facing Sharon at that moment. He did not know what the right words might be.

"She's okay. We got to her in time."

Sharon's eyes darted back and forth at his own.

"Did she say what happened?"

"I wasn't allowed to talk to her. But she was talking."

Sharon shook her head, bewildered.

"How did you know? Why were you there?"

"Luck. Barbara's luck. I told you she was a survivor.... Della went to talk with her last night. I could not explain why in a million years. Just the way Della is. But the store was closed.... Why was it closed?"

Sharon raised her shoulders with her hands out.

"Barbara said she was feeling a little sick. She wanted to go home early."

"She was feeling that bad?"

He knew the doubt was in his voice.

"It was nearly closing time anyway...I am so sorry, now, that I left. I thought it would be okay."

"You left with her?"

"No...we had been arguing. Money problems. She stayed behind. She wanted to finish something, she said. I asked her if she wanted help. She told me to go home. She was still angry with me, I think."

"Then what happened?"

"Karen, one of the part-timers, was there. We left together …And then the police came this morning. The police said there was a note."

"So they said."

Sharon's eyes widened, but there was nothing he could read in that soft blue.

"What do you mean?"

"Barbara is not likely to write a note on a computer. Hell, she even hand-letters her shelf labels. And she's not the type to commit suicide."

"But you found her."

"I found her—on her stomach. Barbara never lies on her stomach. She always said she wasn't comfortable on her stomach. She can't sleep that way. Her boobs are too big. Someone put her down that way. And it saved her life. The rotten bottom of that truck let in enough air for her to survive."

Sharon's mouth opened, first without words.

"I don't understand. You think somebody tried to kill her?"

"I do…"

"Just because she was on her stomach?"

"And the gloves."

"The gloves?"

"She was wearing gloves. It's easy to guess why. Whoever did this was trying to hide their own fingerprints. And Barbara's fingerprints couldn't have been there either. Have you ever seen Barbara wear gloves? I never have. Did you ever see her close the store early? I never have."

"Then you think this was planned?"

She said it with a grimace of horror at the idea.

He let a moment pass. He wondered if "planned" was the right word.

"Yes."

244

Again her lips moved before the word was spoken. "Who?"

She had already lost what color he had seen in her face before. Her lips remained shaped by that last word, as if she might begin to whistle.

"You."

Her eyes went wide again.

"Me? You're kidding! Me?" She smiled oddly and backed away.

He said, "Who else?"

Her shoulders fell and her neck craned forward. "I left! Ask Karen. I was gone!"

"If you did, you came back."

"Why are you saying this?"

"It's the only way it makes sense."

"You're saying I tried to murder somebody. Seriously? That's crazy. How would I get her to stay in the van?"

"I can only guess. Did you drug her? I told the cops to look for her last coffee somewhere around the desk in the office. That's where she did the bookkeeping every night when it got quiet, around six or seven, right? If it's there, I'll bet it has something else in it beside coffee. If it's not there, then there is another reason why."

Sharon straightened her back now.

"Why would I do this?"

"To save your investment."

"But the business depends on Barbara."

"You could sell the books for more than she owes you."

"You're crazy." She said it oddly, like a little girl.

He could not be so sure of the thing that had been on his mind since lying in the woods in Maine. It was far less certain. But it seemed part of a weave of events that all became one fabric now.

"And I think something else that's crazy—about the manuscript. You re-wrote that, didn't you? It was not the same one that Jim wrote, was it?"

Her eyes narrowed. The anger returned. It was in the stiff line of her delicate jaw. It was in the flat line of her lips. They looked very hard to him now. Her eyes darkened, just enough to surprise him. And then it all faded. The lips rounded to a soft pout. The blue of her eyes became jewel-like with tears.

"It was the book I told him to write," her voice was barely audible at first. Her eyes were on her hands, examining the odd cut of her nails. "I did the research. I handed it to him, and he ignored it. He wasn't interested. All he cared about was Scipio. The underappreciated Scipio, he said. There was no history of when Hannibal died. And why would the great general tell so much to an illiterate slave girl? The apparent coincidence in the history was only a lack of our own knowledge, he said. He couldn't see the point. But I had found the real story. I found it first. And then Duggan wrote it…. How could he know? Why did he pick that story? That was no coincidence…I knew she must have told him. Nora was always so smart. She saw it. But not Jim. Jim could be so stupid. So arrogant. It was right there in front of him…." Sharon faced Henry for one moment as if he might confirm her words. Henry had nothing to offer. He felt empty. Her eyes searched his for help. She said, "I am not such a bad person…. You know, I could have stabbed her. They would have thought we had been robbed. So simple. She would be dead now. But I couldn't do it…I couldn't—I saw the thing with the exhaust on some TV show. They said it was painless…. I wanted it to be painless."

She held her hands out again, and looked at the palms. He wondered what she was thinking. He had no idea what should happen next. The weight of his body seemed to growing by the second.

He needed to sit down. He needed coffee.

"Do you want to sit down?" he asked her.

She moved for the couch. He picked up the phone and sat in his chair. She turned again and was out the door.

Mrs. Murray looked up the stairway at him as Sharon pushed her way past. The screen door snapped shut before his hand, and his weight broke the catch loose from the frame. Sharon had parked her car just outside the gate and was in, with her car door locked, as he reached it. The engine grunted. She did not look at him. She appeared to have no expression at all. He hit the roof of the car as it jolted away.

"What happened?" Mrs. Murray called from the porch.

"Call the police. She lives at fifty-seven Phillips Street. She tried to kill Barbara."

The five blocks to Benny's garage to get his truck was in the wrong direction. Henry began to run for Phillips Street. It was easily the farthest he could remember ever running since he was a kid at Brookline High running away from Stuart Maslow. As his breath shortened, he remembered Stuart very well. Where was Stuart now? Was he a lawyer, like Boyle? Henry had lost those fights. Was it two? Three? Some bullies don't run away when the going got rough. Some bullies liked it rough. Maslow had chased him for blocks. And then, at the end, Henry's own father had locked him out. Maslow had beaten him right in front of his own house.

The memory was still so fresh. He remembered the metal taste of his own blood and the ringing in his ears. He took his beatings on the spot after that. It didn't make him a better fighter, but it made him get the confrontations over with. At least he never ran again…That was his freshman year. He would have been fourteen. There were more than a few fights after that.

It began to feel like there was too little oxygen in the air to breathe. A sharp pain suddenly ran up the side of his body, bending him before he could stop the motion of his legs. He staggered, then stood, bent over, hands on his knees in the middle of the sidewalk, until the pain faded. People passing asked if he were all right. He nodded, still catching his breath. He had really always hated running.

Henry walked the rest of the way to Phillips Street. He expected the police would be there before him.

But they were not. Sharon's car was illegally parked at the corner. She did not answer her bell. He rang the other bells. No answers. While he waited for the police, another tenant entered the building and Henry slipped in the door. He ran the stairs to the third floor, his energy renewed by the frustration of waiting.

Sharon did not answer his knocking. There was no sound. He cut the debate with himself short and kicked at the door. Nothing happened. He rammed his shoulder into it. Nothing. And again. Nothing, except a new pain in his shoulder.

His father had shown him something once. Henry sat down in the hallway, braced his feet against the door with his back against the opposite wall, and pushed with his legs. The wood split, cracked, and gave way. He was lying on the floor, looking up, when he first saw Sharon's body.

Pushing the dining-room chair away, he lifted her with his hands in her armpits. She was limp, and her head fell forward above him. Her face was white, almost grey. Her eyes were shut tight. The yellow of her bleached eyebrows seemed artificial against the skin.

Henry held her body up on his shoulder to take the noose away—plain clothesline. She had only tied a simple slip-knot in it. She seemed so light—so thin. It must have been terribly difficult for her to carry Barbara all the way from the second-floor office to the van at the back of the basement.

Her neck was not broken. The thin dark bruise left by the cord could have been painted on. She had choked to death. Her body was still very warm. Her lips, darkened beneath the red of the gloss, were open just slightly to the blue of her tongue caught between the edges of her teeth, as if anticipating a kiss.

The police rang the doorbell just as he put her down on the carpet.

He wondered about it afterward. The hook over the entry to her dining room where she had hung herself was painted over and so oddly placed. What was it used for? Why was it there?

Barbara told him later. She had seen it at a party there once when Jim was alive, before Christmas. It was where they hung the fresh mistletoe.

Chapter Twenty-four

Barbara was released that afternoon. Henry went with her in the cab. He was exhausted, but it seemed like a better idea than going home at the time. She complained of feeling weak but looked fine. She had little to say, and he spoke too much. Her part-timers, Trudy and Karen, were managing the store without her. He told her he would check on things later. He told her a little about Sharon. She did not want to know more. She seemed upset that the store had been opened, under the circumstances. Henry made excuses about her need for money, which seemed inadequate to the events.

He reached home before dark and never undressed. Della was there and held his hand as he fell asleep in his chair.

When he awoke later in his bed, in the middle of the night, Della was still there, and he held her, glad not to be alone.

In the morning, Della called in to work to say she would be late and Henry drove her over to Charlie's on Columbus Avenue for breakfast. Afterwards he drove her downtown to her office, kissed her goodbye, and went back to the bookshop by himself. It was still early, but he tapped on the window and Barbara came to the door.

She hugged him in a full body grip that took his breath away. Then she cried. When she could speak again, she surprised him, as if she was so full of words she could not contain them any longer.

"Do you think Sharon killed Jim?"

She mashed the tears from her cheeks with the palms of her hands.

Henry had never thought about it. Now, it seemed obvious that Sharon might have done that as well.

"Why? For the insurance? How does a person kill someone else and live with it? For so little?"

People did that kind of thing on television shows, all the time, he thought. Barbara pinned her hair back for work. The cat circled her feet expectantly.

She said, "It could have begun with an accident.... You know, when Jim died, the detective questioned me three or four times over the space of a week. Now that I look back at it, I suppose he was trying to pick up on some little thread. He might have guessed she was involved.... They could have argued. She could have hit him with anything—with a frying pan, for all we know. If she could carry me, she could carry him. I was thinking about it yesterday in the hospital.... She never planned things very well. She worried about the details but never the big picture. I even knew at the last moment that she had given me something—put something in my coffee. I had asked earlier about what kind of sugar she had used, because it didn't taste just the same as always. I thought she had used the artificial stuff she likes herself. But I knew for sure when I was passing out in the office, and I tried to get up to the phone—I had fallen, I think—but even then, I was thinking that Sharon had done something. And when I woke up in the hospital—I woke up with that thought as if no time at all had passed. I told the nurse that.... Sharon really didn't think it all through." Barbara knelt and took the cat up in her arms and hugged it like a teddy bear. Homer's motor-like purr scored the momentary silence. "Well, I guess if I had died, there would have been no one to tell, and she would have gotten away with it, but once you pulled me out of the van, I suppose it was all over for her."

Henry told Barbara what Sharon had said about stabbing and robbery. There were no tears left for this. She just shook her head and speculated on all the lives that had been made a mess of. It seemed incomprehensible to him.

"She was so smart. She could write a whole book in a few weeks. Why didn't she just write one on her own?"

Barbara responded quickly with a thought she had obviously gone over in her mind more than once.

"It's the sad part about working in a bookshop like this." She waved her hand at the book-lined walls around them. "Look at them all…. Thousands and thousands of novels by writers who had high hopes and dreams of their own. Not even counting the ones who were never published to begin with. And they're all forgotten. They're like gravestones on a shelf….I remember thinking about that the first time when I was in Rome during college and I took one of those tours down in the catacombs. In those narrow spaces, like aisles in a bookshop, the bones were filed away on shelves." Barbara stopped, looked at him for some answer he did not have, and then continued. "Beyond the money involved, I think she might have been discouraged by all of this." Barbara's eyes scanned the shelves around them now. "There *is* something discouraging about this—about the way people always want to read something new, whether it's better or not. Most people don't even read, but of those who do, very few would even think of buying a used book—'What's new?' I hear it every day—And Sharon was not the type to struggle to write something new and then pin her hopes on the chance of the market."

Henry's thought came out loud. "Taking some of Duggan's money must have seemed like a better bet. What might an accusation of plagiarism be worth to a writer like Duggan?"

This idea silenced them both now. Even the cat appeared to be quietly mulling the possibility.

Barbara suddenly spoke in the voice of his old boss. "You ought to call George Duggan and tell him."

"I should." Henry had not thought of that.

"Go ahead." She handed him the phone. Obviously she felt some guilt over her support of Sharon's cause.

George Duggan answered his phone at Red Hill Camp. Henry explained as much as possible in the fewest words he could manage. Duggan was silent at first, then obviously disconcerted. He asked about Sharon's family. Henry had no idea. He asked about Barbara, and Henry assured him things were well enough.

As they spoke, it became obvious Duggan needed someone to talk to as well. Nora was no longer there. He was alone and his children had left for the summer. He was having trouble starting a new book.

Barbara simply stared at the window from her usual perch by the register, Homer nestled in her lap, until a few seconds before ten, and then she arose and unlocked her door for the day's business. By the time Henry hung up the phone, she appeared tired again. Henry stood in front of her at the desk.

"You know, I could stick around. I'd be happy to volunteer for a few weeks until you can hire someone to take Sharon's place."

Barbara laughed once. Then again, just to be doing it.

"We've been there and done that, kiddo. You're sweet, but you don't belong behind the counter of my shop. Thanks, but Trudy is going to go full time for a few weeks until school starts. We'll get by."

He was relieved.

"At least tell me if there's anything else I can do."

Barbara shook her head.

"It won't be a problem much longer...I think we'll close the store after Christmas."

He had learned long ago not to argue with her. He had never, in his memory, ever won an argument with her.

"I was afraid you were thinking like that."

"I've got to find some form of gainful employment before I get so old nobody will hire me."

Her wan smile showed no conviction. He gave her his best wide-eyed pitch. "You can re-open somewhere close by, in a smaller space."

She closed her eyes at him.

"It won't work."

"How do you know?"

"It's all I know. It's what I know. Everything I've learned says it won't work anymore."

He continued his protest. "But you've been saying that bookselling was a dying trade for years. You don't know if time has really run out. There may be a few years left. Books are still a way to make a living. Just scale down. Don't give it up."

She shook her head. "I'm tired. I've been doing it for too long. Nobody gives a damn. Some reporter will come over from a newspaper and do a piece about the end of a era, or the closing of the book, or the last chapter, or—"

"You are being cynical. That's not you. That's me."

"Nobody gives a damn."

The cat lifted his head to argue. She stroked his chest. Henry tried to modulate his voice.

"Everybody gives a damn. There are people who never shop here who care about this place. This is Boston. It's part of the shtick. People don't read, but they love old bookstores. They really do. They're not lying. It's automatic. They can't help it if they've been sold the sizzle and not the steak. They love the idea of reading more than the crap they're given to read. But there'll always be a few who really do."

"More people come in to pet the cat than buy books." She nuzzled Homer and the cat's eyes half closed in delight.

Henry ignored her. "And there'll always be new students coming to town with clean faces and unsullied hearts who think literature is something special. At least until the professors rape them of their innocence and spread the modern pox—they need you. And you can survive off of that.... Maybe I can't. I can't stand the maroons. But if you give up, there won't be anybody at all left who gives a crap about them. The one person in a hundred who really loves books is going to be left with people like me—someone who doesn't even want to talk to them—who'll deal with them electronically over the internet. They'll have to use a computer to get a book to read. You can't just leave them to people like me. There is no book dust in an email. I won't chat with them about the binding on a Liveright edition before and after Horace sold the last bit of his soul. I won't let them fondle the books in my closet. You'll make me responsible for putting an end to the last remnant of civilization. I would shoot the maroons before I listen to them say another word about how they just love old bookstores as they walk out empty-handed—after they've just bought a sack of DVDs and CDs on their way over to tell you they'll come by again when they have a little more time to browse.... If you give up, I win!"

She smiled at that. She did not answer so much as begin to ignore him as customers arrived. Henry left, worried that his ranting would lose her a needed sale.

In the truck, he took a slim pack of index cards from his shirt pocket and fanned them by date. There was an estate auction preview at one o'clock in Worcester. He was a little early, but there was an old diner near there that had great rice pudding. The process of business would get his mind off things.

At the auction he bought a collection of Lakeside Classics in the red and green bindings. The repetitive cadence of the auctioneer lulled him, releasing the drift of his thoughts. He worked at concentrating on the lots as they came up, but found himself contemplating other matters over and again. He passed on a collection of Philip K. Dick paperback first editions that he was regretting by the time he was driving home. Turnpike traffic kept him from getting back until just before dark.

He dropped the books off at the house before he parked the truck at Benny's and then walked the long way back through the Square. Students were starting to return. The brief and relative quiet of midsummer was past. Clusters of young faces moved hesitantly through the obstruction of tourists holding maps. Uneasy parents followed eager freshman against the flash of crossing lights, through cars drifting slowly, unsure of the traffic patterns. Street hustlers pressed likely victims for spare change. Locals darted around the fringes. Sophomores and juniors, their living spaces already claimed, scouted for familiar faces with whom to rejoice and retell fresh summer tales. An incompetent percussionist, squatting on an overturned milk crate, beat drum-like patterns on an unidentifiable found object at the edge of the pit, where the brick arose in a collar behind the Red Line subway entrance. The fumes of four idling buses drifted over the street.

Henry looked across at the high brick walled enclosure surrounding Harvard Yard with the thought that he had still not visited sweet Ellen at the Widener Library. She would be back from vacation by now. Into his view, only a few feet away, moved the cop who patrolled the area.

Henry remembered the eyes first. He was not as tall as Henry would have guessed, but heavyset. Bull-headed. His cap was pulled low. One thumb hung in his belt by his holstered gun. The cop's eyes stopped, expressionless, on Henry and then moved past him.

Henry kept walking, and then halted, even before his thought was complete. Next to him was Holyoke Center, a small plaza enclosed on three sides by the architecture of cement and glass. Ten feet from him was the bank machine where he had withdrawn the money for Eddy Perry.

Henry turned. The cop turned away.

This was the same man who had been sitting in the car watching Mrs. Murray's house that day, after Sasha had come to his door worried about a stalker. Mrs. Murray had been right. He was a cop.

By the time Henry reached home, he had come to more than one conclusion.

There, in the dark, with the porch light turned off, he found Mrs. Murray sitting by herself, smoking a cigarette.

"I've never seen you smoke." He said from the gate.

"I quit for Sam. He hated it. First pack I've bought in almost twenty years."

"How is it?"

"Not as good as I remember."

She held the pack out to Henry. He took one and sat down beside her.

He shrugged. "Is anything ever as good as you remember?"

She said, "Yes. Some things," and handed him a book of matches and he lit his first cigarette in months.

"Like what?"

"Popcorn. Pretzels. Popsicles. Pizza. Sex."

He laughed, "I'm glad about that…"

Vincent McCaffrey

She exhaled a short laugh with her smoke. Her voice already seemed more husky than he had heard it before.

She said, "Della told me all about…everything. Are you okay?"

"I think so." He smiled, "I guess all I really needed was a cigarette. Now everything is fine."

He smiled at her with the cigarette trapped in his lips and the smoke squinting his eyes. Mrs. Murray seemed to study the darkness.

She said, "What is Barbara going to do?"

Against the streetlight, Henry imaged shapes through the smoke. "She said she's going to close. But she won't. She'll figure something out."

"Good. And George Duggan is off the hook."

"I think so. But he's a little unhappy. He's lost Nora. She ran everything for him. I think he's feeling a little lost in the woods himself. I spoke to him this morning about Sharon, and he sounded a bit depressed by it all. He's up there alone now. But he'll be coming back to Boston next week to find a new secretary. I suppose Nora will keep operating Tremont Press, but she won't be able to get Duggan's manuscripts in shape for publishing anymore. On top of everything else, she was a damned good secretary."

Mrs. Murray's laugh was short.

"She was too young for that old goat."

Henry calculated his answer and tried to remember all the points he had thought of as he drove to Worcester.

"Maybe, but she seemed to be able do it all. Now he needs to find somebody with a command of English grammar, excellent typing skills, and a broad knowledge of literature. Not an easy thing to find, nowadays."

She looked away again toward the street light. "I don't imagine so."

"I told him I would keep my eyes peeled."

"Did you? Busy, busy, busy."

"He's a good guy."

"So you say."

"Della thinks so too."

She smiled and inhaled deeply on her cigarette, ignoring his words. The smoke came back as she spoke.

"So, life will get back to normal."

"No…I don't think so. Not yet."

She did not answer quickly.

"What's wrong?" Her eyes had wandered up to the night sky.

"I think I know something more about the murder of Eddy Perry now," he said.

She stood and stepped onto the strip of grass by the fence, where a tree shaded her completely from the streetlight. A plume of blue smoke reached upward when she bent her head back and faced the stars.

"They say Mars is closer right now than it has been in thousands of years. But I can't see it." she said.

He said, "That's because it's in your hand."

She looked down at the glowing end of her cigarette.

"So it is." She did not laugh. "And what is it you found out about Eddy Perry?"

"I just figured something out…. I'm a little slow, I guess. I'll tell you about it when I know more. First I have to do something about it."

Chapter Twenty-five

Albert drank half his beer before taking a breath, as if anxious about getting it down before he spoke.

"There's not much you can do. Break it down. Look at the facts…There's nothing to link the cop to Eddy Perry except that you saw him on duty that night and he probably saw you give Eddy the money…. I like the fact that he called you a junkie when you surprised him in his car. That makes a pretty clear statement of what he thought of you, and probably explains why he was watching your place that day."

Henry did not grasp this. Something was missing. "I don't understand. Why watch my place, if he thought I was the one buying the drugs? You figure he wanted to steal my drugs?"

Henry had said this very thing on the phone to Boyle as well, and gotten no good answer. Albert swallowed half of what remained in the glass.

"I figure that's something you just haven't figured out yet. It's a piece missing from the board. A rook maybe. If he's tracking down pushers and drug users and taking their stuff, he must have his own game plan."

Tim moved toward them from the sink behind the bar. "What piece? There's another piece?"

Henry said, "There has to be. Otherwise it would all fit together."

Tim looked confused. "Are we talking chess here, or is this some kind of puzzle?"

Albert shook the idea away. "Go ask Alice. She reads that stuff. She knows how mysteries are supposed to work."

This idea appealed to Henry. "What are you having for dinner?"

Tim retreated to the sink again.

Albert stood, as if in response, nearly pushing Henry off his stool. Henry recovered in time to keep his own beer out of his lap.

"Excuse me.… She's out tonight with her buddies. You call her up later and talk to her. In the meantime, I have to take the boys to the mall. They've got to get their stuff for school. Alice told me it's my job this year."

Henry remained sitting but leaned back on the bar. "What's got you so upset?"

Albert twisted his face into a dramatic frown. "Everybody. You. You keep putting your head in where it doesn't belong. Alice, because I get to eat egg salad again tonight. Junior, because if I don't keep an eye on him, he'll buy all the wrong stuff. And now I have to give up a Sox ticket to go to a testimonial. I hate testimonials."

"You're the main speaker. You have to go."

"I'm going to be sick. I'm going to be in front of a hundred people. I'm getting ill right this very minute just thinking about it. I'm getting a violent headache. I'm going to be nauseous. I'll be bedridden. I can't write a speech in bed. Myron Evans doesn't need a testimonial. Myron's wife is the only person who liked him, anyway. Myron had four sons. Let them give the testimonial. Why didn't one of his sons take over the business? Myron was eighty-five years old, for Christ sake—"

"But he's dead."

"Testimonial enough—lucky stiff."

"I thought you said he was cremated."

"A technicality."

"But he started you in the garbage business—"

"Refuse removal," Albert corrected him.

"He started you in the refuse removal business. You owe him! You could have ended up a lawyer like Boyle."

"I owe him for a lot of garbage."

"Refuse," Henry reminded him.

"Refuse! I should have refused when his wife asked me to give the testimonial."

Henry shook his head and held up his hands to stop Albert. "Look. All I need is one thing. I need to know what the missing piece is."

Albert waved his arm in the air as if dismissing Henry's problems as minor, as he backed toward the door.

"Think it over. It's there. I can't stand mysteries. Alice says in the books they always leave the piece right out in the open and cover it with details so you won't notice it. Drives me crazy. Give me a good history book any time."

Henry tried for pity. "I'm just looking for a little help, is all…"

Albert stopped, came back, and handed Henry his Red Sox ticket for the game Friday with Baltimore.

"Why don't you take Tim? He won't mind sitting next to you. He's smelled worse."

Tim looked over from the sink with the mention of his name. Albert knew Tim had season tickets he shared with one of his beer distributors and didn't need another.

Henry stayed at the bar for one more round, after Albert left, listening to Tim expound on the failures of the Red Sox as he walked back and forth behind the bar, cleaning up from the lunch crowd and bringing all the world within earshot up to date with the team's latest attempts to snatch defeat from the jaws of victory.

Henry heard little of it, but nodded or grunted when it seemed appropriate. He found himself thinking about missing pieces.

In the conversation Henry had with Boyle that morning, it was clear that Police Officer Paul Higgins was a real loser. He had been on the force for almost twenty years, and never risen in rank without soon losing it again.

"He is not a trusted man. Probably just waiting for his chance to retire and get his pension." Boyle had said.

Boyle had suggested it might be a sign that Higgins had done something unforgivable, but there was no way to actually know. His sources could not get easy access to Higgins' complete record. That, in itself, was not common. But then, the Cambridge police force was a smaller and tighter group than the Boston Police, where Boyle's brothers worked.

Henry wondered aloud if they could at least gain a partial victory. Boyle had contacted someone at the Internal Revenue Service, but that did not seem enough.

"My guy says the investigation will start pretty quick. Now we have to wait for a nameless bureaucrat to turn up something that might put Higgins in jail. If Higgins has been spending more than he's been making, he'll get nailed. Just like Al Capone."

This might satisfy a lawyer, but Henry was not happy about it. How many men did Capone kill and never pay for? And Higgins was still on the street, in uniform.

Boyle had not called without prompting. His tone had been dismissive and his information short on detail. He had called because he wanted to keep Duggan happy. Henry had spoken with George Duggan again the day before and mentioned there was no word from Boyle. Duggan said he would check with the lawyer and see what was happening.

Henry walked home slowly in the breezeless heat of late afternoon. Even the rush-hour traffic was reduced by the number of people away on August vacation. Things felt like they were coming to a halt, and he was without a clear idea of what he was going to do next. The puzzle was nearly complete, wasn't it? There were not that many pieces to choose from, certainly. But one piece was close at hand.

He found Mrs. Murray in the side yard and spoke to her there. With the house next door still empty, there would be no one else to hear.

She smiled at him broadly as he approached. "You'll never guess what's happened. Unless it's you behind it. Have you been busy again? I got a call this morning from George Duggan. He wants to hire me! He needs an assistant. It sounds like he needs a secretary, but he calls it an assistant. He needs somebody to go over his manuscripts for lapses of grammar and typos and that kind of thing. The publishers don't do that like they used to. I think he just needs somebody to talk to, if you want my opinion. But it's a good job. The kind of thing I can do."

Henry congratulated her.

Green tomatoes nested large among the leaves in clutches, almost as high as her head. The brim of her broad-billed sun hat was bent back so that it was out of the way as she loosened the earth at the edge with a hoe. Henry watched her work a moment before speaking again. He would not have said so aloud, but Mrs. Murray in her hat reminded Henry of his mother in at least that respect. His mother had tried so hard to get things to grow in their backyard. Though never successful, she had always worn a hat just like that. It was an image he had not thought of in a long time.

Henry presented Mrs. Murray with the only facts he knew. It would be up to her to tell him what he could not have known.

264

"Why was Eddy on the stairs that night? Why did he come to see me?" Henry paused, hoping she would say something. She broke another clot of dirt with her hoe. "And why was Higgins watching this house? He couldn't have the time to watch every person he thinks might be buying drugs. He might have known Eddy had been a dealer, sure, but why watch me?"

When she finally stood straight and faced him, she winced, as if the sun had suddenly given her a headache.

"Eddy Perry was an odd little fellow, as you know, but he wasn't a pusher. It was me. I went to him…. After Sam died, I needed something doctors wouldn't prescribe, and Sam had told me once that Eddy was an addict…. In any case, I really had no idea how to get any drugs. It had been so long since I had even smoked a little grass. And even then, after college, I had never bought it. Jer always got it somehow. He was my fella then. Jer of the Golden Hair, I used to call him. He's bald now and teaches political science at Middlebury…. So long ago it seems like another lifetime. Ford was President. Do you remember Ford? Then, it was recreational. Drugs for fun…But after Sam died, I thought I would die too. We had no real friends besides ourselves. We were that close. I had never considered being alive without him. You don't know about that yet. I understand. But maybe you will…" She pulled her leather gloves off and folded them in her hand before she continued.

"Eddy refused at first. Later I went back again and drew him a rather nasty picture of trying to buy a small amount of cocaine from a dealer I had found on the street in Boston. It pained him. He was afraid I would get hurt…Eddy actually sold me what I wanted in order to protect me."

Henry drew a breath. This was much too complicated.

"How did you know him—from his bookshop?"

"Oh, Sam used to buy his reference books from Eddy. Eddy always called Sam when he got something nice...Though I really didn't get to know him until Sam died, when I called him over to take the books away. Eddy looked the books over for an hour or so, and then he sat down—the room was lined with books then, and it was so dark without Sam in his chair by the lamp—"

She stopped her story for a moment, wiping at her cheek with the back of her hand.

"And Eddy said he couldn't afford to buy them. They were too good, and so many, and he didn't have the money...Well, I knew Sam liked him, so I just told him to pay me when he could. It was an odd moment. Eddy sat there in Sam's chair for at least ten minutes without making a sound or a move. It was creepy, really. I didn't know what to do...but then he just said thanks. And then, after a minute, he said it was funny, but his whole life had been like that. He said it made him wonder about God. Whenever he was down to his last dime, someone came through for him..."

Henry looked away, his eyes wandering up toward his own kitchen window as if the answer would be written there in the iron of the fire escape against the white clapboard of the house.

Mrs. Murray studied the broken earth at the end of her hoe.

Henry said, "So you think Higgins was watching you? Could he have thought the money he took from Eddy was for drugs? He might have known Eddy had been involved with that before. And if Eddy was dealing again, he might be dealing to you? Or me? Or both of us? He saw me give Eddy the money for the book that night. He just didn't know it was for a book. Especially if Higgins had not found any drugs in Eddy's apartment after he killed him..."

She shook her head. "I don't know. I let Eddy in that night because he came by to see how I was. Just to see how I was doing. We talked awhile on the porch. You know he wasn't a talker, but he was happy about something—I'm not sure what…. Maybe it was the manuscript. I happened to mention I had another book dealer living here, and he seemed to know you. He asked if he could wait, to ask you about something."

Henry wondered if any of this was important to anyone else but the two of them. Her past was Sarah Murray's business. And there was no need to mention it to anyone else, especially George Duggan. George needed help with his manuscripts, and Sarah had agreed to give it a try. If it worked out, that was enough.

Henry inhaled the thick sun-warmed air, liquid with the smell of the tomato leaves, as if it were better than oxygen.

Duggan called again that night.

He seemed to like talking with Henry, like an older brother bearing secrets. Henry was more perplexed than flattered. For all of Duggan's knowledge and money, he was really just a geek who loved to write. This was something Henry could understand. The man had very few pretensions so long as he was not discussing his work, and Henry avoided the critical assessment of writing as much as he avoided eating eggplant—he had not done either within memory. No, that wasn't right. He had not played the critic since Morgan Johnson was alive. And then it was Duggan who brought Morgan into the conversation.

"I have to make a few decisions. Time is passing. I wish I had Morgan to talk with now. She always had the right sense of things."

Henry hesitated with his answer, worried over stating the obvious, and then decided it was better said.

"She'd tell you to forget what everyone else wanted from you and do what you wanted from yourself."

It brought a silence before the answer.

"Yes. She would say exactly that."

The latest news was that Duggan had hired Sarah Murray to take over Nora's job as his secretary. That was the real reason for the call. Henry didn't mention that he already knew. Duggan was coming down from Maine the next day to Boston to meet with Sarah and Nora at the Tremont Press office. He would be around for the weekend and wondered if Henry could have dinner with him. He wanted to talk about an idea for something he had to write—some kind of introduction to Eddy's book.

Henry had asked what the subject might be.

Duggan had recalled a time in his youth, during the 1960s, when he had tried to live on his own in New York. "I wanted to write plays then.... Now that's a real madness. I was inspired by Sean O'Casey and the lush readings of Siobhan McKenna. I lived on the Lower East Side and went to Off-Broadway theatre whenever I could afford it. I didn't have two cents to rub together. I was working days as a copy editor at Holt, Rinehart and Winston, on Madison Avenue.... And that was just about the time Eddy was shipping off to Germany, but it was much the same city as Eddy described in his book, and his book brought back clear memories of all of it.... And I've decided— I've decided now to use that time as the setting for a new book myself. I owe Eddy a debt. He's given me the push I needed.... He and Morgan."

Duggan especially remembered the old theatres on 42nd Street near Broadway where he had escaped once a week to the double-feature Westerns, all in Technicolor, "like no color anyone uses today. That was the color of real life to me. The world I saw with my own eyes was pale by comparison."

In fact, Duggan had just seen a preview of a new film about cowboys while he was in LA, and it brought back all of those times. He hated LA, but he would have spent the six hours in the plane anyway just to see a good Western again. A real old-fashioned Western. The studio had made him fly out of Portland, because they needed to consult with him for pre-production on *Dreams of Bithynia*. He hated small planes. He hated to be away from Red Hill Camp at all before the leaves were off the maples. He told Henry he would be subletting an apartment on Commonwealth Avenue in Boston over the winter, just so he could be closer to Logan Airport. He'd be going back and forth a lot until the film was completed.

Henry had little more to offer the conversation himself other than a ready ear. He talked a little about first seeing a reissue of *Shane* at the old Orson Welles theatre with Albert. Albert was crazy about Westerns. Henry admitted he had never been much west of the Connecticut river. Duggan encouraged him to buy a motorcycle and just go. Duggan had done that once himself. The greatest summer of his life, just after college. Henry admitted he had never been on a motorcycle. Then, remembering Duggan liked baseball, Henry had offered him Albert's extra ticket without considering the fact that Duggan could probably get special tickets anytime he wanted. Duggan apologized and told Henry he already had an invitation to sit with some "big wigs" out in the new seats over the Green Monster that night, but thanked him for the offer.

"Why don't you take your father?" Duggan had suggested.

That had shut Henry up. He was glad Della had not heard it. Which prompted another thought. He knew his father would not go, but perhaps Della would.

269

Chapter Twenty-six

It was an odd feeling. He did not know why he was awake. He stared at the shadows on the ceiling for most of a minute before he heard noises; then it was quiet again.

These were not familiar sounds. Henry listened harder and heard nothing. He knew Sasha was spending nights with her boyfriend again. Mrs. Murray was in Maine for the week—her first visit there, after a week at Tremont Press with Nora, learning some of Duggan's routines.

Henry got out of bed slowly and went into the living room without turning on a light. Still there was no sound except for the blood rushing in his own ears. He waited.

The small cry of a middle stair was suddenly clear.

Henry moved toward his door, and then quickly away. He suddenly knew that he should move away.

Lifting the receiver on his phone, he began to dial before realizing it was dead, and set it back. He shifted carefully toward the kitchen window.

Someone was just outside his door. He was sure there was more than one.

Henry pulled the window up, lifted the screen and stepped out on the fire escape. His bare feet ached against the iron grate. He pushed the screen down again, knowing it was a minor hindrance, but hoping it would not give him away too soon.

To one side was the roof of the front porch. If he jumped from the porch, he might find them waiting for him. Below him was a drop of fifteen feet or more into the dark of Mrs. Murray's garden and the tomato plants with their wooden stakes.

270

He had never liked heights. Across the side yard was the Phillipson house, still for sale after six months and still empty.

He had already begun the climb to the third floor when he heard the crack of wood from his own door. Adrenalin splintered into his body and made him jump forward. Sasha's window was partly open, as he hoped.

He lifted her screen and then the window and stepped in. The emptiness of her apartment offered a faint echo to his movements as he found her phone in the near-dark. Her phone was dead as well. He was stupid. There was no reason to think her phone might work if his did not.

He pulled out a drawer in her kitchen, and then another, looking for knives in the dark. A can opener fell to the floor. His hand pressed at several empty plastic bags on the top of the counter as he opened lower drawers. Beneath them was loose string—violin string—too thin and too short to offer any hope of carrying his weight. In an odd flash of fantasy, he imagined using it to garrote his pursuers, and, grabbed at this as the sound of movement on the stairs came upward.

Stepping out onto the fire escape again, he thought to yell as loudly as he could, before thinking again that it was more important to put some small distance between himself and his pursuers before they knew exactly where he was, if only because he was very sure they had at least one gun. His toes sank through the grating.

Above him the overhang of the roof was just out of his reach. Below him, the fire escape ended at the lower roof over the front porch. He would have to go past his own window again.

As he stepped down, his hand found the TV antenna wire against the clapboards. It pulled loose but bowed stiffly with old paint as another idea occurred to him. He knotted a violin string to this and tied the other end to the outer rail of the fire escape behind him.

He heard the shattering of wood from Sasha's door. Then he began to yell.

His first "Help" sounded more like a squawk. "Someone call the police. I need help!" He could not bellow quite the way Albert could. He was standing in his underwear on a fire escape yelling for help in the night while being pursued by murderers, and he felt ridiculous.

A light went on in the house across the back yard. He yelled again as he edged further down the stairs. Something moved at his own window just below him. The screen slid up. There was the white of a face in the dark. He kicked at it, using his hand on the metal rail to pivot himself. His toe cracked with the impact on the man's skull, loud enough to echo off the next house. A pain shot up his own leg. There was a curse from the dark below he did not understand.

Someone pushed out the screen from Sasha's window above him and it turned like a dipping kite in the air as Henry vaulted downward past the dark of his own window and onto the roof of the porch. A hand caught at his shirt. There was an explosion of sound between the two houses he understood to be gunfire from Sasha's window. A jolt of pain took his breath as the toe of the foot he had used to kick struck the tar shingles. He was fairly sure the gunshot had missed him. He yelled again for help as he stumbled forward on the porch roof and made the leap he hoped would carry him to the strip of grass below. But he had miscalculated in the dark.

There was another explosion of sound. Henry's bare feet met the cement of the front walk, and his legs collapsed beneath him. Someone barked, "Shit." The low metallic drum of a human body repeatedly striking the iron rails as it tumbled on the fire escape, seemed far away.

His own pain did not feel so bad, but his left leg would not cooperate and move. His ears rang. He felt blood with his hands. He heard the thud of someone dropping down into the dark of the side yard, cracking wooden stakes as they did. Their curses were in Spanish.

Henry tried to roll, and felt dizzy. His fingers struck the metal of the open gate in the dark. The blood on his hands slipped on the metal post as he tried to pull himself up. He could hear someone coming, their feet clapping clumsily at the grass. A hand pushed down on Henry's head as the person passed by him through the gate.

A moment passed, with only the ringing in his ears before this altered to the sound of sirens when the leaves of the trees reflected a pulsing blue from beneath. One police car stopped just beyond the corner, and he heard voices. There was the Spanish again. Another car pulled up at the front of the house and turned a searchlight into the yard, blinding him.

Henry closed his eyes and let the dark absorb his pain.

The two cops who questioned Henry as he lay in the hospital bed the next morning seemed to be in a good spirits. The cause of this was not clear. The smell of the coffee they held in paper cups as they spoke to him was more disturbing.

Judging by the questions they asked, Henry understood some of what had happened, even if they would not directly answer questions themselves. Paul Higgins admitted to nothing. His collarbone was broken in the fall on the fire escape. His concussion was minor. He had been found on the lower roof, unconscious. Higgins was charged with breaking and entering and attempted murder. He was threatening to sue someone for the violin string on the fire escape.

Henry had offered a shortened explanation to the cops for why he thought Higgins had come after him. This did not include Mrs. Murray, only Eddy's known past as a drug dealer and the probability that Higgins had mistaken the transaction that night. Henry insisted that Eddy was off the drugs. Neither of the cops was impressed, but the older of the two was more willing to correct him.

"I don't think so. Your friend Eddy was a bad guy. He used to have some kind of store over in Harvard Square where he kept the drugs for some partner on the janitorial staff at the university. The janitor had quite a business going—a regular network among some of the students and a few professors. Higgins was part of the police unit that took part in that Harvard bust, and knew all about your friend Eddy. But Eddy got away. He'd gotten rid of the stuff before the search. I'll bet Higgins had his eye on Eddy-boy for a long time. He wasn't looking for just four hundred bucks. He was looking for the main stash."

Henry tried to shake his head, but it hurt. "You're wrong," Henry's voice echoed within his skull. He whispered, "You're wrong. Eddy was off drugs. I'm sure of it."

The officers smiled knowingly to each other.

The older one shook his head. "They all go back."

Henry whispered loudly enough to ring in his ears, "Not Eddy. Not this time."

Both cops nodded patiently at his foolishness.

Oddly, an opened packet of heroin had been left on the couch in Henry's living room. The police detective speculated that it probably had been meant as a prop to support the idea that Henry himself was murdered by drug dealers or had been involved in drug dealing as well. Instead, now, it was just more evidence of an additional charge against Higgins.

Higgins' first excuse had been that he was off duty nearby and responded to a call for help. But it was the heroin packet he had dropped on Henry's couch that connected Higgins to the murder of another drug dealer on Magazine Street two weeks before. And it was his partner in crime, a hapless addict from Guatemala, whose testimony was going to keep Higgins in jail without bail.

Henry's own concussion was more serious. He did not remember his head hitting anything. He barely remembered the sound of the ambulance, and nothing else until he had awakened that morning to his father's face looking down at him like he was inspecting a bit of old wiring. The fracture in his leg had required a cast that edged uncomfortably into his groin. A cast on his other foot now held his toe in place. The scrapes on his feet and hands itched beneath bandages.

The police finally left. He hoped he had seen the last of them for the day. The nurse said both Albert and Barbara had been by, but were not allowed in.

Henry slept again and awakened to Della's face. She seemed unusually cheerful. Besides Della's chatting, the only sound was the respirator for the old fellow in the next bed hidden behind the pulled curtain.

Della sat on a chair between his bed and the window and held one bandaged hand as if it were the paw of a dog, unsure how to handle it.

He asked her, "How did you get them to let you in?"

She shrugged. "I told them I was your wife."

He had no comment for that under the circumstances.

Della smiled. "Barbara told me she would take care of your mail orders for a couple of weeks. You don't have to do a thing."

He had to ask, "Who's going to run her store if she's fooling around with my stuff?"

Della smiled again. "I'm helping. I'm going to fill in on Saturday and Sunday afternoons at the store. And I'll wrap your orders in the evenings."

She had been arranging things. He wondered what else.

"The orders should run out pretty soon," he said.

"Not so soon. Barbara wants to put more of her own stock on your site. The other stuff sold so well. Why not?"

All of this sounded fine. Like one big happy extended family. Very modern. Something was bound to go wrong. He had been a Red Sox fan too long to believe otherwise.

She tilted her head, innocently. "And I spoke to your father."

Reluctantly, he asked, "About what?"

"About your moving home for awhile." Her smile had sweetened a bit too much. She knew she was on difficult ground now.

An attempted groan came out of his dry throat as a squawk. "Oh, Jesus. My father can't take care of me."

"No…I would."

Henry fell silent. It was his father who had forced his sister Shelagh to leave home after he caught her on the couch with her boyfriend Rick years ago. If his father had agreed to the idea of Della living with him at the house, there was little else he could find to say. The world had changed, if only a little, and perhaps for the better.

"It might be easier to avoid the stairs for awhile." He said this aloud, thinking of the side room off the hall, where his father stacked boxes of unused electrical supplies.

"And if you're well enough in a month or so, we could go to Budapest." She bounced a little with her words.

"I don't think I could afford it."

Her eyes widened with the joy of the thought. Her voice rose. "It wouldn't cost much. My aunt wants us to stay with them. And I have two bachelor uncles who have a farm somewhere in the Carpathian Mountains. Imagine that! The Carpathian Mountains. And my credit cards are empty. We could go anywhere."

He had a credit card of his own somewhere. He had used it last the night Eddy Perry was killed. Before that, he had used it mostly to rent cars when he needed one, but now he had the truck.

He said, "I don't like the idea of being in debt."

"Well, that's something you'd better get over, kiddo. You don't have any health insurance. You'll be paying these hospital bills for a while."

His debts seemed to have been growing in more ways than he could keep track of. Health insurance? Even after Barbara's problems, he had never given it any thought.

"I suppose."

How could life be bound by such mundane things? All he wanted to do was go looking for good books, and read as many as time allowed. Simple enough. He did not need fancy food. Pastrami would do. His old truck was just fine. He did not even need more than one girlfriend. Della was plenty.

Her face brightened again as if she knew his thoughts. "But then, if we really did get married, you could go on my company health policy."

He looked at her. She was not smiling. He whispered, "Is that what you're proposing?"

"No. That's what I'm supposing. It's up to you to do the proposing.... It's just something to think about. There's no rush. I can wait, at least until you can bend your leg."

But then, Henry thought, he had two legs, and only one was broken.

Acknowledgments

I would like to thank my family for their patience and encouragement. They continue to be my first readers and most constructive critics. The second Henry Sullivan story was the first to be completed, and I was much helped by the criticism of Frank M. Robinson at that crucial stage. And, as before, I must thank Gavin and Kelly and the folks at Small Beer Press for giving it their best.

About the Author

Vincent McCaffrey's first novel, *Hound,* was chosen as a Must-Read Book by the Massachusetts Book Awards. He has owned the Avenue Victor Hugo Bookshop for more than thirty years. He has been paid to do lawn work, shovel snow, paint houses, and to be an office-boy, warehouse grunt, dishwasher, waiter, and hotel night clerk. He has chosen at various times to be a writer, editor, publisher, and bookseller. He is hard at work on the next Henry Sullivan novel.

Find out more at vincentmccaffrey.com.